DEAD FAST

A MIAMI JONES CASE

AJ Stewart

Jacaranda Drive Publishing

Los Angeles, California

www.jacarandadrive.com

This book is a work of fiction. Names, characters, places and incidents are either products of the author's imagination or are used fictitiously, and any resemblance to actual persons, living or dead, business establishments or locales is entirely coincidental.

Cover artwork by Streetlight Graphics

ISBN-10: 0985945567

ISBN-13: 978-0-9859455-6-5

Books by AJ Stewart

Stiff Arm Steal
Offside Trap
High Lie
Dead Fast
Crash Tack

For Heather, and Jamaicans everywhere.

And for Mak Ganim. Keep reading, dude.

CHAPTER ONE

"Freeze!"

I had planned to say the word, or some variation on it, and had even processed it through the old gray matter. But it came out a register higher than mine, and I realized that it was my girlfriend, Danielle, who had called out the order. She dropped her arm from mine and stepped toward the alley. We had often had long conversations about doing stupid things like walking down dark alleys where fights were taking place, but those conversations were usually the result of my actions. But as a sheriff's deputy, Danielle considered herself a protector of people as much if not more than a law enforcement officer. So the fact that we weren't on her patch in Palm Beach but well off it in Montego Bay, Jamaica, didn't even cross her mind. I took a couple of quick steps and came alongside her.

We walked shoulder to shoulder down the alley. The three guys doing the beating had stopped at Danielle's call. A fourth person lay on the ground. They all watched us edging our way down the tight lane. The figures were silhouetted against a white wall that appeared to glow. As we got closer, I realized ambient light was drifting from the other end of the alley, and it got easier to see as we got further in.

"What you *wan', mon?*" said the guy closest to us. He was a big, dark unit with close-cropped hair. "You go now."

Danielle didn't stop walking toward him.

"Step away from the person on the ground," she said in her deputy voice, which I had heard before but only when I, or a perp, was in big trouble.

"You a lady?"

I saw the big guy smile. His teeth shone like a full moon. He turned to his two accomplices.

"It's a woman," he said, slapping his thigh.

I watched the person on the ground out of the corner of my eye. I noted he looked to be a young man, and he crawled back against the wall. The three guys on their feet were giggling, which I didn't take to be a good sign. Grown men don't giggle. They laugh or they snort or they sneer, but they don't giggle. Unless they are on something, in which case they are usually not all that rational.

Danielle stopped just out of range of the first guy. She kept her eye on him but spoke to the one on the ground.

"Are you okay?" she asked him. The guy looked younger than I had first thought, maybe a teenager, and he looked up at Danielle with a mixture of fear and confusion.

The first guy looked me up and down. "Tell your woman to get lost," he said in his singsong Jamaican accent. He still wore the smile, but it wasn't so beaming anymore.

"Pal, I'm not going to do that," I said. "I want to walk out of this alley with all my bits present and accounted for. And if you do too, I'd suggest you listen to the lady real hard." My voice was strong and determined, despite the churning in my guts. Back when I played professional baseball, I learned a thing or two about putting on a performance, about faking it until you made it, about delivering the goods even when the nerves were doing cartwheels in your belly. I sounded convincing enough, but it didn't faze the big guy.

"This ain't your problem, mon."

"Three on one?" I said. "Yeah, it's my problem."

The big guy nodded, almost imperceptibly in the darkness, but we all heard the sound of a switchblade opening. It wasn't a happy sound, and for a moment I wondered how I got myself into these situations. I wasn't in Jamaica to die in a knife fight. The snap of the switchblade bounced around the hard surfaces of the alley. I couldn't see the knife, but I could tell by the way the guy held himself it was in his right hand. We stood in silence for a moment, them waiting to see if the sound would drive us away, us waiting to see if he was prepared to use it. The answer to their query was *no*, the answer to ours was *yes*.

The big guy lunged at me and parried the knife at my chest. It was a long, loping move, clumsy in its execution, like a team mascot winding up and pretending to throw a fastball. All drama and no substance. He turned side on as he lunged, so I turned as well. But not where he was expecting. My former partner and mentor, the late, great Lenny Cox, had always told me that the human brain works in patterns. We search them out, even when we don't mean to, and once we have hold of them, they are difficult to dispel. Traffic lights were the perfect example, he said. He had spent some time in Asian countries where the traffic lights were just red and green, no yellow. The GIs tasked with driving couldn't get their heads around it, and at every traffic light there was either a sudden stop that sent the troops in the back flying, or there was an accident. Lenny said if you could disrupt the pattern, the enemy could be confused long enough for you to gain the advantage, as long as you didn't also follow the patterns ingrained in you.

I coupled this advice with some basic sports science I had picked up in ball club training rooms over the years. The big unit lunged with the knife on the right, and the pattern of things told him that I would do the same—move to my right, so as to keep the knife furthest away from me and to keep him face on. Like a dance move. So I didn't. I stepped in on my left, straight at the knife, which had slowed at the end of his parry so I could easily grab hold of his arm and keep the knife away from me. I held his arm, cocked my left leg, and rocked back on my right leg as though I was winding up on the mound, and then I kicked out my left foot and cracked the big guy in the side of the knee. It was basic human physiology. Some guys are big, some guys are small, but knees are knees. His kneecap slid sideways, his leg buckled under his body weight, and the big guy crumpled in a most unbecoming fashion. As he hit the dirty alley, I thrust out my heel and landed on his wrist. He yelped with pain, perhaps at the wrist but just as likely from the knee, but either way his hand opened, and the knife spilled to the ground.

As I watched it tumble from his grasp, I heard a guttural scream, and the second guy charged. The thing was, as he came at me I realized from his motion and the sound he was making that he wasn't a *he* at all. It was a girl, maybe twenty years old, with shoulder-length dreadlocks and a thin, chocolate-colored frame. There was a cluster of stars tattooed on her chest above the tank top she wore. I generally have a life rule against hitting women. True, I tried to extend that rule to all people as often as I could, but I rarely broke it with women. I'm sure at some college in the Northeast they would call me sexist for not hitting a woman, and a misogynist if I did, but I was okay with my position on it on a day-to-day basis. Today, however, I would likely disappoint them all, because despite my feelings on the matter, if a woman charged at me—possibly armed with a knife—she was going down. No sexism. I just hate knives.

It didn't matter either way. The girl came at me, shrieking, but didn't quite make it. Danielle took two quick steps forward and thrust an open palm into the girl's chest. The heel of her palm hit the girl in the breastplate, just below the neck, and she almost flipped right over, landing in the dirt with a thump that belied her slight frame. She was sucking hard for air, the wind knocked out of her as I grabbed the first guy's knife off the ground. I stood and moved shoulder to shoulder with Danielle, and we faced off with the third guy. This one was definitely a male, tall and thin, more dreads, with limbs that waved in the breeze. He took a moment to consider us, and his buddies lying in the dirt, and then he turned and ran. The kid who had been copping the beating reached up off the ground toward the running guy and let out a deflated moan, then dropped back against the wall. Danielle and I went to the kid. His facial expression was not one of eternal thanks.

"You let him get away," he said, in his thick Jamaican lilt.

"Don't worry about him," said Danielle.

"Don't worry? What are you, Bobby Darin? He has my shoes, *mon*."

I looked down, and indeed the kid had bare feet. But it was his bleeding head I was more concerned with. Danielle told him to stay still, that he might have a concussion, but he brushed her off and said he could sit his *own damn self up.* I turned and cast my eye on the two attackers, but they were both still lying on the ground in considerable distress.

"We should call the cops," I said.

Danielle smiled. "I'm glad you think so."

The kid laughed. "Yeah, mon. That gonna happen."

"Why?" said Danielle.

"Tourist like you get tonked, maybe *dey* come, but not for me." The kid put his hand to the back of his head, and it came away bloody. He had split it when he fell, and although it didn't look too bad, it did warrant attention.

"Then we should get you to a hospital," said Danielle. Her voice was soft and caring, and I wanted to go to the hospital with her, even though there was nothing wrong with me. But the kid wasn't feeling it.

"I ain't going to no hospital. And I *don* need no more help from you." He tried pushing himself up, got halfway, and wobbled as if he was going to fall. I caught him before he did, which earned me another dirty look. I could just as easily be done with the grumpy kid, but I had suffered my share of beatings here and there, and they almost always put me in a bad mood, so I was prepared to write off some of his attitude to that.

"Then at least let us help you home," I said. "You've had a bad knock on the head."

The kid tried to hold himself up but couldn't, so he let Danielle take one side and me the other. The girl Danielle had hit was regaining normal breathing, and the big guy propped himself up against the cinderblock wall, holding his knee and no doubt wondering how he was going to get home with only this bird-framed girl to use as a crutch.

"Don't come back here, mon," said the guy through gritted teeth.

I looked around the alley, the trash and patches of hardy weeds.

"Yeah, because it really demands a repeat visit," I said. I turned, and like competitors in a three-legged race, we hobbled out of the alley.

"My name's Miami," I said. "Miami Jones. This is Danielle. You got a name, kid?"

"Markus. Markus Swan," he pouted.

"Well, let's get you home, Markus. Someone's probably worried about you."

"Yeah, I'm worried about me."

I nodded back to the alley. "You worried about those guys?"

"No, mon. I'm worried 'bout my momma. When she finds out I lost my shoes, she gonna kill me. *Tanks* to you."

As we helped the kid out onto the dark street, I wondered what I had done to deserve him, and why I had bothered to get out of my beach lounger in the first place.

CHAPTER TWO

That morning we had been living the full Jamaican vacation experience. We were lying on loungers looking over the tranquil waters of Montego Bay because once again, Danielle had beaten me in a bet. This time it had been a run on the beach on Singer Island a couple of months previous, but she hadn't let me forget the wager. She never did. I had been on the losing end of plenty of bets with Danielle and had been subjected to alcohol-free months, weeks of vegetarian menus, and even a series of yoga classes. So a wager where my losing resulted in me taking an island vacation seemed a no-brainer. As a result we found ourselves doing exactly what we did pretty much every evening on our back patio overlooking the Intracoastal Waterway on Florida's east coast, only our margaritas had been swapped out for rum drinks of a variety I had no idea existed, and we sat at an all-inclusive resort where it was socially expected to begin drinking before lunch.

They say relaxing on a beach with a good book is the perfect way to recharge one's batteries. After a swim, a few hours reading, and then passing on lunch for another swim, my batteries were oxidizing from lack of use. I glanced over at Danielle, in a one-piece swimsuit and doing everything for it that the designers envisaged, palm shadows dancing across her as she frowned at a novel. She must have felt me looking at her, as she turned to me.

"You okay?" she said.

I held up my plastic mug filled with rum and cola. "Can't complain. You?"

Danielle glanced around the small cove where the hotel sat, raked sand falling gently into an azure Caribbean Sea, and then out to a reef that kept the deeper emerald water at bay. The sky was clear, one solitary cloud adding some variety to the canvas. A gentle breeze wafted in from Cuba, keeping things pleasant, and the sound of the wind rustling through palm fronds completed the calming effect. It was postcard perfect. I watched Danielle take it all in, and a smile crept into the corner of her mouth as she did. She finished her assessment by coming back to me.

"Don't hate me, but I'm bored," she said. And that was just one of the many reasons I loved her.

The concierge threw all kinds of tour ideas at us, but traipsing around a rum distillery with a bunch of snowbirds from Michigan wasn't our idea of a good time.

We decided to wander into town and meet some locals, which the doorman thought was a terrible idea.

"If you must go, you should take a taxi," he said with a smile. "Walking is not for you."

A beat-up minivan took us from the resort and dropped us on Gloucester Road in return for a king's ransom. The area looked like Bourbon Street. Buildings of bright greens and oranges blocked the view of the water, each offering touristy drinks in a uniquely American atmosphere. I didn't fly to the Caribbean to sit in an American chain restaurant, so we wandered past a sign that told us we were at Doctor's Cave beach and headed for something more authentic. I like authentic. At home on Singer Island, most of the houses had been razed in order to build minimansions on the water. My place was on the water, but it was authentic down to the wood paneling and shag rug.

We found authentic in the form of a joint called the Pork Pit. It was a rundown-looking place with a view of a barren park proclaiming itself as *Dump Up Beach*. Neither the bright yellow building nor the park screamed *come in and stay awhile*, but the smell of jerk chicken and pork wafting from outdoor grills was enough to make up our minds. It was my kind of place, offering cold beer, generous smiles, and helpings of the most delicious meats. They clearly weren't trading on their location, and Danielle and I enjoyed a late lunch. I cornered our server and told him we were looking for a local spot to listen to some music and enjoy a beer or two, and he directed us to a small place off Falmouth Road. It reminded me of a few joints I'd visited in Lauderhill, a Jamaican enclave back home, that had some of the best people and music one could hope to while away a few hours with. This place was no different, except that the building looked like it might blow down in a decent breeze. Two guys were in a corner playing acoustic guitar, with a third occasionally joining in on the steel drums. There was some Marley, some Beatles, and what I guessed was some original stuff, and the mood was easy and exactly what we were looking for. Except for one guy at the bar who looked like Colonel Sanders, we were the only white people in the place, which earned us a few grins and plenty of high fives. Danielle got me on the floor for a few slow dances, which weren't a lot different from the fast dances. It was laid-back, and as the afternoon turned to evening a cloud of ganja smoke spread out across the ceiling. I wasn't feeling the beer, but the atmosphere I was breathing was going to my head. I told Danielle I needed some air, so she paid the check and met me on the steps of the bar.

"Shall we take a walk?" she said, looping her arm through mine. The sun was in its final throes, dropping with a mystical burst of green into the ocean. We walked away from the water, up through the town that was already more asleep than awake, and then cut back around toward St. James Parish Church. The palm trees and the water didn't feel so different from Florida, but something about the air was dense and unfamiliar. My head cleared and Danielle stayed tight against me, and I felt good. We crossed a dark section of town, wood shutters closed, lights doused. That's when Danielle stopped. She tugged me back, and her eyes focused my attention down an alley between two crumbling cinderblock buildings. I saw several men, three or four, silhouetted by the whitewashed wall behind. One was separate from the others, the focal point of their geometric wedge. We stood in silence watching, then in a flash, punches were thrown, and we ended up helping an ungrateful kid home to his mother, and our Jamaican vacation took a turn onto the pages they don't put in the tourist brochures.

CHAPTER THREE

The building Markus's family called home looked like they had moved in six months before completion. It was exposed cinderblock, no stucco, no paint. One side looked finished to lock up, a door and windows, while the other end bore only one wall, like the ruin of a Roman fortification, with a concrete slab poured below. Markus pushed the door open and we stepped into a dark house. There was light coming from a back room, and the smell of something hot and spicy permeated the air. Markus called for his *mudda*, and a woman in an apron appeared in the light of the rear room. She wore a substantial frown already, but upon seeing Danielle and me, the frown managed to deepen. She had a point. We probably weren't the kinds of faces that appeared at her door with good news very often. She looked me up and down first: tall, lean enough for my age, and wearing chinos and a shirt featuring palm fronds in a repeating pattern. It might have looked like the kind of gear an American tourist would wear in Jamaica, except that I dressed that way more or less every day back home. The woman then turned her gaze to Danielle. She wore a dress that matched the turquoise of the Caribbean waters, and her shoulder-length brown hair was tousled just enough to look like she'd done it on purpose.

"*Wot 'appen ya*, boy?" said Markus's mother, wiping her hands on a towel that hung from the apron tie.

"*Nuttin'*," said Markus.

"Nuttin', my eye," she replied, looking at us, maybe for answers, or maybe because she'd never had white folks in her home before. I left the talking to Danielle. She was better than me at plenty of things, and diplomacy was one.

"Mrs. Swan?" said Danielle. "My name is Danielle Castle. We found Markus being assaulted in town."

"Assaulted?"

"In a fight," said Danielle, to clarify.

It must have clarified it some. Mrs. Swan slapped her son hard across the cheek. His head snapped back, and the sound cracked off the cinderblock.

"No, Mrs. Swan, you misunderstand," said Danielle. "He was attacked. It appeared to be a robbery."

Mrs. Swan continued to frown at Danielle. I wasn't certain the cop-speak was getting through.

"Ma'am, it wasn't his fault," I said, not sure at all that this was the case but feeling that I could sort that out after the tension had been removed from the room.

"Who you, *mista*?" she snapped.

"My name is Miami Jones."

"Miami? *Wot* kinda name be Miami?"

I shrugged. It was a fair point. I wasn't born with it, but I'd had it longer than I hadn't, so it was as much me as my furrowed brow and my sandy hair.

"He has a cut on his head," I said, skipping her question.

The frown didn't ease, but she followed my eye and looked over the cut on Markus's head, and then she directed us toward the kitchen.

"Come, yah," she said.

We helped Markus into the back room, the only one with light. It was a small kitchen, with a wooden table and stackable plastic chairs. The source of the spicy aroma was a pot on an old stove. We deposited Markus in a chair and stepped back as his mother took a woven basket from a shelf and then used some cotton buds to dab bright red ointment on the boy's head. It looked worse when she was done, but I figured it was some kind of antiseptic, which would help. As I watched her work I realized she looked younger than me, which felt way too young to have a teenage son, and it made me feel old and crusty. When she was done she packed her things away.

"Wash up now," she said to Markus, and he stood and walked out the back of the house to the area that appeared to still be under construction. We heard the splashing of water, and Mrs. Swan turned to Danielle.

"Wot 'appen?"

"We were walking in town," said Danielle, "and we saw Markus in an alley with three others, and they hit him. One of them ran away with his shoes."

Mrs. Swan nodded to herself and dropped the frown a little. For a moment she seemed far away, and then she was back, and so was the frown.

"*Tank* you," she said.

"You're welcome," said Danielle.

"You should not be walkin' about dis place at night. It's not safe fo' da tourists."

"With all respect, Mrs. Swan, it wasn't us that was in trouble," I said.

"No, but you watch it, all da same."

"Don't worry, ma'am," said Danielle. "I am a law enforcement officer in the US."

"Police?"

"Yes, ma'am. Do you know why these people would steal Markus's shoes? Were they worth a lot of money?"

"Some money, yah."

Markus came back inside, wiping his hands. I noted that his feet were still bare.

"Markus, were they your only shoes?" I asked.

He glanced at his feet and then back at me.

"Nah, mon. You let him runweh wit my Nikes. Now I gotta run in me gym shoes."

Markus shook his head and walked away, out the front, not bothering to put on any footwear.

"He has to run where?" said Danielle.

"He da runner," said Mrs. Swan, stirring the pot on the stove. "He run da fast races."

"Fast races?" I said. "You mean sprints? Like Usain Bolt?"

Mrs. Swan smiled for the first time since we'd arrived. "Dot's 'im."

"And someone stole his racing shoes?" said Danielle.

"Looks dot way."

"Does that sort of thing happen a lot?" I said.

"If *don dada* say so, den yah."

"Don dada? Who is he?"

"Not who, what. *Don dada* be de boss man. Whichever boss man *don* get his way."

"Boss man? What do you mean?" asked Danielle.

Mrs. Swan shrugged and put a couple of old coffee mugs on the table.

"Tea?" she said.

Danielle smiled. "Sure, thanks."

I nodded. I wasn't much of a tea drinker, especially in hot climates. I'd heard the tales about drinking hot beverages to increase your internal temperature, which in turn made you more comfortable. That was complete garbage. I didn't care how many scientists said otherwise, hot drinks made me hotter, end of story. On a broiler of a summer's day, nothing quenched me like a nice, cold beer. But when I find myself in a foreign land like Jamaica, or Mississippi, I found it the gracious move to accept their hospitality.

Mrs. Swan poured hot water from a kettle into a chipped china pot and sat as we waited for the tea to steep. She didn't seem to be actively avoiding the question about the robbery, but she wasn't in any hurry to answer it.

"Do you know why this happened, Mrs. Swan?" asked Danielle. I could see Danielle had kicked into sheriff mode, and she could smell trouble.

Mrs. Swan poured the tea into our mugs and then sat back and assessed Danielle, as if she could read her character just by eyeballing her. She gave Danielle a good long look, and it wasn't so much the silence as the glare that drifted into uncomfortable territory. But eventually she must have seen something that prodded her forward.

"It's da sports. Da athletics," she said. She sipped at her steaming tea and then continued.

"Dare's no much for da boys to do, no' much future here in MoBay," she said, looking around at the bare cinderblock walls. "Sports be da way out. Da way to make some kind a life, udder dan workin' in da hotels."

Danielle and I both nodded, but Mrs. Swan didn't pay me any mind. She and Danielle sipped their tea. I was waiting for mine to drop below the ambient air temperature.

"So this thing with Markus, it's competitive," said Danielle.

"Dot's right. Dare be a lot of pressure. If a child can run, or play cricket, or even da football, a lot of folks want to jump on dem coattails. You get it? E'rybody want a free ride outta town."

"So how does it end in a beating in an alley?" I said. For the first time since she had sat, Mrs. Swan looked me over, fortunately with less intensity than she had when we had arrived.

"E'ry boy dot makes it, ten udders do not. And da boys wit talent, dey find demselves wit a benefactor. Like it or not."

"A benefactor?" said Danielle.

Mrs. Swan nodded economically. "Da equipment is no' *someting* we can afford, but dare are always mon who can give da gifts, like my boy's runnin' shoes." She spoke the latter half of the sentence like her tea had just been spiked with salt. "But dees mon, dey not always the best mon. Maybe my boy run too fast, an udder boy's benefactor maybe try da dirty stuff. Steal his shoes, maybe hurt him, so he can run no more."

I leaned back in my plastic chair and watched Mrs. Swan's face. I guessed if I had kids in this environment, worried about whether they were going to get home safe from training, I'd have a frown permanently etched across my face too. And on me, that would mean furrows a farmer could grow potatoes in. But I knew a little about her plight. Even in the States, promising athletes had a lot of people trying to grab hold of their limited coattails. I had been approached by agents while at college, which was against the rules of the National Collegiate Athletic Association, and I saw guys get kicked out of school every year for infractions. I'd had college boosters, supposedly supporters of the school, threaten me with harm if I didn't play a certain way or attend the opening of their used car lot or condo development. And when I made the pros, long-lost acquaintances came out of the woodwork as though we'd shared a womb. Personally, I never had a problem telling people to crawl back into the hole they came out of, but for some guys, it was more than their coattails could handle.

As we sat considering what Mrs. Swan had told us, Markus came bustling back inside. His mother stopped his motion dead just by lifting her palm up to him.

"Where ya be?"

"Algy's house. He gotta phone."

"Who ya callin'?"

"Mista Richmond, who you think?"

"Don't you be sassin' me, child."

Markus hung his head. "Sorry."

Mrs. Swan jutted her chin at her son. "Wat he say, Mista Richmond?"

"Dunno. I didn't call 'im. Algy not home. His phone neither."

"Who's Mr. Richmond?" I asked.

"He gimme da shoes," said Markus, with a look that said I should have known that.

"Benefactor," said Mrs. Swan, with raised eyebrows.

I nodded and looked at Markus. "They were racing shoes?" I said.

Markus nodded. "Ya, mon. Spikes an' all."

"And you need them?"

"Trials comin' up. Course I need 'em, mon."

"And how do we get another pair?"

Markus said nothing. His mother smiled, but she didn't seem happy.

"Mista Richmond," she said.

"Okay," I said, pulling my cell phone from my pocket. "Call him."

"You don understan', mon. He in America."

"So? I have an American phone." I handed the cell phone to Markus. "Call him. Call your Mr. Richmond."

CHAPTER FOUR

Markus knew the number by heart, and he paced around the kitchen with my phone to his ear. It wasn't that big a space, so he looked like a hamster in a wheel. I heard him ask for Mr. Richmond, and that was the last I understood. Clearly he had reached some kind of minion because he waited on the line for a long time, and I watched those roaming charges ticking over like the gauge on a gas pump. Eventually Mr. Richmond must have come on the line because Markus started talking, listening, and then talking again. It was all gibberish to me. I love the Jamaican *pat-wah*, a singsong, pared-down version of English, spoken at a pace and with an accent that was like the Enigma code for non-Jamaicans. It was like listening to French jazz—melodic and enjoyable, but thoroughly unintelligible.

After a lengthy conversation, which I assumed was a play-by-play of what had happened in the alley, Markus listened, frowned and then held the phone out to me.

"He wanna speak to you."

I took the phone and held it to my ear.

"This is Miami Jones."

"Yes, *Mista* Jones. Dis is Desmond Richmond." He made a big deal of pronouncing the O's in his name. "I believe I am indebted to you, suh," he said. He had the Jamaican lilt, but it had been smoothed around the edges by years away from the island.

"We've never met, Mr. Richmond. You don't owe me a thing."

"Well, you saved my charge, from what I hear. So I thank you."

"Not necessary," I said. "Markus was the one we helped."

"And he thanks you too, suh."

"Not so far." I glanced at Markus, standing directly behind where his mother sat. "What is it I can do for you, Mr. Richmond?"

"I wish to hire you, Mista Jones."

"You what?"

"Yes, I know of you, suh. You see, I am based in Fort Lauderdale. I have seen you in the newspaper. You are *the* Miami Jones, yes?"

I had been something of a small-town legend during high school in Connecticut, my football and baseball exploits getting my picture in the local rag back when there still was a local rag, and on local television in Miami when my baseball took me through college. I'd even made it onto ESPN when I was promoted from the minors up to the Oakland roster, back in the day, and I still rated a mention every now and then, when they ran stories about sports people who had made it to the top of their competitions but never actually got to play a top-flight game. They were pity pieces that always missed the point, but they and my occasional high-profile case meant that more people knew me than I ever thought my life merited.

"I suppose I am," I said. "But I don't see what it is I can do for you, Mr. Richmond."

"Mista Jones, you are in Montego Bay. You can see for yourself. There are many happy people, but there are also many desperate people. People who will do *anyting* to get out. Even hurt young men like Markus so they can ride their own athlete out of town."

"Who's riding Markus out of town?"

"It be a fair question, Mista Jones, to wonder of my motives. But am already out, suh. I got out under my own steam, and all I want is to help *udder* athletes do da same."

It sounded like a fair argument, but I had only heard the case for the defense, so the jury was still out on Mr. Richmond's motives.

"So how can I help?"

"In a few weeks, Markus will run in da under-seventeen Jamaican trials. This is an important race.

Making the national team, even at this level, opens many doors, like races in Europe and the United States."

"You want me to run it for him?"

"No, Mista Jones," said Richmond, laughing. "I want you to protect him. Make sure he is not hurt. Get him to and from trainin' for the next few days. I will be flying into MoBay in a few days, so until I am there, I want to hire you to protect my boy."

It seemed like a reasonable request. We did the odd spot of protection and bodyguard work, usually the rich and famous jetting into Palm Beach or Jupiter, wanting the paparazzi or their wives or husbands kept well away.

"I'm not cheap, Mr. Richmond."

"Nor am I, Mista Jones. Have your office here call me. I can arrange a retainer."

I cupped my hand over the phone despite the presence of a mute button I could never fathom, and leaned into Danielle.

"He wants to hire me to protect the kid."

Danielle nodded. "Do it."

"For a few days, until he gets here."

"Do it," she repeated.

"But our vacation?"

"We've been here a day, and I'm bored out of my mind, MJ. Do it. It'll be a good way to see the real Jamaica."

I wasn't sure the real Jamaica was what the tourist board wanted us to see, but I dropped my hand from the phone.

"Okay, Mr. Richmond. I'll watch Markus for you." I looked at the boy, and his body deflated. No doubt being escorted around by a white Yankee was going to do wonders for his street cred.

"I just have one question for you. Who wants to hurt him?"

"Markus won't tell me exactly who it was beat him. He said he didn't see them. Did you?"

"I did, but I can't say much more than they were some black dudes with dreadlocks, and that pretty much nails the entire country."

"Not to mind, suh. I am sure I know. You should watch for Mr. Winston's boys."

"Winston."

"Yes, suh. Cornelius Winston."

"All right, thanks. I guess we'll see you in a few days."

"Yes, suh, you will. Keep my boy safe."

I hung up the call and looked at the three pairs of eyes on me.

"So looks like we're gonna be watching over you for a few days," I said.

"I don need no watchin' over, mon," said Markus.

"All evidence this evening to the contrary."

"Well," said Mrs. Swan, long and slow as she pushed herself up from the table with the effort of an eighty-year-old woman, when to my mind she was well short of forty. "If yo gonna be stayin', we best get some dinna on."

CHAPTER FIVE

Dinner was an all-star affair. News of Markus's altercation had traveled fast, and a procession of friends, family, and other hangers-on paraded through the house, inspecting Markus for damage and checking out the *whities* that had been put in charge of his safety in a country where we knew no one and Markus was surrounded by a small army of folks who wanted him safe. But everyone offered us generous smiles and shook hands with Danielle and me. Someone fired up a grill in the portion of the house that was still under construction, and the bubbling pot that Mrs. Swan had been tending was moved out to a trestle table, along with bowls of food that people arrived with. Reggae tunes were cranked up from a speaker attached to an iPod. I wasn't sure if it was a planned party, an impromptu get-together, or just a communal way of eating, but either way it was delicious and fun. I was still pretty full from the beers and jerk pork, but I was offered a small plate of rice and something and felt obliged to take it. Danielle took hers with a smile, obviously keen to try this real Jamaica she spoke of.

"What is it we are having?" she asked the young woman who had handed her the plate.

"Ackee and saltfish, wit rice and beans." She beamed, in a way that suggested she had made the dish.

Danielle nodded a thank you, and we both took a bite. The ackee and saltfish was an acquired taste, and the rice and beans were a touch spicy but delicious.

"What is ackee?" I asked the young woman.

She smiled again, the kind of grin that could have been harnessed by a power company.

"Ackee is a fruit, comin' from Jamaica. It is poison if you don know what you is doin' wit it." I hesitated to put another forkful in my mouth, but the woman's smile grew even deeper.

"No problems, suh. I know what I is doin'."

Everyone around me was eating without fear or hesitation, so I figured her word was good. I ate in silence, watching the group grow to twenty or more people, most of whom inquired after Markus. Many of the men gathered together at the end of the concrete slab, away from the house. There were frowns and as much gesticulating as one could manage while holding a plate of food. Clearly folks were not happy about what had happened to Markus, and I couldn't blame them for that, but this was more than discontent with the safety of the streets in their town.

"You got try dis, brudda," said a young guy, thrusting a bowl of whatever had been cooking on Mrs. Swan's stovetop. He was smiling, which seemed to be a pretty common condition in these parts, and he had hair shaved the consistency of Berber carpet. He handed me the bowl, took my plate and then sat on a plastic chair beside me. He jinked his head at me, urging me to try what was in the bowl. I decided not to bother about its toxicity level as it smelled fantastic. I took a spoonful and chewed on it. It was a meaty stew, spicy but not overly so, and full of flavor.

"What is it?" I asked.

"Mannish wata, mon."

"Mannish water? Tastes like spicy stew."

"You got it, mon. Goat stew."

"Goat?" I said, chewing. I'd never eaten goat, but it was like gamey lamb. The young guy leaned across me and looked at Danielle.

"Missus?" he said, nodding at my bowl.

"Yes, please," said Danielle. The guy jumped up, danced his way over to the pot, and returned with a steaming bowl for Danielle. She dove in with the gusto I generally reserved for mirages in the Sahara. She was the fittest person I knew, beat me in pretty much every physical endeavor short of throwing a fastball, and she didn't eat a lot. But she ate well, and I guess that made all the difference. In the past few months we had made an effort to get in better shape, and I looked as good in my board shorts as I had when I was playing A-ball in my early twenties. Danielle looked like Danielle, which in my eye was something like if Nike had commissioned Leonardo da Vinci to paint an ad for women's sportswear. I watched her eat for a moment, and then I turned to my new friend.

"I'm Miami," I said, offering my hand.

He took it, and we shook. His hands were supple, and his grip was like a velvet glove.

He smiled. "Markus's cousin, Garfield."

"Like the cat," I said.

He half frowned and then laughed, slapping his hand on his thigh.

"Nah, mon. After da cricketer."

"Okay," I said. I didn't know much about cricket, other than the players wore croquet uniforms and games went for three weeks. I had no idea who Garfield the cricketer was.

"You play cricket?" I asked.

"E'body heah plays da cricket, mon. You?"

I shook my head and ate. "Uh uh. Baseball."

"That cool, mon. That cool."

I glanced at the group of men that formed and saw the mood hadn't eased any. I turned back to Garfield.

"Those boys don't look happy about what happened to Markus."

"Nah, mon. No brudda 'appy 'bout dot. But dots MoBay."

"This sort of thing happens a lot?"

Garfield shrugged.

"Seems a lot of people are banking on Markus."

"Can say dot. A boy show some talent, no matter a' what, cricket, runnin', *footboll*, den folks a set demselves on him. Hopin' he make it big, and some o'dot rub off on dem."

"Coattails," I said.

"You got it, brudda."

"And is Markus that good at running?"

"Dead fast."

"So his competitors might want to hurt him?"

"Nah, no competitors, mon. The benefactors. *'Ot steppas*."

"Hot steppers?"

"Yah, mon. De bod man. Gangstas. Dey rich, and dey wanna piece a da action."

I noticed that Danielle had stopped chewing and was listening to us.

"So let me get this straight," I said. "There are bad guys backing each athlete, supplying their equipment."

"No e'body a bod man, but e'body want sum'ting for hisself."

"Right. So they help the athletes with shoes or whatever, then maybe they get a cut of future earnings."

Garfield nodded, his movements fluid, like a puppet with no strings.

"Or maybe these guys want athletes to run bad in a certain race, or throw a cricket game?"

"Maybe, mon." Garfield had lost his smile, and he looked older for it.

"But they need their guy to get to the top before they hit pay dirt," I said.

"Yo gettin' it."

I nodded. I was getting it. I looked around the space, the one finished wall, the half house. These were happy people with very few possessions, who, like most of us, were laboring under the assumption that more stuff was going to make them happy. I lived in a county that held some of the richest people on the planet, and there weren't too many smiles driving down Worth Avenue when I cared to look.

"You like living in Jamaica, Garfield?"

"Yah, mon. Is paradise."

I couldn't argue with that. "But you want to get out?"

"Nah, mon. I just wanna fass car."

"A fast car?" I smiled. "A fast car won't necessarily make you happy."

"But yo have a fass car."

"How do you know that?"

"Only a brudda wit a fass car tell a brudda he don need a fass car."

There was no getting around his logic. It was easy to preach when you lived in a fully finished house.

"So the Swans, they don't have the money to finish off their home?"

Garfield glanced around as if he'd just been teleported in. "Dot's a Jamaican yard."

"Yard?"

"Yah, mon. We don got dem big banks like you Americans. We make some *coil*, we built a li'l bit more yard. Den we gotta wait, make some mo' coil."

"You just build the house a piece at a time?"

"Dot's it, mon."

"That's one way to do it."

"In Jamaica, dot's da only way."

"So I guess Markus is under pressure to make that happen?"

"True 'nuff."

"From those guys?" I said, nodding at the group of men.

"Yah, mon."

"And his mom and dad?"

"His *fadda* long gone, but his mudda, sho' she wan' 'im be big-time."

"His dad's not around?"

"Nah, mon. Him was cricketer, yah. Good one. Lotta people wan' a piece a him. Him no take it good and do a runna."

I nodded. It made sense that a kid could fall in with a bad crowd if he was searching for a father figure. If I had turned a different corner and not met Lenny Cox while I was in college, I might have gone the wrong way after my dad died.

"Those guys," I said, looking at the men, "are they going to cause trouble?"

"Nah, mon. Dem angry, but dey not gonna do nuttin' against Mista Winston."

"That's the second time I've heard that name. Is he behind what happened?"

"Markus no tellin' it, but e'body know it."

"I need to meet this guy."

"Mista Miami, me take ya to da trainin' *di morrows.* You see Mista Winston all right."

CHAPTER SIX

It was still dark when we arrived at the Swan home to take Markus to training the next morning. Another overpriced taxi ride back to our resort had given us a few hours of sleep, and I woke to the sound of gentle waves lapping on the beach, which for me was the sound of home. They do massive meals at all-inclusive resorts, as if the guests didn't get to eat at home and needed to load up for the winter. The breakfast buffet we had seen on our first morning could have fed a marching army, but only if the army rose at a decent hour, because the other thing about resorts is they are not designed around early risers. So Danielle and I dressed, her in shorts and a tank top, me in cargo shorts and a shirt, the blue one with palm tree prints on it, and we crept like cat burglars through the open-air foyer of the resort, past the darkened restaurant to the hotel entrance. It turned out we were even too early for the taxis, so the doorman made a call on his desk phone, and in fifteen minutes we were in another rusted-out minivan bouncing into town.

Garfield, he named after a cricket player and not the cat, was standing outside the house, waiting. "Good mawnin'." He smiled, handing us each a warm paper bag. Inside was something that was halfway between toast and an English muffin.

"Is called *bammy*," said Garfield, anticipating Danielle's question. "Is made from cassava."

I bit into it. It was crunchy on the outside but soft and buttery inside. I nodded my approval to Garfield, and he led us into the house. Markus was sitting in the kitchen, putting on a pair of runners that looked to have worn out two owners previous.

"You train in those?" I said.

"Ot steppa got me udder good shoes," he said, raising his eyebrows and lacing up his runners.

We walked across town in the dark, Markus and Garfield laughing and chatting, oblivious to any danger, but Danielle and I each took a side and kept our eyes open. It occurred to me that there was no danger, that with his good running shoes gone, Markus was no threat. But I wasn't getting paid to assume the world was golden, and I knew that out there somewhere, in the sleeping town, was a big guy with a busted knee who was probably in a great deal of discomfort. And if there was one universal rule in life, it was that big guys rarely came in sets of one.

The sun was hiding behind the mountains when we got to the training facility—and training facility would be a pretty fancy description of what I saw. It was an oval of patchy grass, some parts bare, other parts in desperate need of a mow. Around the outside of the oval was a ring where the grass had been shaved so close as to be almost non-existent. Running lanes had been painted along one side, but they petered out around the bend. There were a couple canvas pop-up shelters, under which men were sitting in lawn chairs, watching youngsters stretch and jog and generally warm up.

Garfield led Danielle and me over to the chain-link fence that surrounded the oval, and we leaned on it as Markus joined a group warming up. The mood seemed light and carefree, joking and laughing, just some kids out for a jog, a bit of fun. Then a stocky guy with a whistle took the field and the smiles disappeared, and the group came to a laconic form of attention. The coach blew the whistle, and the runners took off slowly around the perimeter of the oval. I glanced over at the men under the pop-up shelters, passing around coffee and what looked like some kind of cake.

"Who are those guys?" I asked Garfield.

"Yo might call dem interested parties." He gave a knowing smile.

"Interested parties? Interested in what?"

"Interested in da form of dare horses." He nodded out to the track. I had a vision of old men in hats, standing by the fence in the cool morning dew at Gulfstream Park, watching jockeys and thoroughbreds going through their paces, taking notes and trading tales about previous wins at the distance.

"They bet on the races?"

"No," said Garfield. He smiled his conspiratorial grin. "Dot wouldn't be legal."

"Who are they?"

"Some dem family, distant family most. Some dem business mon, of a sort. You know?"

I knew. Wherever there was a chance to lay a bet, there were always businessmen, of a sort. We watched the athletes finish their warm-up, and then they spent some time working on their starts, exploding out of the holes they had dug in the ground to simulate blocks, again and again.

"Are all the facilities this sparse?" I asked Garfield, looking around at the sad grass and the lack of any kind of change rooms.

"No, mon. It depend on yo school. Da good school, dey got da asphalt track, electronic timing, all dat jazz. Our school, we got dis," he said, looking around.

"So the kids compete for their school?"

"Dot's right. Summa da good school, dey recruit da good runners from da bad school, so da rich always run good."

Danielle leaned toward Garfield. "If Markus is a good runner, why isn't he at a school with better facilities?" she said.

"Dot's 'is mudda. She don't allow it."

Markus and his teammates gathered at the end of the straight and took some instruction from their coach, and then the coach ambled down the straight and stood on the inside of the track where I assumed the finish line for one hundred meters would be. A man wandered out from under the pop-up canopy and stood at the chain-link fence, opposite the coach, and pulled out a stopwatch the size of a donut, the kind that I remembered coaches using in my own high school days. Six boys lined up at the start line. There were no starting blocks, just the holes, so the boys each crouched in their own preferred style, and then there was a pause where the whole island seemed to go quiet. Then the blast of an air horn, the coach holding the canister high above his head. The boys kicked away from the start and ran. They looked to be moving in slow motion, arms pumping, legs lifting, the first few paces still in a semicrouch, then gradually standing tall and running hard. They were all long and lithe, wearing the onset of musculature that would fill out in the coming years, leaving them strong and explosive. As they charged down the track they seemed to get faster the closer they got to us, and by the time they hit the finish, they weren't much more than a blur. The sound was thunderous, feet on grass and heaving breathing sounding more like charging bison than I would have thought possible from a half dozen kids. As they flew by, both the coach and the guy by the fence hit their stopwatches. The coach made a mark on his clipboard, and the other guy turned to the pop-up canopy.

"Tenay," he called.

I turned to Garfield. "What was that?"

"He's timing da winner. Ten point eight second."

I didn't know much about track, but that seemed pretty quick. I recalled somewhere under ten being some kind of record, so under eleven on grass, with no starting blocks, had to be some kind of effort. The herd came to a stop by the fence at the end of the straight, and then wandered onto the infield to walk back to the start. They were breathing about as hard as I do bending over to pick up a penny.

Everyone's focus turned back to the start line and the second group of runners. Markus was among them, jumping up and down in an inside lane, loosening up. The coach called out, they all got into their crouch, and the air horn pierced the air once more. The slow-motion start was repeated, and a couple of the outer lanes pulled out fast, gaining yards in but a few steps. Then it seemed as if Markus wound up. He stood tall, his long, thin legs reaching out and dragging the earth beneath him. By the halfway mark he had caught the early leaders, and then in a flash of color and cacao-colored limbs, Markus hit the finish with daylight to second. I snapped my vision to the guy by the fence. He was looking at his big stopwatch, and then he turned.

"Tenfo," he called.

I turned back to Garfield and noticed Danielle was waiting on Garfield also. Garfield just nodded.

"Ten point four second. No bod."

The coach yelled something at the runners, and they turned and headed back to the start. As Markus walked past the coach, he barked something more, but he didn't sound impressed by 10.40. Coaches were coaches. They were never happy. I guess that was part of the job.

As the boys walked toward the start, all heads on our side of the fence turned as one at the sound of a deep rumbling across the gravel. A gray Rolls-Royce crawled into the park, moving slow like a lion across the savannah. The car looked massive, as only a Rolls can do, and it edged to a stop in front of the pop-up canopy. A driver in a pressed shirt and trousers jumped out, ran around the back of the car, and opened the rear door. The rear doors of a Rolls open nice and wide, in case you wanted to carry an armoire back there. But there was no furniture inside, just an old man. The man wore salt-and-pepper hair and a goatee, and his dark skin was a couple of shades lighter than most of the other people around him. But he had the unmistakable fluid gait of a Jamaican. He slipped out of the car and stood, surveying the scene and smoothing the lapels on his cream-colored suit. As if he were some kind of deity, the sun broke the peak of the mountains behind us and spread golden light across the man and his car. His driver slammed the door home and took up station by the car as the man ambled over to the pop-up canopy that was now offering some value to those under it.

The man was clearly known, but known was not the same as liked, and the men under the canopy parted as the cream suit wandered by. The old guy wore a big smile and nodded a lot, the way politicians do.

"Who is that?" I asked Garfield.

"Mista Jones, you ask to see Mista Winston. Dot be 'im."

"What is he doing here?"

"He da chairman of All-Schools Athletics, so he visit all da trainings. In truth, he wanna see da competition."

"He's here to spy on Markus," I said.

"And one or two udders, yah, mon."

Winston shook a few hands and made chitchat, all the time his eyes moving, taking in faces and names and who knew what else. His eyes drifted out from the shelter and crossed mine. He did a double take, perhaps surprised to see white faces at a school athletics training session, or perhaps he had heard that the minions he dispatched to steal Markus's running shoes had come home a little worse for wear. I gave him a slight nod, and his eyes moved along, as he spoke with the men under the canopy.

The coach rearranged the groups of students and then set up another race. The six boys sorted themselves into lanes; then the coach called, and the air horn blasted. The start was slow again, but I must have been getting acclimated to the speed because the race didn't appear to pick up pace at the halfway point, and by the finish, a couple of boys looked as if they were almost jogging. The man by the fence clicked his stopwatch and turned to the men.

"E'lemtoo."

I turned to Garfield.

"Eleven point two," he said, not taking his eyes off Winston.

I watched the second group, which included Markus, sort themselves out. Then the horn blew, and they jumped out of the non-existent blocks. Markus never got out of third gear, and hit the finish in about fourth, give or take. The stopwatch guy called the score.

"E'lemfor."

"Eleven point four," said Garfield, without me asking.

"That's a good second slower, even more for Markus."

Garfield nodded. He jutted his chin toward the group of men, and I turned to see Winston break away and amble in our direction. He took his sweet time.

"I don't believe we've met," he said on approach. His voice had that unmistakable Jamaican singsong accent, but he didn't use the patois.

"I don't believe so," I returned.

"Cornelius Winston," he said, extending his hand.

I took it. He had a strong, lively handshake for a guy who had to be well into his sixties.

"Miami Jones," I said. "And this is Danielle Castle."

Winston took Danielle's hand and bowed his head.

"It is a pleasure, madam." He stood himself up and smiled. It wasn't the same smile I'd seen around the place, that unabashed, genuine flash of the pearly whites that seemed to emanate from most Jamaican faces. This one seemed practiced.

"So what brings you folks to our paradise?" he said.

"Exactly that," I said. "We heard it was paradise."

"Do you not agree?"

"Oh, I agree. But even Eden had snakes," I said.

Winston nodded gently. "We don't get too many tourists at *atletics* training."

"We're not really resort people," Danielle chimed in. "We were looking for the real Jamaica."

"Well, it may not be flash, but this is certainly the real Jamaica. We do love to run."

"That you do," she said. "So what brings you down here, Mr. Winston?"

"I am chair of the Inter-Secondary Schools Sports Association , you see. We run "Champs." That is, the high school athletics championships. Part of my role is to visit with each of the schools."

"Do other schools have a proper running track, or are they all like this one?" I asked.

"Just like the United States, we have schools with better facilities and worse facilities. I lobby all I can, but ultimately this is a government issue." He gave me the smile again. "So what is it you do, Mr. Jones?"

"I'm an investigator," I said. "Danielle is a sheriff."

He nodded as if this greatly impressed him, which I doubted it did.

"And from where in America do you come?"

"Florida. Palm Beaches."

"Of course. I have been to Florida many times. A lot of strip malls."

"That's for sure. A few beaches too."

"Well, it is always nice to have such esteemed visitors to our humble little island. In fact, I'm actually having a function this evening, to celebrate the upcoming championships. If you would like to meet some locals, as you say, I would be delighted to invite you."

"Mr. Winston, that's awfully kind of you," said Danielle.

"Not at all, my dear. I suspect you'll be quite the talk of the evening." He raised an eyebrow, and if I didn't know better, I'd have said the old guy was flirting with her.

"It sounds like we can't afford to miss it," said Danielle.

"Indeed," he said, making to turn away. "Rose Hall, seven o'clock." He eyeballed me up and down, giving my shirt a good look. "Dress is nothing too formal. I look forward to seeing you then."

He nodded his farewell and walked back to his car, where his driver opened the door. I turned to Garfield, whose jaw had settled in the dirt at his feet.

"You going to this party?" I said.

Garfield shook his head. "No, mon. No one I know ever go to Mr. Winston's party. He's a rich mon."

"And yet I don't feel quite as esteemed as he suggested," I said.

"You know what they say," said Danielle. "Keep your friends close."

I nodded. "And your enemies closer. Say, Garfield, do you know where this place is, this Rose Hall?"

"Yah, mon. I know Rose Hall. Is the home of the White Witch."

"The White Witch? Well, that just sounds like a hoot."

After training we walked Markus and his friends to school. The school yard was surrounded by a six-foot-high concrete fence, and the guard at the driveway boom gate wasn't giving us as much as a smile, let alone entry onto the grounds, which made me feel comfortable about leaving Markus for the day.

"Do you work, Garfield?" I asked as we wandered away from the school.

"Yah, mon. Da ganja don buy itself." He smiled. "I work at one a da beach resorts, behind the bar. I don got to be in til lunchtime."

I nodded. He seemed like the kind of chatty guy who would do well behind a bar. I felt my stomach rumble and realized all I'd eaten was some bammy, and I longed for a cool drink.

"So what about this Rose Hall? Is it here in town?"

"Nah, mon. Rose Hall be outta town a bit. You can get a taxi, no problem."

"Yeah, those taxis are pretty rich. Is there a car rental place around?"

"Yah, mon. But drivin' in Jamaica not for everyone."

"I don't plan on driving across the country."

"What you want?"

"Just something to get from A to B."

Garfield thought about this and then smiled.

"I know just da ting."

CHAPTER SEVEN

"How am I going to do this in a dress?" said Danielle.

"Just hitch it up, missus," said the guy in the Rasta hat, standing by an old black Yamaha motorcycle. We were in a service garage. A small jeep was up on racks, and the guy in the Rasta hat had been changing the oil when we wandered in. Garfield had offered a series of high fives and fist bumps that looked like the handshake of a secret society and then told the guy we needed transportation. The Rasta hat had walked us over to the motorcycle. It was about the same age as me, a seventies special, and, like me, had a classic look that had gone in and out of fashion several times over the years.

Garfield nodded. "Better dan a rental car. Nowhere you can't go on a bike."

"How much per day?" I said.

The guy shrugged. "It no for rent."

I turned to Garfield and put my arms out as if to say, *What the?*

"Nah, mon," said Garfield. "He be sellin' it."

"How much?"

"Two hunnerd," said the guy.

"US dollars?"

He nodded.

"One hundred."

The guy laughed like I was Leno and slapped his thigh. "I like you, mon. Let's say one-se'nty five."

"One-fifty. And some gas."

"Okay, mon. One-fi'ty. Da tank is full."

Garfield left us to walk home, and we saddled up and took the coast road back to our hotel. The Rasta had loaned us two helmets, which I was grateful for when we were nearly sideswiped by a dozen minivans on the ride back. The doorman at the hotel wasn't too sure what to do with the bike. Most guests never left the resort, and those who did were on tours. We ended up leaving it by a royal palm beside the service road that headed into the resort, and we made for the restaurant. The buffet was over, and staff was cleaning up and prepping for the lunch trough, but they were generous enough to find us coffee and bagels. As far as breakfasts went it was more Jamaica, New York, than MoBay, Jamaica, but it filled us up. We spent the rest of the morning lying on loungers on the beach. The bartender at the beach bar asked me to repeat my order three times when I asked for cola *without* rum, but I wasn't sure what to expect at Rose Hall nor what to expect on the ride there, so I elected to keep my wits about me and stick to the soft stuff. In my mind I could see my business partner Ron back in West Palm Beach, shuddering at his desk and not knowing why. A bar on the beach with free beer would be Ron's version of a *Field of Dreams*.

Danielle disappeared during the afternoon, and I wandered the grounds for a while. It really didn't make sense that we would take on a client while on our vacation, but sometimes downtime helps you learn a little about yourself. I had come to realize that I, and my lovely partner along with me, really didn't do downtime so well. Sure, an evening on the back patio of my place on Singer Island, watching the sun beat a retreat into the mainland housing estates and the Everglades beyond, was my favorite way to end a day. But when leisure was the only point of the day, I started to get itchy feet. I thought about this for a while, and when the train of thought petered out, I did the only thing I could think of and went back to our room for a granny nap. When I woke, Danielle was sitting on the balcony, reading a paperback.

"Hey," I said. "Where'd you disappear to?"

"Just moseying around the boutique. Good snooze?"

"Vacation mode." I smiled. "I'm just going to go collect Markus from school, make sure everything's okay. You all right here?"

She looked out from the balcony, across the beach and blue water, as a catamaran glided past.

"I'll manage for an hour," she said, offering me a wink.

I took the motorbike from its spot under the palm tree, got smiles and head shakes from the doormen at the resort, and then puttered back into town. I reached the school without event and was sitting on the bike waiting when Markus appeared at the gate.

"Where you get dot, mon?"

"A guy can't walk everywhere. Hop on. I'll give you a ride."

Markus smiled wide and took the spare helmet from me. There's something about teenage boys. They can be surly as hell, but get them on a motorcycle and suddenly you're Santa. I gave the engine a good rev, attracting plenty of attention, then peeled away and sped down the potholed road toward the Swan home. I left the bike out front and walked in with Markus. His mother was inside, cooking something in that same pot, the smell of ginger and Scotch bonnets permeating the house.

"You're not going out tonight, right?" I said to Markus, making sure his mother heard me.

"Nah, mon. I got a school project to do."

I nodded and glanced at Mrs. Swan, who gave me a nod in return. I felt comfortable that Markus wouldn't sneak out without me. Despite my sense that any danger had abated, I was still being paid to do a job, and I also knew that danger had a habit of jumping out of the shadows just when you thought it had left town.

"I've been invited to a function at Rose Hall tonight. By old Mr. Winston."

I saw both Markus and his mother raise their eyebrows.

"I'd like to check him out, see what he's about. But I don't like the idea of leaving you alone. If he's the one causing you trouble, then he knows I'm helping you, and he might try something while he knows I'm not with you."

"Mista Winston no try someting in our home," said Mrs. Swan.

"How can you be sure?"

"Take a look outside," she said, turning back to her stovetop. I wandered back down the hall and stepped outside. While I'd been delivering Markus inside, half a dozen men had appeared in front of the house. They were some of the same men who had been at the impromptu party the night before and had been upset at what had happened to Markus. Now they stood guard in front of the Swan house. They noticed me and each offered a small nod, which I returned as I checked them over for weapons. I didn't see anything, which made me feel better. When weapons get introduced into a story, they have a habit of being used. I turned and went back into the kitchen.

"Those guys aren't armed, are they?" I asked Mrs. Swan.

"Wit what?"

"Anything."

"Dey not armed. Dey just gonna stand out dare like the Queen's Guards." She shook her head like she would never understand the motivations of men. Oddly, the thought of the guys standing outside made me feel better.

"Okay, I guess that helps. But it's still best if Markus stays in tonight."

Mrs. Swan turned to me. "You go to yo party. Nobody comin' in here tonight, and Markus not be goin' out."

I nodded thanks and told them I'd be back in the morning for training, and then grabbed the bike and headed back to the resort. The doorman took the bike from me and rolled it over to its new home beneath the royal palm, and I ambled through the open foyer. The whole building was designed to take advantage of the sea breezes, and it was working, as a gentle air moved through the whispering tendrils of the palm trees. There was a bar to the side that opened up to the obligatory postcard view, beach and sky and water, a head of clouds drifting in, the scent of marinara sauce wafting through as the kitchens prepped for the onslaught of the starving masses crawling up from the beaches and pool loungers, hungry for all-you-can-eat pseudo-Caribbean cuisine.

I kept moving along the path to our room. Danielle was no longer on the balcony. I dropped the helmets on the bed and watched the view for a moment. Standing in Jamaica, I was still closer to Key West than Key West was to Jacksonville, and so much of the place felt like home, yet at the same time foreign. The beaches, the tint of the sky, and the way the clouds moved unabated through the picture were the same. Even the sound of the breeze through the palms was familiar, the sound that put me to sleep most nights on Singer Island. But it was different. The sea was a different shade of blue and emerald green out beyond the reef. The air felt heavier, and the smells, even away from the jerk chicken of the kitchens, held a spice to it that was anything but Florida. A lanky guy climbed a coconut palm, using a cloth to wrap around the trunk and lever against as he walked his way up, where he hacked at the fibrous balls.

I was watching another guy on the ground catch the falling coconuts, when I heard a sound behind me. Danielle came out of the bathroom in a long dress, tropical flowers that reminded me of Gauguin, with thin straps across her tan shoulders. The dress was casual but elegant and hugged her firm, strong body like a second skin. I smiled and looked down at my palm tree-print shirt and khaki shorts.

"You trying to make me look bad?"

"Oh, you aren't going to a party in that," she said, looking me up and down.

Danielle stepped aside and revealed some clothes she had laid out on the bed. I wandered in off the balcony to inspect: a white linen shirt and simple tan trousers were on the bed. There wasn't a palm tree-print to be seen, but they looked good nevertheless.

"Where did this come from?"

"I did a little shopping. Try it on."

I washed up, tossed on some aftershave despite not shaving, and put on the clothes. They looked good, even on me. Together we looked like those island people in magazines, as if we had not a care in the world, and this casual look was as dressed up as we ever needed to be. I offered Danielle my arm.

"Shall we?"

"Why, thank you, sir."

CHAPTER EIGHT

When we arrived at Rose Hall, the valet gave us the same amused smile we had gotten earlier from the doorman at the hotel. Danielle took off her helmet and shook out her hair, and then she turned to me and ran her hands through my mass of sandy-blond locks. The valet pushed the bike away, and we took in the building. It was a stout-looking Georgian manor home, grand but showing its age. The Hall sat on top of a hill that led way down to the ocean, perhaps a half mile below. I had an idea of what the scene must have looked like when Rose Hall was in its prime, a stunning view of sprawling lawns and distant ocean that was diminished only slightly by the addition of a Hilton resort down by the water's edge.

The sun was in its last throes as we headed for the steps up to the grand door, where a dark man in top hat and tails checked our names off the guest list. We were led into a candlelit foyer flanked by rooms filled with antique furniture and roped off like a museum. Young women in white blouses and black skirts stood guard in each room, offering smiles and explanations of the room's historic contents for anyone who cared to listen. As we were ushered through, it seemed no one was taking them up on the offer, but our guide suggested we do so later.

We wandered out of the grand home into a rear garden, where a large marquee had been erected. White lights were strung on poles to lead the way. Inside the marquee we were offered champagne, which we accepted. I was still on the alert, but I didn't want to stick out by not holding a drink. A wooden floor had been laid over the grass, and tables were set up like a wedding reception was about to take place. Everyone was well dressed, but no one more so than the waitstaff. The guests ranged from linen suits with sky-blue ties to one guy in a palm tree shirt and chinos. I fell somewhere in the middle of the sartorial stakes, and Danielle matched any of the women. We wandered through the marquee toward a band playing acoustic guitars and steel drums. We were enjoying the music when I heard the voice behind me.

"Mr. Jones and Officer Castle," said Winston. We turned to see him, dressed in a tan suit, impressively cut and perfectly matching what I guessed were alligator skin boots.

"I am glad you could make it." He smiled, and I noticed his teeth had yellowed through the years. I wondered if he was a smoker.

"We are humbled by your invitation," I said, suddenly finding myself talking like someone from *Downton Abbey*. Grand old homes could have that effect on me. I was a riot when I visited Carolina tobacco plantations.

"It's a wonderful venue," said Danielle, not bothering to correct Winston on her title. Police officers and sheriff's deputies were often protective of their titles, unless it paid for people to not know the difference.

"It is a magnificent old home, is it not? Much history here. Not all of it good, but history nevertheless."

"History can be like that," I said.

Winston nodded. "Indeed, suh. You must be sure to tour the home before the evening is over." He leaned toward me as if about to share some great secret. "Especially the dungeon." He flashed the yellow smile again.

"We'll do that."

"Well, if you will excuse me, I must greet some people. I hope you enjoy yourselves." He bowed his head and turned his smile on another couple entering the big tent. Danielle and I gave each other raised eyebrows. We left the marquee and strolled around the garden in the twilight. The house was lit from within, and long, jagged shadows were cast from its walls. We stood watching the shadows play across the grass and exterior of the building.

"One of the most haunted places in the world," said a voice from behind us. We turned to see an older man in a linen jacket and trousers and pale-blue open-neck shirt.

He had swept-back hair the color of brass, and purple veins punctured his bulbous nose. Unlike all the other voices around us, his lacked the easy swing of the Jamaican patois.

"That right?" I said.

"American?" he said.

"British?" I responded, in an eloquent tit for tat.

"Of course, old boy. Arthurs is the name," he said, shaking our hands.

"Miami Jones, Danielle Castle."

"First time at Rose Hall?"

"First time in Jamaica," I said.

"Well, let me tell you about Rose Hall. The whole place was once a sugar plantation, back in the seventeen hundreds. Made a fellow called Palmer an awful lot of money. Before your countrymen made their fortunes on the backs of poor, wretched slaves, my countrymen were doing it here. Story was that old Palmer got himself a lovely English wife, by the name of Annee. That was his error. He allegedly died of, shall we say, unusual circumstances, as did her two subsequent husbands, and if you believe the stories, several lovers. It was said when she tired of a slave lover she would send him out here in the backyard to have his head lopped off, whilst watching from that second-floor bedroom up there."

"That's horrible," said Danielle.

"They didn't call her the White Witch for nothing. Folks around here believe her to be in contact with dark forces."

I felt my spine tingle, and Danielle took a step closer to me.

"Today we might suggest she had some serious mental disorders, hmm?"

"Some," I said, my eyes fixed on the shadows coming from the bedroom Arthurs had pointed out.

"Now they say her spirit haunts the old hall, and that perhaps her spirit is itself haunted by the spirits of those she killed."

"That's a sad story, Mr. Arthurs," said Danielle.

"It's all poppycock, of course. There is no evidence that any of it actually happened, at least not to those folks. But most of it probably happened at some point to someone here. Jamaica's history is not all sunny beaches and rum punch. Speaking of rum, have you been to the pub under the house?"

"There's a pub under this house?"

"One of the old storage areas, yes. It is charming old spot. I'd be happy to show you."

In a way, Arthurs reminded me of my business partner, Ron, and not just in his love for a drink. As I was pondering this, a voice called out across the lawn.

"Ladies and gen'men. Dinner be served," boomed the baritone by the marquee entrance.

"Perhaps after tea," said Arthurs, offering his arm to Danielle. She smiled and took it, and I affirmed my belief that Arthurs was Ron's long-lost English brother. Arriving back at the marquee, we were greeted by the smell of something roasted and porcine, and Arthurs directed us to a table. As we reached our destination, Cornelius Winston appeared.

"Ah, Arthurs, a pleasure as always," said Winston, with very little pleasure in his voice. "Mr. Jones, Officer Castle, I'd like you to meet Assistant Commissioner of Police Harrow and Mrs. Harrow."

A stern-looking man in a dark blue uniform shook my hand—gripping me as though he was about to place me in cuffs—and then did likewise to Danielle. Mrs. Harrow nodded politely from behind her husband's shoulder.

"I thought you'd have much to talk about over dinner, all being law enforcement folk. Well, if you'll excuse me. Enjoy your meal."

We took our seats, and exchanged introductions with the other couple that joined us, the director of *Tennis Jamaica* and his wife. I'd never heard of a Jamaican tennis player, and the words Tennis Jamaica brought forth an image of four women playing doubles before a lunch of salad and Perrier. I didn't think verbalizing that thought was prudent, and he didn't seem that chatty, so I turned to Arthurs.

"So what is it you do on the island, Mr. Arthurs?"

Arthurs grinned like the proverbial cat. "I am what you might call a man of leisure. I was formerly with Her Majesty's Foreign Office. I was posted here in Jamaica for a few years and always vowed I would return. So in lieu of the rain and a tiny garden in Kent, I came back to paradise."

I nodded. It was as good a reason as any to go somewhere. Arthurs spoke about Jamaica like Ron talked about Florida, and the idea of a familial connection popped into my head again. The interesting thing about it was that Ron had been born in Jamaica, and his father had also been a diplomat for the US Department of State, but I couldn't recall Ron ever coming back since I'd known him.

"So, Officer Castle, which department are you with in the United States?" said Harrow.

"I'm actually with the Palm Beach County Sheriff's Office."

"Oh, I see. I thought your sheriffs were known as deputies."

"Yes, Assistant Commissioner, you are correct—I am a deputy."

"I see. And what brings you to our fine island?"

"Initially, a vacation," she said. The *initially* hung in the air, and we all waited to see whether Harrow would take the bait.

"Initially? How curious." Assistant Commissioner Harrow was more a nibbler than someone prone to swallowing the bait whole.

"Yes. A friend of ours was attacked the other evening, so we are helping to ensure he doesn't come to any further harm." Danielle had her cop voice on, and she sounded like she was about to hand out a speeding ticket. Clearly something about Assistant Commissioner Harrow had her hackles up.

"A friend of yours?" said Harrow. "An American?"

"No, a local."

"And did your friend report the event to the constabulary?"

"I don't know. But I do know he seems very reluctant to offer IDs on his attackers."

"Well, Deputy, I am sure you know as well as I, without the cooperation of the victim, investigation, let alone prosecution, is most difficult. We do what we can, as I am sure you do, but just like America, there is crime in Jamaica. We fight as well as we can with the resources we have."

"I'm sure," Danielle said with a smile. It wasn't the kind of smile I ever wanted her to give me.

"And just like it is for you, it does not make our job easier having vigilantes roaming our island, taking the law into their own hands."

"Of course not. If something happens, we'll be sure to call you."

"Do that," said Harrow, and with a curt nod, he signaled the end of the conversation, the way only a superior officer can do. I figured Arthurs was going to be better for intel.

Dinner was served, a fish plate, no options, which was just fine with me. If I could see the ocean, seafood was always my go-to. In Omaha, I'd pass on the seafood buffet. Either way, the snapper in butter sauce with peppers and onions was delicious.

"So what exactly is this function in aid of?"

Arthurs sipped at a tumbler of Appleton Estate rum and picked at his snapper. "That is a good question. Let's call it a fundraiser, shall we?"

"Fundraiser for what?"

"I feared you'd ask me that, so I fear I'll have to tell you. I believe in the United States you would call it political fundraising."

"Winston is running for office?"

"Of a sort. He is currently chair of the Inter-Secondary Schools Sports Association of Jamaica, and on the board of the Jamaican Athletics Association. These are quite prestigious roles in Jamaica. As I suspect you've seen, athletics is quite the deal here on the island."

"I've noticed."

"So positions like those which Mr. Winston holds are highly prized themselves. But they are small cheese when compared to the big prize."

I could see old Arthurs enjoyed stringing out the tension in his tales, so I went with it.

"And what might that big prize be?"

"The International Olympic Committee representative. A life of first-class travel, the finest hotels, visiting sports facilities." Arthurs glanced at Assistant Commissioner Harrow and then continued. "And arranging . . .how can I put it . . .deals beneficial to Jamaican athletics." He raised his eyebrows and dipped his head to his rum. "It's quite the pork trough."

"I think it would pay you well, suh, to keep such commentary to yourself," said Harrow.

"Of course, of course," said Arthurs, winking at me. "Regardless of my baseless opinions about the luxury requirements of our sports officials, it is surely the most coveted position in Jamaican sports. And therefore the most difficult to attain. One must bring a lot to the party."

"Like money?" said Danielle.

"Well, yes, that. But more than that, a pretender to the throne must show how he would lead his kingdom into a glorious new tomorrow," he continued, taking another sip. I couldn't help feeling his story was going off the rails.

"How does he do that?" I asked.

"Winners, my boy. He produces winners. He brings the next tranche of champions under his wing, and he delivers Jamaica more gold medals."

I had more questions for Arthurs but decided to keep them to myself until I had a less public forum. An emcee, who moonlighted as the guitar player, tapped the microphone and called our attention. Cornelius Winston took the mic and thanked us for attending and for supporting Jamaican athletics. It occurred to me that Danielle and I hadn't paid to attend, and I wondered if we'd get an invoice in the mail. I figured we were supporting Jamaican athletics by making sure one of its athletes got to the starting line in one piece, and that counted for more in my book than feathering Winston's nest.

Winston asked us to charge our glasses, and he toasted Jamaica, her athletic heritage, and the Queen. I figured the last one to be the queen of England, which surprised me a little, given half the marquee's population was probably descended from slaves who had been brought to the island under the English. Regardless, the room stood and toasted Queen, country, and running, and then Winston handed the mic back to the guitar player, who broke into a soulful tune that sounded remarkably like Johnny Cash. I gave Danielle a puzzled frown.

"Yes," said Arthurs. "It is Johnny Cash. He and his wife lived close by on Cinnamon Hill. He even wrote a song about Annee Palmer, the White Witch."

Thoughts of white witches were more than I cared for, so I whispered to Danielle that I was going to seek out the little boys' room, and I made my way out into the night. Tiki torches lit the path from the marquee to the house. I wandered alone across the lawn and up into the house. The girls who were standing about when we arrived seemed to have disappeared. I wondered if they were on dinner break, when a giant of a man appeared at my side. The floorboards in the house creaked like a schooner in a squall, but the big guy had moved silently. He was a good foot above me, which pegged him at a decent seven foot. He didn't smile, and I wasn't completely sure that his face was capable of it.

"Can I help you, suh?" he said in a deep voice that fit his stature perfectly.

"Bathroom?"

"Downstairs, suh." He pointed to some stone stairs, and I nodded my thanks and headed down. The stairs were barely shoulder width, and the further down I went, the darker it got. By the time I reached the bottom, I was in near blackness. The air was a good few degrees cooler, and musty. I stepped across an uneven stone floor and brushed my hand along the wall, looking for some kind of light switch. Maybe it was the stories I had heard earlier, but I felt a presence, as if someone was in the dungeon-like space with me. I was going to speak, to ask if someone was there, but the words were sucked from me as the hefty door behind me slammed closed, dumping me into total dark. I stood for a moment, trying to get my bearings, trying to sense whether I was indeed alone, when I felt a shiver of breeze wrap around my neck like a scarf, and a voice whispered from the ether.

"*Miami . . .*"

CHAPTER NINE

"Miami," the voice said again. It was a woman's voice, with a definite Jamaican lilt even in that solitary word. I stood frozen, holding my breath, and wondered if the White Witch of Rose Hall had come to visit me. There's that willful suspension-of-disbelief thing. With the stone house, the cool dungeon, and the darkness, my brain was going along with the whole ghost thing, despite my better judgment. But then the White Witch started giving me life advice and ruined the mood.

"*Leave da boy. Leave da island,*" she whispered.

"What boy?"

"*Leave da boy. Leave da island.*"

I let a grin creep over my face. It was too dark for anyone to see it anyway. "Yeah, I hear you. But what boy are you referring to?"

There was a long pause, then: "*Da runna boy. Richmond's boy.*"

Richmond's boy. Markus. I took a moment to ponder how the White Witch knew about Markus. I supposed that there was a pretty well-connected spirit network out there. But all set-dressing to the contrary, I concluded that the voice wasn't really a ghost but rather someone under the influence of Cornelius Winston. I suppressed a chuckle at the idea of using ghost stories to scare someone away. It all seemed so damn hokey.

"Is this the White Witch?" I asked, deciding that I wasn't in imminent danger and I should have some fun with it.

"*I be Annee Palmer.*"

"Great. Annee, it's a real pleasure to meet you. Now, you've lived here—sorry—existed here for a long time. Where would you recommend as the best place for jerk chicken around town?"

Once again there was silence. Perhaps Annee was tossing over her favorite chow joints, or, more likely, whoever was trying to put the fear of God into me was scrabbling as their plan went south.

"Tell you what. You think on that, and get back to me."

I'd had enough standing in the dark talking to vapor, so I edged back along the wall until I reached the stairs. I hit the heavy door and then felt around until I found a large iron lever. With a push it clicked, and I drove the door open with my shoulder. A small set of steps led up to the main level, where the giant who had sent me down was nowhere to be seen. The girls offering tours of the various rooms had reappeared, and some partygoers had wandered inside to take in the Georgian style of the grand house. I did the opposite. I strode back out into the fresh air, glad to be out of the cellar, and I shook out my shoulders. Our table was empty, the assistant commissioner and his wife nowhere to be seen, and Arthurs and Danielle were on an impromptu dance floor in front of the band. They were playing Christopher Cross, not my kind of tune, so I took to the bar, asked for a rum, shot it down, and asked for another. I might not have believed in ghosts, but the experience still gave me the heebie-jeebies. I watched Danielle dancing with Arthurs, then the song finished, and they joined me at the bar.

"Is that rum?" said Danielle. "Don't forget we're riding a motorcycle home."

"For medicinal purposes only," I said, and I recounted my adventure in the dungeon of the house.

"Do you always make yourself so popular?" asked Arthurs.

"Usually, yes," I said. "Seriously, does this sound like something Winston might do? Invite us to a fundraiser at a haunted house to scare us off the island with spooky voices? It's like amateur hour."

"I wouldn't have given him credit for such creativity, but I guess anything's possible."

"And what about seating us with the police chief?"

"Assistant commissioner," said Danielle. "I didn't like that guy at all. If you ask me, they were trying a one-two.

Scare us off in an official capacity, then follow it up with an old-fashioned scare." Danielle looked at me. "Were you scared?"

"Honestly, I was freaked out at first. Total darkness will do that. But I wasn't buying the ghost act. It's like a *Scooby-Doo* episode, for crying out loud."

"So what should we do now?"

"I think I've had my fill of Rose Hall. I say we head back to the hotel, get some shut-eye, and make sure Markus is okay for school tomorrow."

"So you're not staying away from the kid, then?" said Arthurs.

"Not a chance," said Danielle.

I shook my head.

"Good for you," said Arthurs. "Just be careful. Ghost stories might be one thing, but in Jamaica, if they really want you away from the boy, things can get a good deal more serious, and how."

"Thanks for the advice," I said. "You staying on?"

Arthurs nodded. "I have a driver and a bottle of someone else's top-drawer rum." He winked us a farewell, and we headed out of the marquee. I didn't fancy going through the house, so we walked around the side. When the valet saw us coming, he dashed forward with our helmets and then retrieved the bike.

"G'night, suh," he said.

I thanked him and squeezed ten US dollars in his hand, and then got on the bike. There were a number of other cars being valeted, and we followed a sedan down the hill to the main road, where the car turned into the darkness to the right, and we turned into the darkness to the left.

CHAPTER TEN

I took the ride easy, having had a couple rum shots, and we didn't see much traffic. The headlight on the bike was more a suggestion, and the road had its fair share of potholes. I heard the engine of a vehicle coming from behind, and I assumed it was another guest from Rose Hall, making their way back into MoBay. We passed a resort, spotlights pasting an eerie glow on the palm trees out the front, and then we moved on to a dark stretch, no doubt a rocky part of the coastline not conducive to a resort beach, so left undeveloped. I saw the headlights grow larger in my mirrors, and I moved to the side of the road to let the faster vehicle pass. As it reached us I saw it was a minivan, equally beaten as every other one, and for a moment I was surprised that a guest at the kind of function we had just attended would be going home in such a van. A dark face peered out of the open window, but I saw no features, no eyes, no smile. The van moved ahead a little. Then it swerved.

The van shot violently to the side, almost taking us out. But the driver had assumed our speed to be greater than it was, and despite my rums, I had time to brake and pull in behind the van. Just as suddenly as it had jerked to the side, the driver hit the skids, and the van fishtailed in front of us. In the fraction of a second I had to think about it, I was convinced we were going to run right into the back of the van, so I yanked the bike into the darkness beside the road. The headlight gave us a preview of a grassy channel, and I felt Danielle tighten her grip around my waist, no doubt sensing that things were about to get dicey. The bike left the road, and I pulled up on the handlebars, lifting the front wheel slightly, and we dropped several feet down into the channel. The landing was smoother than I expected, then the front wheel hit some thick grass that wrapped around the spokes, and the bike lost all momentum. Unfortunately, we didn't. I was launched over the handlebars, Danielle clinging to my back like a baby monkey on its mama. As we fell toward the ground, we separated and I tucked, trying to roll as best as I could on impact.

I took the hit on my shoulder, softened by the long grass, then I flipped over, legs up in the air, like an out-of-control gymnast, and I dropped over and hit the ground flat out on my stomach. I took a second to brush away the shock, and then I took a quick inventory. Adrenaline was keeping the pain at bay, but I felt for breaks and found none. I lifted my face up from the grass and looked for Danielle. All I saw was more grass. I heard the van, which had taken some time to stop, backing up. For a moment I wondered if they had hit an animal, causing them to swerve and brake. Then a pair of feet landed in front of me.

"You okay?" whispered Danielle, laying her hands on my shoulders. She had discarded or lost her helmet.

"Yeah, I think so. You?"

"Yes. Thank goodness for grass, hey?" She looked up, alert, as if she had just bounced off a bed, rather than been thrown over the handlebars of a motorcycle.

"They're coming back," she said.

I pulled up onto my hands and knees. "Was that an accident?"

"What do you think?" she said, but her tone told me she had no doubt it was not. "Come on, get up."

We stood, staying crouched, and moved to the back of the channel, where we heard the doors on the van open and then slam shut. The headlights of the van gave us some vision, and three silhouettes appeared above us. They were looking down into darkness, so one of them lit a flashlight and scanned the channel until he found us.

"Hello," said one of the men, an incongruent joviality in his voice. The flashlight guy stayed on the road, spotlighting us, and the other two clambered down the embankment into the channel of grass. Even in silhouette it was clear they carried big clubs, like baseball bats on steroids. To my dismay I realized they both held cricket bats, big wide chunks of lumber with handles. The two men came toward us. The angle of the channel made it impossible for them to move side by side, so one came before the other. I felt Danielle behind me, and she put her hand on my shoulder.

"What do you think?" I whispered.

"You're going to have to take one for the team."

We waited for them to get closer, just out of reach of their big bats, and then we moved. I charged like a blocker on a football field, paving the way for my running back behind me. The first guy saw me coming in the spotlight, and he pulled his bat back and swung. I'd been hit by sports equipment before. It's surprising how many thugs like sports equipment as weapons. I'd copped baseball bats, hockey sticks, even bowling balls. None of them were fun, but at least those experiences had taught me a thing or two that might prove useful now. Plus I had the added benefit of still wearing my helmet.

The cricket bat came down hard, and I moved with it, down and away, turning and tucking my head to hopefully save myself from a smashed cheekbone. The bat connected across my shoulder blades, pain searing down my spine. But it was a glancing blow, knocking me forward into the grass but at least not splitting me in half. The follow-through of the swing brought the bat down with me, and that was when Danielle sprang into action. She charged—this I knew because she stepped on my butt as she ran forward, trying to get to the guy before he could raise his bat again.

She made it. I heard the sound of a fist connecting with a nose, a sickening, crunching sound, and I rolled onto my back to see the guy stagger but not go down. Danielle was well trained, fit and strong, but she wasn't taking down a big guy with one punch. But then that wasn't her plan. The guy put one hand to his bloody nose, a natural reaction to one's face exploding in a mass of blood and snot, and as he did, Danielle went for the bat. She grabbed it midshaft, in the thick part, and wrenched it up, pulling the handle out of the guy's hand. He must have felt it go and tried to regather, leaning away in case she swung at him. But she didn't swing. She used as little movement as possible and thrust the bat like a pool cue, crashing the end point of the handle into the guy's crotch. He gave a muffled yelp, oddly more noise than he had made when his nose was broken, and he bent over. That gave Danielle the time to flip the bat through the air, like a baton twirler, catching the handle, winding up and swinging for the bleachers, or whatever one swings for when playing cricket. The wide chunk of wood clocked the guy in the chin, and his head snapped up, and then he fell backward like a giant redwood meeting its end.

The second guy watched from behind, powerless to intervene, but now he held out his bat, down in front, like a Jedi knight. I thought I caught a smile form in the edges of the flashlight's beam. Danielle raised her bat up, across her shoulder like a baseball batter. The guy took a small step forward. Despite his buddy's demise, he was clearly confident he could take this skinny little woman in a sword fight of sorts. But Danielle wasn't about to parry with him. She slowly dropped the bat, down behind her back, elbows up. The guy held his bat out front but stayed out of range. Then Danielle jagged her elbows down, propelling her bat over her shoulders in a chopping motion, and let it go. The bat flew from flashlight to darkness, impossible to track with any accuracy and probably so fast it didn't matter anyway. It spun like a Seminole tomahawk, over itself, until it connected with the head of the second guy, and he dropped like a skydiver with no chute.

Danielle jumped forward to make sure the guy wasn't coming back for more, but I was pretty confident based on the sound alone that he wasn't waking up anytime soon. The flashlight followed her, and she kneeled by the fallen guy. I took the moment of darkness to get up and use the grass to pull myself out of the channel. The guy on the road was flicking the light between his two buddies, probably in shock. He collected himself and realized that discretion was the better part of valor, and he turned to run back to the van. Only he turned straight into me. His mouth dropped open as if I had materialized out of nothing, his eyes went wide, and he dropped the flashlight.

"The White Witch says hi," I said, then I pushed him backward, and he fell down into the channel. I grabbed the flashlight and found Danielle pulling herself out of the grass, and I helped her up onto the road.

"You okay?"

She nodded, but was shaking. "Think I need a rum," she said.

I hugged her gently, sure her body had to be hurting as much as mine. Then we heard the third guy call from down in the channel.

"You kilt dem!"

"They're not dead," said Danielle. "They just won't be getting up for a while. You prop them up, they'll be fine." Then she turned to me. "So, that rum?"

"The bike?"

"I'm not trying to fish a motorcycle out of there," she said. "And I lost my shoes, so I'm not walking back. I'm sure they won't mind if we borrow their van."

I threw the flashlight into the scrub and tossed my helmet down in the general direction of the motorcycle. Then we got in the van, and I piloted us home. I pulled into the front of the resort, we gingerly got out, and I tossed the keys to the valet.

"It's a loaner. See that it gets back to its home, will you?"

CHAPTER ELEVEN

The morning dawned like another postcard, cloudless and mild. My shoulders still ached despite half a dozen ibuprofen, and Danielle had a nasty purple bruise along the triceps on her right arm, but we were glad to be done with our adventures at Rose Hall. Danielle suggested a hot tub, so we went down to the pool and sat boiling like a couple of lobsters. The pool area was like a land grab in the Old West, people claiming loungers with towels in the predawn darkness before retreating back to their rooms. The hot tub loosened up my muscles some, and once we were sufficiently cooked we went back to our room. I was feeling particularly feisty despite, or maybe because of, my beating, so I collected all the towels off the vacant loungers and dropped them in the used towel bin as we left. Danielle just shook her head and smiled.

Markus didn't have an early training session, so we were able to grab a plate of tropical fruit at the breakfast buffet. Then we went to the doorman and asked for a minivan into town. I had to chalk up the motorcycle as a bad investment. The van took us to the Swan home, but when I tried to pay, the guy gave a shake of the head.

"You keep dot boy safe."

I nodded and said that was the plan, and then we collected Markus and walked to school. It appeared that news of us arriving back at the hotel in someone else's van had spread through the grapevine, and the rest of the story had been pieced together. As a result, Markus seemed more impressed with us than he was before, as if he hadn't been convinced we would actually protect him, if push came to shove. We dropped him at the school gate, and then I let out a deep breath and looked at Danielle as if to say, *Well, what now?*

"Let's get a coffee. I want to go see our esteemed assistant commissioner, and I am betting he's not in the office this early."

Danielle was right about that. We ventured down to the constabulary offices, a featureless, squat building behind wire fencing, at about nine thirty, and we were sitting in the lobby for half an hour when Harrow marched in. He didn't look overjoyed to see us.

"Mr. Jones, Deputy Castle, what can I do for you?"

"We'd like to report a traffic incident," said Danielle.

"I am sure the desk officer can help you with that."

"And an attempted murder."

Now Harrow frowned. "That's quite the accusation."

"It is. Shall we document it?" said Danielle. She was standing tall and clearly in no mood for Harrow's prevarication. But we all knew that now she had made the statement, Harrow had to at least hear her out.

"My office."

His office turned out to be a large space with walls that had been painted white a couple of decades earlier. Slow-moving ceiling fans shifted air around that smelled like cinnamon. Harrow sat behind his large but plain desk and invited us to sit opposite.

"Would you like to make a formal complaint?" said Harrow.

"I don't know," said Danielle. "Will it do any good?"

"Excuse me? Deputy, I don't know how you converse with your superiors in Palm Beach, but here we expect a greater level of respect than what you are showing."

"In Palm Beach we earn respect, we don't expect it. That being said, we already told you about an assault that you suggested was a funding issue, so I am just trying to ascertain if tourists being driven off the road and beaten with cricket bats falls into the same category or if we should contact the US embassy."

Harrow took a shallow breath that seemed more for show than for air and steepled his fingers together.

"Your embassy is in Kingston, at the other end of the island. Regardless, I assure you we take all matters regarding tourist safety very seriously. So why don't you describe the events for me?"

Danielle gave a law enforcement version of the previous night's adventures—just the facts, ma'am. Words like *assailants* and *brandishing* and *deadly force.* She left out my ghost story, which seemed the prudent move.

"So how did you get back to your hotel?" said Harrow, looking between Danielle and me.

"In the van," I said.

He frowned. "You stole their van?"

"They suggested we could borrow it, and we asked the valet to see that it was returned."

"Well, it seems you do know how to attract trouble."

I couldn't debate that point, but I wasn't sure that was what Danielle wanted to hear.

"We can take matters forward, if you wish to make your complaint formal," said Harrow.

"I just gave it to the assistant commissioner. How much more formal does it get?" Danielle frowned. She was really bruising for a fight, and I wasn't convinced she wouldn't leap across the desk at Harrow.

"If you wish to make it in *writing*," said the assistant commissioner. "We have procedures. But I will offer a pound's worth of advice for a penny. You are guests here on our island, *temporarily*. You have come to avail yourself of our resort hospitality, and you have chosen to forgo such hospitality and venture into matters that should not concern you. Local matters. Now, Jamaica can be a dangerous place. Beautiful but dangerous. It does not serve you to disrespect a man like Mr. Winston. If I came to your country and made vicious accusations against your president, how welcome do you think I'd be?"

My guess was in parts of Florida that would earn you a street parade, but I decided to keep that to myself.

"So my advice to you is to be thankful you suffered no serious injury, and enjoy the rest of your vacation in the safety of your resort."

Danielle gave Harrow a steely look, which I was surprised to see dissolve into a soft smile. It was like a switch had flicked inside her, and it was seriously Stepford.

"Assistant Commissioner, I apologize. We did come here to enjoy a relaxing vacation, and we have, as you rightly point out, strayed from our purpose. I am sorry to have wasted your time."

Danielle stood, and I followed suit. The assistant commissioner didn't get up. Danielle thanked him again, I gave a nod, and we left. I waited until we were on the steps of the building before I spoke.

"Okay, that was weird. You just giving up now?"

"Hell, no," said Danielle, with a look that might have turned a lesser man to stone. She shot the look back at the constabulary building. "He's the worst kind of cop. We've got them at home too. Jaded, maybe corrupt."

"You spend enough time swimming against the tide, maybe it wears you out," I said, playing devil's advocate for reasons I didn't understand.

"No, you swim upstream, it brings out your character. You make it, or you don't, because of who you are." She turned back to me, the look gone. "You know when I went to the law enforcement leadership conference in

Atlanta? I met plenty of high-ranking people who'd been in as long as Harrow. But they hadn't given up. If anything, the fight made them more determined. I'm sure not all cops here are like him. I'm sure there a plenty who give a damn."

"I give a damn," said a voice from behind us. We snapped around to see a girl standing on the steps who appeared all of sixteen years old, dressed in a dark blue police uniform that looked like a Halloween costume on her.

"And you are?" I asked.

"Corporal Lucia Tellis, Jamaican Constabulary Force."

"Corporal? What are you, twelve years old?"

"I'm twenty-four, suh."

I noted she had an accent, but it wasn't nearly as pronounced as some. "Twenty-four? If you say so."

"What do you give a damn about, Corporal?" asked Danielle.

"I give a damn about the JCF motto, ma'am."

"And what is your motto?"

"Serve, protect, and reassure."

"And what about your boss, the assistant commissioner?"

"Between you and me, ma'am, he's not exactly my role model."

Danielle smiled. "I like you, Corporal. My name is Deputy Danielle Castle. This is Miami Jones."

"Yes, ma'am. I know. I know all about it. And I want to help."

CHAPTER TWELVE

Corporal Lucia Tellis took us to a small coffee shop a few blocks from the police station. She had ebony skin that glowed in the sunshine, smooth as a bowling ball, and her frame was delicate, like fine china. Her eyes told another story altogether. We were the only people in the coffee shop, save the woman who had been wiping the grime from the front windows before following us in and bringing us coffee.

"You know we produce some of the best coffee in the world, right here in Jamaica," said Corporal Tellis, and she earned a beaming smile from the woman, who was pouring the coffee from a large pewter pot. We all took a sip and nodded our approval to the woman, who smiled again and then retreated behind her small counter.

"So, Lucia, that's a nice name. Are you named after the island Saint Lucia?" asked Danielle.

"I'm named for the saint after which the island is named."

It was a nice name, and the coffee was fine, but after wasting the morning on Assistant Commissioner Harrow, I was itching to get to the point. "Corporal, what's the deal with your assistant commissioner?"

Tellis didn't miss a beat. "You have to understand, not everything in Jamaica is like the tourist brochures."

"We kind of picked up on that."

"Like many islands in the West Indies, we are both rich and poor, and the difference between the two is great. And with such disparity comes disruption."

She was well-spoken, and I found myself impressed by her. It occurred to me that I had assumed she wouldn't be. That everyone on the island would have the laid-back attitude, and the singsong speech, and that the poverty I had seen meant a lack of education. I felt bad about having made the assumption. After all, I worked in Palm Beach, one of the richest places on the planet, and it was proven to me every day that wealth did not necessarily equal intellect.

"What do you mean by disruption?" asked Danielle, sipping her strong black coffee.

"Excuse me, I sound like a politician. I mean crime, Deputy. People who have nothing often resort to crime."

"People who have everything do it too, trust me," I said.

"Of course, but it is different. In Jamaica, we have one of the highest homicide rates in the world. There are drug problems. Not just the ganja, but we are also used by cartels in South America as a trafficking point into America. That brings its own violence. And we don't have the budgets to fight it. The rich choose to hide from it, in gated communities or in resorts, and as long as they are not affected, all we can do is stem the tide. We have no power to stop it."

"You don't seem ready to give up, Corporal," said Danielle.

"No, ma'am. I am not. I am not a fool, I don't claim it to be easy, but we can do it. Any organization gets its energy from the top. A dynamic leader results in a dynamic rank and file. Did you know our new commissioner is the first ever to have a PhD in criminology? He got it in your country. He is the new model. Integrity and energy."

"Unlike Assistant Commissioner Harrow," I said.

"Yes, unlike him. He is the old school. Using privilege to insulate himself rather than to help others."

"He's a cliché. And he's not the first one we've run into. Do you know what happened to us last night, Corporal?" I asked.

"Yes, suh, I do. My cousin works at your resort. You were run off the road?"

"We were, but that I can handle. It was being attacked with cricket bats that didn't fill me with joy."

A sorrowful look washed over the corporal's face, like she took personal responsibility for us having a less than stellar opinion of her homeland.

"And it happened directly after we left the event at Rose Hall. An event hosted by Cornelius Winston. An event during which I was warned off helping Markus Swan."

Tellis sipped her coffee but remained silent.

"So it seems a little more than laziness that your assistant commissioner, who we met at the party, would be less than interested in investigating an attack on us. Given, as you say, we are the very tourist dollars that Jamaica depends on."

The corporal sipped her coffee, then gently placed the mug down and lifted her chin to me. "Mr. Winston is an unusually powerful man."

"Unusually?" said Danielle.

Tellis nodded. "Yes. He is a powerful man in Jamaica, for certain. He has many business interests, some of which are not exactly legal, but many of which now are. His businesses have become more legitimate over time."

"So how is he unusual?" I repeated.

"You must understand, that for these men, they are older, so they are perhaps considering their mortality, their legacy. Of course, they could all become philanthropists, but they are not the sort of men to let their legacies get in the way of their lifestyles. Rather, one should complement the other." She sipped her coffee and continued.

"Mr. Winston is an important figure in Jamaican athletics. This is a considerable deal in Jamaica, where sports, especially running, are held in the highest regard.

But he is not at the top of the totem, nor do his responsibilities give him much leverage outside the region. But for some reason, he does have quite a profile abroad. He is often in the company of influential people in other countries, like America or Britain. He has quite the international network for a man with no international position."

"What does that mean, Corporal?" asked Danielle.

"I don't know," she said. "All I can tell you is that men like Assistant Commissioner Harrow might benefit from Mr. Winston's activities. So he has an incentive to assist Mr. Winston and not you. What that incentive is, I do not know."

Maybe she didn't know, but I knew. Arthurs, the old Englishman at the Rose Hall function, had told me as much. Winston was making a play for an IOC role. And I could see how an international network might be helpful in gaining such a position. I could also see how a man in that position might need security advice on international venues, and how that perk might be attractive to an old cop sitting in a cinderblock building in MoBay. I resolved to keep these tidbits to myself until I felt it was necessary to share with the young officer.

"So, Corporal, we all agree no one will help us," I said. "But we do this for a living. We'll cope."

"Yes, suh. I don't mean to suggest otherwise. But the two of you . . ." She leaned back and looked me up and down, then did the same to Danielle. "No offense, suh, but you don't exactly blend in here. I knew about your accident last night before you woke up this morning. If I have eyes and ears about, Assistant Commissioner Harrow does too. Same for Mr. Winston."

It was a fair point. With my sandy hair and predilection for palm tree-print shirts, and Danielle looking like a Nike model with a few years of Krav Maga under her belt, we didn't exactly meld into the background anywhere in Montego Bay.

"No offense taken, Corporal," I said. "Your point is well made. So what do you suggest?"

"I can help you. I know most of the gangs that do occasional work for Mr. Winston. If you can get an ID from Markus Swan, I can track down who attacked him. And that may well lead to whoever attacked you."

"And confirm who hired them," said Danielle.

"Precisely, Deputy."

"I'm on vacation. Call me Danielle."

"All right, Danielle. Please call me Lucia." She turned her gaze on me. She was pretty, but that wasn't the most arresting thing about her. It was the determination in her eyes that grabbed me.

"So what say you?"

"All right, Corporal. We could use your help. We'll chat with Markus, see what we can get out of him."

CHAPTER THIRTEEN

Lucia left us in the coffee shop to walk back to the police station and returned with a clean, almost-new-looking Suzuki Jimny in JCF livery. It was a toy model of an SUV, two doors and not a lot of leg room in the back, but it beat walking. Lucia made a call en route and discovered that our motorcycle and helmets had been retrieved from the channel and were presently sitting in the very workshop where we had purchased the bike in the first place. I wasn't too keen on getting run off the road again, so we left it where it was and took our police escort to the Swan residence.

We left Lucia to return the car and knocked on the door. I heard a call of *come in*, so did just that. Mrs. Swan was in her usual spot, boiling something or other on the stove, and she gave her usual frown as we entered.

"Markus is fine," said Danielle. "He's at school."

I saw the frown loosen some, and she nodded for us to sit at the table. She offered us tea, which we declined, still full on coffee.

"Mrs. Swan, do you have any clue who attacked Markus?" I said.

"You was dare," she said. "'Ow would I know?"

"I just thought Markus may have said something."

"No, suh. Markus don say nuttin'. But I don need no hearin' to know it was Mr. Winston behind it."

"What makes you say that, ma'am?"

"He's a bod man."

"Maybe, but I've been wondering. If he's so powerful in the athletic community, and he's willing to go so far as to injure Markus in order to basically conscript him, then why not just go with him? Why not accept his help instead of the help of some joker who isn't even in Jamaica? What's Richmond got that Winston doesn't?"

"Pfft," she said, shaking her head. "Richmond. He no shinin' light, dot I tell ya."

"So why let him help Markus?"

Her shoulders sagged, and she turned and poured some water into a kettle, which she put on the stovetop. Then she joined us at the table.

"Mista Jones, somebody got to help. We don got da money to buy fancy shoes and da like."

"I understand that, ma'am. So why not go with Winston? I'm sure he has access to plenty of Nikes."

Her face softened, almost sad to look at, and for the first time I could see the woman she had been, before life wore her down. The kettle blew its siren call, and she stood and made a solitary cup of tea, then she returned to sit with us.

"My husband, Mista Jones, was a cricketer. He could run too, dot for sure, and dot is how he come to the eye of Cornelius Winston. Mr. Winston was not such the big mon as he be now, but he knew what he wanted, even den."

"And what do you think he wanted?" asked Danielle.

"He want control. He want power." She looked into her tea, and then up at Danielle. "He want my husband." I watched her sip her drink, searching for words or canvassing memories. "Mr. Winston want my husband to run for him. My husband tell 'im no, he want to play cricket. Den Mista Winston want my husband to play cricket for him, to throw matches dot Mr. Winston want to bet on. My husband refuse, and he get beaten. Again and again. Den Mista Winston threaten me, threaten our boy, Markus."

She took another drink and looked into the mug. For a moment I thought she might shed a tear, but it never came.

"One night, men came. Dey held me and my baby boy. Dey was going to do tings, bod tings. You know?" Mrs. Swan looked at Danielle, who nodded.

"My husband come home, find dees mon, and he fight dem. He kill one a dem. Kill 'im dead. Da udder mon run away. Den we hear, the police, dey gonna take my husband away to jail. He cannot do dot, so I tell him run. So he run. He run away."

"Where did he go?" asked Danielle.

Mrs. Swan shook her head. "I don know. I tell 'im, never call, never write, or dey find you. So he never did."

"Never?" Danielle raised her eyebrows. Mrs. Swan glanced at her like she was going to share something, but she dropped her eyes.

"No, never."

We sat in silence for a time, each in our own thoughts. My head was with Markus, growing up without a father, knowing or not knowing about why he left, why he wasn't there to take his boy to those early morning training sessions, to watch him run like the wind. I was at college when my dad died, although I lost him years before when my mother surrendered to the cancer. In a lot of ways he had let me down when I needed him most, so I couldn't wait to leave, to run from Connecticut and never go back. Baseball and football took me to college in Florida, then baseball took me to California and back to Florida, and I landed with a new mentor in the late, great Lenny Cox and a new direction in life. And it wasn't until I was back in South Florida, the baseball career come and gone, that I realized that I had let my dad down every bit as much as he had me. And I wondered at what thoughts were coursing through Markus's mind. Without a father figure to bounce our thoughts off, our minds have a nasty habit of turning on us. Which gave me an idea, and I unfurled myself from my seat.

"I'm just going to step outside and make a call," I said.

Danielle nodded.

Mrs. Swan did not.

CHAPTER FOURTEEN

I wandered outside, where the breeze had picked up and clouds gathered around the mountaintops like old men around a bar. I took out my phone and called West Palm Beach. The number rang three times before it was answered.

"LCI," said Lizzy, my office manager. When Lenny Cox, the founder of the firm, died, he left me the business, and it was suggested that I change the name from Lenny Cox Investigations to something more apropos. But we already had the stationery, so I declined.

"Lizzy, it's me."

"Why are you calling here?" Lizzy was my self-appointed guardian angel. She seemed to see her role as being in charge of both my religious salvation, which was a task as destined for failure as an antidevelopment politician in Florida, and in conjunction with Danielle, my health and work/life. The latter role manifested itself in all kinds of torture, not limited to but including removal of all the liquor from my office during one particularly zealous cleanse. Lizzy had ordered me to not call while on vacation and had almost commandeered my phone for the duration.

"I just need to talk to Ron."

"No, you don't."

"It's not a work thing, honest." I felt a small twinge of guilt about lying to a devout Christian but figured I could deal with any given deity. A month of stony silence from Lizzy was too much to bear.

"He's not here."

"Is he at Cassandra's?"

"No."

"Thanks, Lizzy."

"Are you at least having a good time?"

"It's a blast. Like Florida, without the snowbirds."

"Don't drink too much. I know what those all-inclusive resorts can be like."

"You do?"

"I've heard. Say hi to Danielle."

"Will do. I'll see you in a few days."

I hung up and dialed another number. It rang and rang again, but I knew it wouldn't go to voicemail.

"What?" answered the gruff voice at the other end.

"Mick, it's Miami."

"This can't wait til you get here?"

"I'm on vacation, Mick. In Jamaica."

"Why?"

It was a fair point. I lived by the water, currently drove a convertible Porsche around in the sunshine, and spent my down hours sharing a few drinks in the outdoor bar of Mick's place, Longboard Kelly's. Except for the jerk chicken, Jamaica really wasn't all that different.

"Is Ron there?"

"Do cats taste like rabbit?"

I didn't bother trying to respond to that, given I ate so many of my meals out of Mick's kitchen. Instead I listened to the scratch and bang on the line as Mick took the phone to the bar. I could picture Ron, my business partner, drinking partner, and best bud, sitting under the palapa shade on his stool, silver mane shining in the afternoon light, chatting with Muriel the barmaid and just being, the way one can in Florida.

"Miami, how goes my birthplace?" Being born in Jamaica meant Ron could never be president, but he still held onto the hope that his beloved Florida would break away from the union and form its own republic, complete with daily state-mandated happy hours.

"Hey, Ron. It's more like Florida than I'd have given credit."

"Why do I get the feeling you've not being lying on the beach?"

"We did that. The other day."

"And since then? What trouble have you found?" I could hear the smile in his voice.

I gave him the abridged version of our vacation, from the assault in the alley to Markus and his benefactor,

Richmond, and Winston and Rose Hall and getting run off the road and attacked with cricket bats.

"So par for the course," said Ron.

"Yeah, even including the complete apathy of the local cops. If these thugs are connected to Winston, then I don't know how we get anywhere, because the local cops are completely in his pocket. Except for one young officer, and I don't know how much she can help."

"Can I advise going back to your resort and keeping your head down?"

"You sound like the assistant commissioner. But I'm not worried about me and Danielle. I'm thinking more long term. This kid can really run, and all this corruption might not only prevent him from running—it might end a lot worse than that."

I heard Ron take a sip of what I was sure was a beer.

"Well, I'm afraid I'm not that well connected in Jamaica anymore, and anyone I do know is in Kingston. MoBay was never really my haunt. But there is one avenue you might pursue."

"And that is?"

"The State Department."

"We thought of that, but the embassy is in Kingston. It's nowhere near here."

"True, but I'm pretty sure there's a US consulate in Montego Bay. You and Danielle are US citizens who have been assaulted. If the cops won't help, maybe the consulate will."

"A consulate? Worth a shot. But I'm not sure how that helps Markus."

"You say he can run? Really run?"

"Dead fast, as they say here."

"Then there's one other idea. Get him out. Get him away from the bad influences."

"I've been thinking about that."

"Are his grades okay?"

"Think so."

"You still know the athletic director at UM, don't you?"

I nodded to myself. "I do."

"They offer scholarships for running?"

"I suppose so."

"So maybe he could run his way into an education."

"Yeah, that's an idea. Thanks, Ron. Keep my seat warm."

"This is Florida, my friend. That's what the sunshine is for."

I smiled and hung up, then looked once more to the mountains behind me, green turning to black in the shadow of the clouds. Perhaps Ron was right. Perhaps I could get Markus away from his problems, away from a fate like that of his father. The question was, could he really run as fast as he needed to?

CHAPTER FIFTEEN

The men at the athletics track were gathered under their canvas pop-up shade, but unlike the previous morning, it was actually earning its keep. We met Markus at the school gate and walked with him to the track, where he warmed up with his teammates. I watched the men under the shade, still assessing the boys like livestock, and I couldn't help but think of what Mrs. Swan had told us about her husband being pushed to throw cricket matches.

The boys did some laps around the long grass, their coaches barking in the patois that I couldn't decipher. When they came to line up again to run some sprints, the men in the shade stood, the timekeeper with the stopwatch took his place, and Danielle grabbed my phone and flicked it on to video record the run. I stood by the guy keeping time, using my watch to keep time of my own. Markus was jogging up and down on his toes, sending small plumes of dust into the air.

The head coach wandered down to the finish line with his air horn, called the boys to be ready, and held the canister in the air. Markus bent down, looking like he was in motion just by the way he held himself, and waited for the blast. The coach pressed his button, and the sound of a foghorn pierced the afternoon sunshine. All eyes were on the boys, a mishmash of colored singlets and dark flailing limbs. Markus started as he had the last time, slow out of the blocks, but by the time he was fully upright, he was a quarter of the way done and level with the fastest starter. By the three-quarter mark, he had the thing won. He hit the line in a blur, and I punched my stopwatch and looked at it, and then glanced up at the other timing guy, who was looking at me.

"Ten thirty-five?" I said.

The other guy smiled wide and glanced at his own watch. "Yah, mon," he said, nodding and turning to the men under the shade. I looked at Danielle.

"You get that?" I said.

She nodded. "Yep. He's quick."

"Dead fast," I said, taking my phone and looking up a number. Danielle turned her attention to Markus, who was laughing with some friends. I saw him look our way, and Danielle nodded. Markus grinned.

I placed my call and wandered away from the fence, looking around as I watched for any appearance of Cornelius Winston.

"University of Miami Athletic Department," said the voice on the other end.

"Aaron Katz's office, please." I waited as the call was transferred, and I repeated my request to Katz's assistant.

"May I ask who is calling?"

"Tell him it's Miami Jones."

Again I waited, and the air horn blew again and startled me. I turned to see another group of boys charging down the dry running track.

"Jones?"

"Hey, Aaron," I said distractedly, watching the race finish. From the look of the timekeeper, it wasn't anything special.

"Sorry, Aaron. How are things?"

"Busy, as always. What can I do you for?"

"Do you guys do athletic scholarships?"

Katz laughed. "You been drinking? What do you think paid your way through college?"

"No, I don't mean football. I mean athletics, as in track. Running, specifically."

"Sure we do. Why, your beach runs improving?"

"They are, as it happens, smart guy. But no, I'm talking about a kid. In Jamaica."

"Okay. Sure, we've had a few study here. They produce more than their share of fast runners."

"They do. I'm in Jamaica now, and I've met a kid who is quick. Seriously quick from what I can tell."

"How quick is quick?"

"Couple minutes ago he ran a hundred in ten thirty-five, on a dirt-and-grass track with no spikes."

"Decent. Our scholarship consideration standard is ten fifty."

"I've got video. You want to see it?"

"Sure, send it through. I make no promises, but I'll share it with the track coach and see what he says."

"It's coming your way."

"Right on. I got another call. I'll catch you."

I hung up, and Danielle came over and helped me fire the video off in an email to Katz. Markus didn't run again, and the coach sent him and couple of other boys to practice their starts. Danielle and I leaned on the wire fence and watched. A practice session of cricket started up in the middle of the field. The bats were familiar, the game not so much. One big guy wandered away from the middle with a red ball in his hand, and then he turned and sprinted back. When he got about the length of the pitcher's mound from home plate he swung his arm high over his head and flung the ball at the batter, who was wearing some kind of padding on his legs but no helmet. The ball bounced halfway to the batter, cutting viciously up at the batter's face, where he simply rocked back and hit the ball to the side, perpendicular to the stretch of hard-packed dirt between the batter and the pitcher. It was like smashing a foul ball on purpose, except that it seemed to be totally within the rules, as he took off running toward the pitcher.

"You like cricket?"

I turned to see Garfield, Markus's cousin, joining us against the fence.

"That guy just pitched one that bounced at the batter's head."

"He no pitcha, he da bowler."

"Bowler, whatever. You guys don't wear helmets?"

"Only for da fast bowling."

It looked plenty quick to me, so I turned from the imminent bloodshed to Garfield. "You play, Garfield?"

"Sure, I play."

"That's right, you said you were named after a cricket player."

"No a cricketer, da cricketer. Da best ever, Suh Garfield Sobers."

"He was good?"

Garfield made a *pfft* sound that suggested my question was redundant. We heard another crack off the bat, and a fielder ran away, chasing the ball along the grass.

"Do you know what happened to Markus's dad?" I said, not bothering with a time-wasting segue.

Garfield frowned and shuffled his feet.

"You best talk to Mama Swan 'bout dot."

"I did. She told me. I want to know if you know."

He nodded. "I know."

"So that's why he's not with Winston."

"Dot's why, yes, suh."

"What do you think she would say if there was a chance he could get into a US college, fully paid for?"

"I tink she'd give you her arms to get Markus outta dis," he said, looking around at the patchy grass field.

"What about you?" said Danielle.

"Me?" Garfield smiled ruefully. "I don get into no trouble, an' I no atlete, so nobody cause me no problem. I do my work. I live in paradise, mon." He nodded. "You tink he can get into university?"

"I don't know yet," I said. "I'm making some inquiries. But there's one other thing. I need to know who the guys were, the ones that attacked Markus?"

"You saw dem."

"We did, but two guys and a girl isn't a very helpful description. I think he knows exactly who they were."

"Dare was a girl?"

"Yeah, a mean piece of work. She had tattoos on her chest."

"What tattoos?"

"Stars, I guess, maybe five or six, right here." I pointed to my chest, just below my Adam's apple.

Garfield nodded and glanced toward the field.

"Dis won't hurt Markus?"

"No, Garfield. It will help him. And anyone else who is getting hurt by these thugs."

"Oh, dey no *tugs*, Mista Miami. Dey Rastas who lost *dare* way. Dey do work fo' Mr. Winston all right, on da side."

"On the side of what?" said Danielle.

"Mostly dey just grow ganja."

"They grow marijuana?" she said.

"Yes, ma'am."

"How much?"

"A bit."

"Where?"

Garfield turned his gaze to the mountains behind us, thick with foliage, tall and dripping with moisture from the daily gathering of white clouds.

"We need names, Garfield," I said.

He looked at me and lost his genial face, like the skin had tightened on his bones.

"I give you names, suh. But dis come back to hurt my cousin, you can no get off dis island fast enough. You got dot?"

CHAPTER SIXTEEN

The next morning we escorted Markus to school. He seemed to be getting used to our company, and although it wasn't necessarily the beginning of a beautiful friendship, it wasn't openly hostile either, and that I could live with. We left him at the gate and wandered back into town to visit the garage where we had bought the motorcycle. The guy who owned the shop smiled wide and handed us the same helmets, which I hoped were not damaged from our previous accident. The bike sat in the corner of the workshop, a little scratched but otherwise showing no ill effects from landing in the channel.

"She'll run okay?"

"Yah, mon. You jus' keep on da road dis time, okay?" He laughed at his own hilarity, gave us a wave, and returned to his work. I started the bike, and Danielle got on behind.

"You okay with this?"

"Of course," she said. "Say, didn't you have a motorcycle at home at one point? What happened to it?"

"It's like this one. It prefers the company at the workshop."

"Well, there aren't so many grassy landing spots on I-95. I think you should get rid of it."

"I think it got rid of me, but I couldn't agree more."

We puttered our way back to the resort, where we went for a swim and then had coffee by the pool. It was another monotonously glorious morning. Our server recommended the ackee and saltfish, but I declined and stuck with coffee. We were biding time. We knew that Markus's benefactor in the US, Desmond Richmond, was coming in tonight from Lauderdale, and at that point our engagement with Markus would officially be over. I felt uneasy about that for reasons I couldn't pin down, other than there being a lot of loose ends left hanging. I got the sense Danielle felt the same from the way she kept shifting in her seat, like she just couldn't get comfortable.

We took a walk along the beach and came upon a woman selling wood carvings off a blue plastic tarp. She gave us a beaming smile and welcome, and we chatted with her for a while about the knickknacks she was selling. I'm not much one for souvenirs, useless garbage that people would never normally buy but feel compelled to purchase on vacation, so they can take it home and fill up their garages with anything other than their car. But the woman was warm and friendly and not in the slightest bit pushy, and Danielle took a liking to a wood carving of a green bird with a long, thin tail twice the length of its body. It looked like a hummingbird with streamers coming out its backside, and the woman told us it was called the Doctor Bird, Jamaica's national bird. I jogged back to our room to grab my wallet, and then back to pay the woman. She sent us on our way with another smile and a wave. We trekked back along the beach, biding time.

"You know, we haven't been for a run since we got here," she said.

"It was a run that got us here, remember?"

"Not my fault. You lost the bet."

"I did. But I should also point out, we have been in two fights, so it's not like we've done no exercise."

"That's true," she said, looking away across the azure water. "You want to get some lunch?"

It seemed that eating was the major event at the resort, and we were being sucked into it. We stopped back at our room before heading down to the buffet lunch. As Danielle set the bird in her suitcase, I glanced at my phone. There was a message on it, so I picked it up. It was Corporal Lucia Tellis, calling to tell me that she had looked into the names I had gotten from Garfield, and she had tracked them down to a location on the outskirts of MoBay. She added that they were known to have a sizable marijuana plantation up the hill and that she'd call back when she had more news.

Apparently it was IHOP day at the lunch buffet, because lunch consisted of pancakes, sausages, and burgers. I took a rum and coke and a plate of fries and played with my food as we took in the view. Danielle got a Bloody Mary, which was food as far she was concerned. We sat in silence again for a while. It wasn't just Markus on my mind. I looked over at Danielle, using her celery like a hockey stick on the ice in her drink. We had come to Jamaica on the back of a bet, but we both knew there was more to it than that. We had dated for a few years now, but only recently had she moved into my house, after she had been shot by a drug dealer. Although the injuries weren't life threatening, they hurt deep and brought up thoughts about mortality and the future for both of us. At the time the silence between us had grown uncomfortable, and I had resolved to communicate better. For a while I had. Now the silence was back, and it wasn't just walking away from Markus that was echoing in the void.

"You okay?" I asked. It wasn't the greatest icebreaker, but I never claimed to be Shakespeare.

Danielle shrugged. "Yeah, you?"

"You don't look like you're enjoying your vacation."

She looked me in the eyes. "Are you?"

"I'm happy to be here with you," I said.

"That's not an answer," she said.

I wasn't sure how the tables had turned, but now she was asking the questions. "I'm worried about what happens to Markus when Richmond arrives and the job is done."

Danielle dropped the celery into her drink. "Me too. What do you normally do if a job ends but the case isn't resolved?"

"You know what I do."

"You stick your nose in where it isn't wanted anymore."

"I do. But I'm not so sure that's what you want me to do."

She frowned. "Why do you say that?"

"The law of unintended consequences."

Danielle nodded, leaned forward, and reached for my hands. I gave them to her and felt her soft grip.

"I told you, MJ, I trust you. I know you don't always take the conventional route, and although I'd rather not think about it, probably not the legal route at times. But I also know you'll do what you think is right. And despite what many people think, I know your moral compass points in the right direction." She took a deep breath and looked away at the line of people waiting patiently for recently frozen patties on a bun. I got the sense that Danielle had more to say, so I held my tongue. She turned back to me and gave me the half smile that always sent an irregular rhythm through my heart.

"MJ, life is the law of unintended consequences. When I left Eric, I didn't expect to wind up on a case that would lead me to you, and I sure didn't expect to lose my heart to a scruffy beach bum. I didn't expect to get shot, and I didn't expect that to lead to us living together. It's all unintended. It's not about avoiding the unexpected—

it's about how you react to the events that life throws at you."

I smiled. "How did I get so lucky?"

Danielle let my hands go and leaned back in her chair. "Don't get too comfortable, buddy." She smiled, this time the whole way.

"So you're not bored?"

"With you?" she asked.

"No—here, on vacation. Why, are you bored with me?"

"You, no. Here, out of my mind."

"You wanted to come here," I said. "You won the bet, remember?"

"I wanted to come to Jamaica, yes. But this?" She glanced around the room. I did the same. It was filled with people who clearly worked hard, saved up their precious money and their even more precious vacation time, and took a week to step out of their lives to live as the other half lived. I couldn't blame them. Life could be a grind if you let it get you down. But I discovered that a long time ago. It was why I had never returned to the Northeast. In Florida I had found what I was looking for. Not utopia, not by a long stretch. There was corruption, murder, and mayhem as much in South Florida as anywhere. Maybe more. But there was also brightness, the sun washing care from my back, watching people fly into Palm Beach International to get a week of what I got every day. I worked hard, I played hard enough, and I was surrounded by the best people I'd ever met in the world. I suddenly wondered why I had even left, and I looked back to Danielle.

"I don't need a break from my life, MJ," said Danielle. "I just need to live it."

"Maybe next time we should go skiing in Tahoe. Mix it up."

Danielle shrugged. "I've never skied."

"All the more reason. But that doesn't do us much good now. We're in Jamaica. And we're not doing her justice."

"In any way, shape, or form. So what do you think?"

"I think we should do what we do best. Stick our noses in where they are no longer welcome."

"So, what shall we do until we pick up Markus?" she said, chomping on celery.

"Well, Lucia said she'd get back to us, so I guess we wait until she finds something. Otherwise, I don't know. Another swim?"

Danielle looked at me with a face that reminded me of a black panther I saw as a kid in Connecticut. We went on a school field trip to an awful zoo, and I remembered standing in front of the hurricane wire cage that looked like it was the playground of an elementary school in a bad area more than any attempt at a wildlife environment. The panther just walked from one side of the cage to another, back and forth, like a prisoner who had been in solitary for way too long. The big cat gave a constant guttural growl, as if its confinement were slowly, inevitably, driving it insane. That was what Danielle looked like now.

"Ron suggested we try the US consulate. Maybe we should visit."

Danielle dropped the celery back in her glass and smiled.

"Let's go."

CHAPTER SEVENTEEN

The US consular agency office turned out to be hidden away in a newish office/shopping complex between our resort and Sangster International Airport. It was designed to look tropical in that Key West way, if Key West had been designed by Walt Disney. We found the office in a pastel-colored building opposite a Burger King. There was no signage other than a small silver nameplate by the front door, and the whole place gave the impression that it really didn't want to be found.

A woman at the reception desk told us that yes, the office was open for consular business, but no, the consul agent himself was out of the office and therefore not available. He wasn't expected back anytime soon. We thanked her for her help and wandered out into the near-vacant parking lot. The whole area seemed designed for tourists who were encouraged to never visit it. There was a tour office, a souvenir shop, and what looked like an insurance agency, a sandwich place, and an automotive supplies store. I nudged Danielle and walked over to the auto store where I grabbed a couple of quarts of brake fluid and a can of spray paint. I took my goods in a drawstring bag with an oil company logo on it and walked back into the sunshine.

Danielle stood waiting in the shade of the patio of the building, and I glanced at an older man sitting back in the shade of a palm tree by the auto store. He wore a gray beard and no shirt and was thin as a pencil. He smiled and nodded at me.

"You be wantin' da ambassador," he said.

I was pretty certain the ambassador was sitting in much nicer digs in the capital, Kingston, but I got his meaning all right.

"Yeah. She says he's out of the office."

"Dot be sure, mon. He always out a da office."

"You know where?"

"Yah, mon. You be wantin' Gloucester Avenue. *Margaritaville*."

"Margaritaville?"

"Yah, mon. Trust me. Dots what you be wantin'."

I gave the old guy a ten for his trouble and went back to the bike.

"He says if we want the consular agent, we should check out Margaritaville. What do you think?" I said.

"You'd rather go back to the buffet?"

We cruised by the airport and followed the coast until we reached Doctor's Cave beach, and the road where the taxi had dropped us the first time we had come into town. I slowed down, the lunch traffic hardly rush hour, but the relaxed speed was more in line with the pace of the street, and we puttered by all the gregariously colored bars and eateries on the water until we came to the one named after Jimmy Buffett's finest work. I'm a Buffett fan. We dressed from the same tailor, I loved his tunes, and I even saw him in concert at Cocoa Beach one time. But I was not a fan of mass-produced, lowest-denominator Americana. We parked the bike and stood looking at the building, two stories with a waterslide shooting out from the back of the top level down into the warm ocean below. It was more Daytona than Caribbean, and I shuddered in my shirt with little surfboards on it.

The interior was as exterior as inside can get, breeze wafting through at will, keeping things mild and relaxed. Alan Jackson was playing on the sound system, and the brightly colored lunch tables had been mostly vacated but remained unbussed. A bar ran along the side, above which was a big flat-screen television. A solitary man sat at the bar, looking up at a college football game on the flat screen. He was sitting on a beer and was demolishing a chicken wing.

"Mr. Lambert?"

The man looked along the bar. He wore a blue oxford shirt, and a cream jacket was hanging off the backrest of his barstool. To my eye, he looked a lot paler than a man living in a sunny place like Jamaica ought to look.

"Can I help you?" he mumbled through a mouthful of chicken.

We stepped toward him, and I couldn't help but notice him give Danielle a good looking over. I couldn't blame him for it—I caught myself doing the same thing more often than I should, but most strangers were at least a little furtive about it. Danielle grinned. Not because she liked being ogled by a lech who should have been at work rather than drinking at a bar, but because she knew, before she even opened her mouth, that she had his measure.

"Mr. Lambert, my name is Danielle Castle."

"American?"

"Yes, sir."

"If it's consular business, the office is in Whittier Village."

"Yes, sir, we went there. It was actually you we wanted to talk to."

"Please make an appointment at the office."

I knew this guy. Not literally, but I knew the type. He was an American who had found life as a big fish in a tiny pond more palatable than life in the big pond back home, where he would never have made it past the middle of any totem pole he climbed. He wasn't a State Department employee. He probably managed some local office for a US company and kept his head down enough to never get noticed and moved on. It happened to a lot of expats. And this one had finagled his way into a part-time gig as a consular rep in an office that saw little business, the odd

PR task representing the US to the local government, but mostly handling complaints from US citizens who had lost their passports while on snorkeling trips. Working too hard was definitely not on his agenda.

I pulled my phone out and flicked it to video, and scanned a shot of the bar and the football on the television, then panned down and pointed the phone at the consular guy.

"What do you think you are doing?" he said, scowling.

"I'm taking some vacation video. I call this one *Our Nation's Diplomats Hard at Work*. I thought my friends in the State Department might get a kick out of it."

"I'm not a diplomat."

"No kidding."

Lambert dropped the wing on his plate and wiped his mouth with a napkin that was covered in sauce.

"What do you want?"

Danielle took the seat next to Lambert, and I the next one along. The bartender ambled over, and with a nod I ordered two beers.

"Our situation can't wait for an appointment, I'm afraid," said Danielle. I couldn't see if she was batting her eyelids, but it felt like she was.

"What situation is that?"

"A friend of ours was assaulted," said Danielle.

"Is your friend a US citizen?"

"No."

"Then they should talk to the local authorities." Lambert eyed the basket of wings but didn't take one. He glanced up at the television. It was Georgetown against Brown. It wasn't exactly the Orange Bowl, so I wondered which of the schools Lambert had attended, and decided my money was on Brown.

"We were then driven off the road the other night, and we were also assaulted."

"Like I said, you should talk to the local constabulary."

"We did," said Danielle, sipping her beer. "They weren't very interested."

Lambert dragged his attention away from the football and looked at Danielle.

"Look, miss, what can I tell you? Jamaica is a safe place for US citizens to visit, but the Department recommends you stay in your resort and visit tourist destinations through approved tour companies."

"How safe can it be if you tell people to stay locked up in their resort?"

"Safe enough. Like any country with poverty, there is crime. But crimes against tourists are rare, if you act accordingly."

I leaned my elbows on the bar and looked at the television, but I spoke to Lambert.

"So the State Department's position is if US citizens get in trouble, they're on their own?"

"The Department's position is that you should not go looking for trouble."

"What if trouble finds you?" I glanced back at him and raised my eyebrows.

Lambert frowned at me. "I'm sorry, I didn't get your name."

"Jones, Miami Jones."

"Miami? That's your name?"

"Beats the hell out of *Brown Bear*," I said. Brown University was a member of the Ivy League, and they had gone with the imaginative moniker of Brown Bears for their athletics teams.

"How did you know I was a Brown alum?"

"Educated guess. You're watching a football game that no one but alums of the schools would care about, and if you had gone to Georgetown you'd be a lot better at your job."

"Mr. Jones, you can insult me all you like—"

"Great."

"But it is not my job to run interference for troublemakers who have been offered the finest local hospitality yet keep wanting to search out the worst in people."

"Finest hospitality?"

"I know you were at Rose Hall the other night. I remember you," he said, looking again at Danielle. I was pretty sure it wasn't me he remembered. He licked chicken grease from his lips before continuing. "And I know you tested the hospitality of more than a few important people. Our business is diplomacy, Mr. Jones, not assisting bullies."

"We're talking about an otherwise defenseless young man, and you're talking about the rich and powerful. Seems to me that your diplomacy *is* helping bullies."

"I believe we are done." Lambert finally picked up a chicken wing and bit into it, signaling an end to the conversation, at least in his mind. I generally find people expect me to leave the room at such a juncture, so I swiveled to the bar and sipped my beer. Danielle watched me and then joined in. We drank in silence, letting Lambert wiggle in his seat. He glared at the television, chewing on his chicken wing like it was uncooked grits, doing everything in his power to not look at us. Eventually he lost. They always do. I can sit in silence and stare someone down for hours. Lambert wiped his mouth with the same dirty napkin, smearing his face rather than cleaning it, then dropped off his stool and threw the napkin into his plate. He gave me his best dirty look, but the effect was nullified by the buffalo sauce that ringed his mouth. He opened his lips to say something but must have thought the better of it, and he stormed out, leaving his lunch, his beer, and his football team behind.

We let him go and finished our beers. I asked the bartender to change the channel to a real football game, and he flicked it over to English Premier League soccer, which wasn't quite what I meant, but he seemed happy about it, so I let it lie. We ignored the screen and moved to a view of the water. As we watched a skiff glide across the water, my phone buzzed. I picked it off the table, didn't recognize the number, but answered anyway.

"Miami Jones."

"Mr. Jones. This is Corporal Lucia Tellis."

"Lucia. I got your message."

"Yes, I wanted to let you know I have reliable information that the assailants whose names you provided are recuperating at their residence."

"So you're going to pick them up?"

"Not yet. I also tracked down the marijuana plantation that they run, on the mountain."

"And?"

There was a pause before Lucia continued.

"Are you doing anything tonight?"

CHAPTER EIGHTEEN

As it turned out, we were doing something that night. We stayed at Margaritaville enjoying the view until it was time to collect Markus from school. He was pensive as we made our way home, he and Danielle walking together, me straddling the bike and kicking alongside, my drawstring bag on my back. We arrived at his home, where a gathering of friends and family was already waiting for us. There was an expectant buzz in the air, people chatting quietly, food and drinks being brought in, like preparation for the arrival of royalty. We walked through the group in front of the house and took Markus inside. A woman I didn't know was sweeping the floor and gave me a harsh look for traipsing dirt in. We found Mrs. Swan in the kitchen, sitting at the table. A couple of other women were tending pots at the stovetop. Men were setting plastic chairs around the open slab of concrete outside. Mrs. Swan looked indifferent to the activity. She gave a soft smile to Markus, and he touched her shoulders before retreating to his bedroom.

"A lot of hubbub," I said.

"Yes, suh."

"When does his highness arrive?" I said.

Mrs. Swan smiled. "At his pleasure."

The crowd had swelled, and a party was well underway when word filtered through to us in the backyard that Mr. Richmond had arrived. Darkness had fallen, and I was eating some kind of delicious curry dish, the flavors of which I couldn't replicate if I had the rest of eternity to figure it out. Mrs. Swan was in the kitchen, and Markus had gone out to meet Richmond. There was quite a welcoming line, because it took Richmond a good ten minutes to make it to the kitchen. I saw him greet Mrs. Swan, who didn't stand from her chair. They talked for a time, then Richmond was presented with a drink, and he continued along the line of people, everyone wanting to shake his hand, everyone clambering for a space on Markus's coattails.

Richmond took his time getting to me. Obviously I knew who he was, and given that Danielle and I were still the only white faces in the place, he knew who I was. He shook every hand in the yard, making his way around the concrete slab, smiles and backslaps like he was the Second Coming. When you play top-flight college sports, you meet plenty of boosters who know how to work a room. The number of smooth operators doesn't go down at the pro level, but Richmond worked a room as well as any of them. He was different from Cornelius Winston in almost every possible way. He was younger, for a start. Maybe fifty, give or take, and his close-cropped hair was all black. He wore a thick black mustache, beneath which beamed the kind of smile that can be produced only by a high-priced orthodontic practice, a variety of which did a roaring trade in South Florida. But the thing that struck me most about him was that despite looking like everyone else around him, even down to the casual shirt and gray trousers, he wasn't like them.

The proof was in his eyes. I'd seen plenty of eyes like them. Playing in the minor leagues, I saw all kinds of eyes, with all kinds of intensity. And in my major league adventure, twenty-nine glorious days with the Oakland A's, almost all the eyes held a level of focus and determination that most folks were incapable of. Richmond had those eyes. Focused, like he was capturing everyone's face on a hard drive hidden in his brain. But Richmond's eyes were also dark and mean. His smiles told you that you were the center of his world for that moment, but his eyes said that in any other moment, he wouldn't care if you were dead or alive.

He finally reached Danielle and me, we stood, and Richmond gave me the pearly whites. He did a good job of keeping his eyes on me when everyone else preferred looking at my girlfriend. I offered my hand, and Richmond took it with a grip that could have pulled the skin off a snake.

"Mr. Jones, it is good to finally meet you."

"You too, Mr. Richmond. Good flight?" No one could say I wasn't a master at meaningless chitchat.

"Like riding the bus. But I must thank you for looking after my charge in my absence."

"We were pleased to help."

Then *we* gave Richmond the opportunity to cast his eye over Danielle. He shot her the pearly whites as well. "Desmond Richmond," he said.

"Danielle Castle."

"Miss Castle, my humble thanks. My charge has been much safer under your eye."

"I agree. Which makes me wonder what happens when we leave."

"I am here now, of course."

"But you live in Florida, is that right?"

"It is. But I will take steps. I assure you of that." Richmond turned to a younger man who stood five paces off him. The young man dropped a thick envelope into Richmond's hand, which he passed to me.

"For your time," said Richmond. It felt like cash, but the currency and amount was anyone's guess. I didn't look in it. I agreed with Kenny Rogers. You never count your money when you're sitting at the table.

"Thank you," I said.

"No, thank you. I know you interrupted your vacation to take this job, so I don't wish to keep you any further. Please enjoy the rest of your stay." He stepped aside as if to let us out, and I got the sense he thought it was time we left. But we weren't there for him—we were there for Markus, and Mrs. Swan.

"Thank you, Mr. Richmond, but we are enjoying our vacation just fine." I smiled and sat back down, and Danielle joined me. Richmond almost frowned, but he caught himself and tacked into the smile, the whole time watching me with those dark eyes. He nodded and moved on to the next coattail jumper. He was giving everyone he spoke to the impression that the coattails were really his, not Markus's, and he was the one who decided who came along for the ride. Eventually he completed the circle, and he disappeared back inside. Danielle and I ate some jerk chicken, drank some beer and chatted to some smiling, happy people who proved, if ever it was needed, that money did not buy happiness. Which made it all the stranger that they were all trying to climb aboard the Markus train. Perhaps money didn't buy happiness, but it could buy a finished home.

I saw Garfield wander into the yard, moving like a reed in the breeze. I winked, and he smiled and came over.

"Mista Miami," he said, slapping me a low five.

"It's just Miami."

"A course, mon."

"Good party."

"Oh, yah, mon. E'body bring out dare best fo' Mista Richmond."

"I've been meaning to ask, what's his story?"

"Mista Richmond?"

I nodded.

"You don't know?" Garfield smiled and slapped his thigh. "Oh, you'll love dis one, Miami." He took a sip of the juice in his hand and leaned in like he was about to share the location of the Ark of the Covenant.

"You 'member da *Cool Runnings*?"

"The bobsled movie?" said Danielle, who was leaning in from my other side. I felt like Switzerland.

"Dot's da one. Da Jamaican bobsled team, nineteen eighty-eight. Mista Richmond was on dot team."

"He was one of the bobsledders?" Danielle seemed impressed by this news.

"Yah, mon. Sort of. He was what ya call da alternate. He wasn't in da team at first, but one mon got hurt, and he was da backup. He never actually raced in da 'lympics, but he done turned it into someting."

"How did he turn it into something?" I asked.

"At first, dare was not such a big deal after da 'lympics. No one in Jamaica pay much notice to da Winter Games. But den dare was da movie. Now it become a big deal." Garfield nodded his head to emphasize how big a deal it was, and then sipped his drink. "All da team become famous, but Mista Richmond, he work it good. In America e'body wants to see da *Cool Runnings* boys, and Mista Richmond, he a guy wit a lotta charisma. You know? He go to America, he on TV, he do shop openings, he become a celebrity."

"And then what?"

"Den he smart. He use his celebrity to get bidness. He landed in Fort Lauderdale, and I hear dare is many Jamaicans dare. So he do bidness."

Garfield was right. Lauderdale, and specifically Lauderhill, west of Lauderdale, had become one of the biggest Jamaican communities outside of Jamaica.

"What sort of business did he get into?"

Garfield tilted his head like he didn't want to tell, but it didn't stop him. "Lots of bidness. Not so legal bidness, dot's what I hear."

I could imagine the business. Drugs, loan sharking, protection, good old racketeering. It all happened in varying degrees in the shadows of Lauderhill.

"So if he's so well set up in the States, why is he messing around with school-age athletes in Jamaica?"

"He wan' what no coil can buy. Prestige."

I nodded. It fit with what I'd heard from Lucia and Arthurs. Richmond had made his fortune the hard way in the US, doing goodness knows what kind of dirty stuff, and now he wanted to come home and be the BMOC. Big Man on Campus. He was just like Winston. They both wanted to be seen as legitimate, as heroes to a nation. And just as Arthurs had said, Winston needed to foster winners to get his IOC position, so Richmond was doing the same. Maybe a few years behind, but the same track. And then it occurred to me. What if he wasn't a few years behind? What if Richmond was climbing the ladder faster than Winston? What if Richmond also coveted the same IOC position, and Winston knew it?

Lucia had told us that Winston had been setting up a network outside of Jamaica that didn't completely make sense to someone with no real international positions. But it did make sense if Winston thought that Richmond was already in the States and had built a network out of Lauderhill into the wealthy and connected homes of South Florida and beyond. That might be driving him. And it might be a reason why Winston's goons had assaulted one of Richmond's athletes.

I thanked Garfield for the background and went for a mosey through the house. People were relaxed in the yard, and less so in the kitchen. By the time I got to the living room, I felt the tension. It was like Richmond was a planet and his gravitational pull was putting stress on those bodies closest to him. He nodded from a matted sofa, where he was holding court. I edged through and sat on the armrest of the sofa, next to Richmond.

"Markus is a good runner," I said.

"Yes, suh, he is that."

"You know, there are colleges in the US that offer athletes like him scholarships. He might be good enough to get one."

Richmond smiled. "He don't need no scholarship, Mr. Jones. He just needs to run."

"Sure. But college athletes get to run, and they get some of the best coaching in the world. Great facilities and a degree at the end, if the running doesn't pan out."

Richmond shook his head. "That might be the American way, but that's not for a Jamaican. For us, there is already a path. Races here, races in Europe. The Diamond League. Not more school that Jamaicans cannot afford. We need to stay hungry, to race for our lives. That is why we win and Americans do not."

"Maybe you're right. But I can't help think Mrs. Swan would like to know there is that option."

"Mr. Jones. Let me tell you something." The smile disappeared, and the eyes bore into me. "Mrs. Swan don't need some crazy ideas being put into her head. She knows what is best for her boy, and she knows that I share her desire for her boy to make the best of his gift." Richmond edged himself around so he was facing me. "I thanked you for your help, but now I must insist that you leave the poor woman alone and not put unrealistic ideas in her mind."

His sharp eyes underlined his insistence, and I didn't think it wise to push it, so I nodded my agreement.

"Perhaps you're right."

"I am, Mr. Jones. I am."

I excused myself and wandered back through the party. I noted as I moved through the throng that Richmond's man, the guy who had handed him the envelope full of cash to give to me, was following me. The house wasn't that big, so he might have just been going to the kitchen for a drink, but I saw Mrs. Swan in the corner of the kitchen, and Richmond's guy took up position between Mrs. Swan and me.

As I passed out of the kitchen, I noted some butcher's paper that had been wrapped around some meat that had arrived earlier that day. The meat was now roasting over coals in the yard, and the paper had been discarded so I tore a piece off. I went outside and asked Garfield if he had a pen, and he disappeared and came back with a lead pencil. He stepped away, and I wrote a quick note, which I folded and handed to Danielle. I whispered in her ear, like we were exchanging sweet nothings, and we were interrupted by Garfield clearing his throat.

"Sorry, Miami."

"That's okay, Garfield."

"No, I mean, dare is someone at da front door fo' you."

"Someone?"

"Da police."

Danielle and I got up. I thanked Garfield and told him not to worry. I returned the pencil, and we weaved our way out. Markus was in the kitchen, and I collected my drawstring bag, thanked him for the party, and wished him well for the upcoming races. We shook hands, and for the first time, he looked me in the eye.

"Tank you," he said.

I shrugged like it was nothing, and I made for the hallway. Danielle was giving Mrs. Swan a hug, and as she did I saw her press my note into Mrs. Swan's hand. Danielle thanked her again, then stepped around Richmond's man and joined me in the hallway. We walked out, saying our goodbyes, and I offered a wave to Richmond, who was still on the sofa. He returned my wave with one of his own and a smile that looked more like relief that I was leaving. But I might have been reading too much into it. We stepped outside. The evening was cool but not unpleasant. A group of partygoers was smoking out front, as they do, and we walked through them to the road, where Lucia Tellis stood waiting by a dark blue Suzuki Vitara.

CHAPTER NINETEEN

The road into the mountains was less a road than a riverbed. The mountains were so green because the tropical clouds gathered on an almost daily basis and dropped their bounty on the foliage. But the water then ran down the manmade gravel roads, washing them away in rivulets of mud. We bounced around in the Suzuki Vitara, but it was better than a motorcycle, and better than the other option Lucia said she had, which was the tiny Suzuki Jimny she had gotten from the motorpool last time. At least the Vitara had a proper back seat and actual four wheel drive. As it was, it took over an hour of careful driving by Lucia to reach our destination. The thick canopy of juniper cedar and pawpaw trees kept the moonlight at bay, so only the headlights showed us a path through the maze of ferns and orchids. Lucia stopped a couple of times to check her notes and then continued on.

The headlights captured a broken-down shell of an old car, and Lucia slowed as we reached it. She passed me a hefty flashlight and told me to point it out past the wreck. I did so, slowly panning across the green blanket until I reached what looked like a small logging hut. I held the beam on the hut. It was a hundred yards from the road and looked as though it was being consumed by the forest around it.

"This is it," said Lucia, and she cut the engine.

The noise of the engine was replaced by a chorus of forest noises, insects and creatures moving through the brush and across the branches above us. Lucia checked her notes again.

"My information is that the gang you named, Winston's thugs, has a ganja plantation here. The cabin there is the marker. The plantation is behind it."

Danielle leaned forward from the back seat. "Can I ask a question? Why do you not raid it if you know where the plantations are?"

"Resources," said Lucia. "And motivation. Ganja is part of the Rastafari culture, so it's part of Jamaican culture. In small lots it is therefore tolerated. But you've met the assistant commissioner. There is not a lot of motivation to do more unless the problem starts spilling out onto the streets of MoBay or Kingston. Lots of the stuff grown here will leave our shores and end up in your country, so the feeling is that it isn't really our problem."

"It's ours," said Danielle.

"Precisely. There are occasional raids, but the growers just move from one spot to another, and half the time the raids are on old plantations because the growers knew we were coming."

I turned to Lucia. "But these guys don't know we're coming, right?"

"No. There's no paperwork on this little tour."

"Good," I said, punching the lever and opening the door. The sound of the forest was louder outside of the car, like a white noise machine turned all the way up. There was no single discernible sound, just a mass of organic chatter. I grabbed my drawstring bag and headed off into the forest. There wasn't a track to speak of until I got well past the car wreck, and then I happened upon a thin line of crushed foliage, which I followed to the logging hut. The hut was made from wood that I assumed was local and had worn to a dark, dank brown by the years and the almost constant moisture. I shone my flashlight across the hut as Lucia and Danielle arrived with flashlights of their own.

"Do they use this hut?" I said.

"Maybe," said Lucia. "For rest, when they are working the crop. But I doubt they would store anything in here."

I scanned the hut and found a door, from which hung a large, rust-colored padlock. I considered the lock for a moment. I learned a trick to pick a padlock with a cut-up soda can, back when I was doing my graduate program in criminology, but I didn't have a can on me.

"If we break in, they'll know we've been here," said Lucia.

"Is that a problem?"

"Not to me."

"Good. 'Cause they're gonna know. One way or another." I shone the light around and, not seeing another way in that didn't leave a mark, I turned to Lucia.

"Let's see this crop."

Lucia led us around the hut and into a wall of thick greenery—ferns and banana trees and vines hanging like Tarzan's drapes. To the eye it looked impenetrable, but that was just an illusion. Lucia pushed her way into the foliage and disappeared, like a wormhole in a science fiction movie. I glanced at Danielle and then followed Lucia in. The sheet of greenery was a veneer, and I swept it aside as easy as a thick blanket. On the other side, Lucia stood shining her light across a field of more green. But this green was different. It was lower, the canopy having been hacked back to offer the plants below access to the sunlight. The space was wild, yet cultivated. And it was all one species. The long, thin, distinctive leaves of *Cannabis sativa*. Marijuana. Ganja.

The field was large, but with just three shafts of light it was difficult to conceive how large. The open canopy above might have offered more moonlight, except for the thick clouds that hung above like a ceiling.

"This doesn't look recreational," said Danielle, sweeping her light across the field.

"No," said Lucia. She turned to me—although I couldn't see her in the darkness, I felt her voice directed at me. "What now?"

"This definitely belongs to Winston's guys?"

"One hundred percent."

"And is he involved?"

"My intelligence says not directly. But who knows. They are getting this stuff out of the country, and Winston is making all kinds of connections in America."

"You think he's working a drug network?"

"I don't know. There's no evidence of it, and at his age, I'd have thought those days were behind him. He wants to be legitimate. His legacy, remember. But tigers don't change their stripes easily."

That was true, but it didn't matter. The guys growing this stuff didn't just grow; they used. And that meant their loyalties could be divided. I slipped the drawstring bag off my shoulder and dropped it to the moist ground. The ladies shone their lights downward, and I pulled out two bottles of brake fluid.

"Brake fluid?" said Lucia.

"Faster than Roundup. Works in the wet too."

"Works to do what?"

"When I was a kid in Connecticut, we had a neighbor growing weed in a hothouse by our side fence one summer. My dad called the cops, and they blew him off. So one night he took a ladder, some shears, and some brake fluid and he poured it over the plants. It started raining while he was doing his thing, but it didn't matter. Those plants were dead before morning."

"You want to kill all these plants?" said Lucia.

"As many as we can, yeah."

"Okay."

"Danielle and I will take a bottle each and work from the outside in. Lucia, you stay and direct us with your flashlight."

"You don't want me out there?" she said.

"You're a cop, and this is your turf. You shouldn't be doing this, even if it is a drug. This way you're just holding a flashlight."

Danielle and I made our way to the edges of the plantation, where the jungle immediately took over. We were about the width of a football field apart. We opened our bottles and walked away from Lucia, pouring a little brake fluid on each plant as we went. About a half-length of a football field later, I hit the jungle. I waited until Danielle's flashlight reached the same point, and then we walked back toward Lucia, her flashlight like a beacon on a New England shore. We marched up and down two more times before our makeshift weed killer ran out, accounting for about two-thirds of the crop, at a rough guess. It wasn't as good as I had hoped, but it would send the message well enough. We packed the empty bottles back in my bag and left the crop to die. When we reached the wooden hut, I stopped.

"One second," I said, reaching into my bag and pulling out the spray paint I had bought. The lock was too substantial to break, but a lock is only as good as its door. The wood that made up this door was hardy stuff, but the hinges were rusted, and the screws holding the hinges in place more so. I kicked at the door with the heel of my boot. It took a dozen good kicks to get movement and ten more for the lower hinge to give way. Then I put my shoulder into it, and on the third drive I was flung onto the floor of the hut as the door opened the wrong way, the hinges busted and the door now hanging by the padlock. Inside the hut was basic. A couple of wooden chairs and a table. It seemed whatever they brought up with them, they packed out again. The Sierra Club would have been proud. Danielle and Lucia stepped inside and lit the wall up. I shook the spray can and painted a message in lemon yellow, to underscore the point made in the field out the back.

Work for Winston OR grow ganja. Can't do both, mon!

"Nice color," said Danielle.

I looked over the can. "I thought it was white."

Lucia stepped up to inspect my work. "They'll probably drive themselves crazy trying to figure out what the yellow means."

"I can live with that. What I want is these guys off our backs and away from Marcus. Let them focus on what is happening to their ganga business."

We pushed our way out and marched back single file to the car. Lucia did a K-turn and pointed the Vitara back down the mountain.

"I should feel bad about this," she said. "We did just break the law."

"No, we did that. I told you. You were just holding the flashlight."

Lucia let the car idle as she looked at me. "You didn't finish the story about your dad. Didn't your neighbor know who had killed their ganja?"

"Of course. But what were they going to do? Call the cops? *My neighbor killed my illegal weed crop.* I don't think so. No, they knew. So they also knew who to mess with and who not to mess with."

"What did they choose?"

"Doesn't matter. Either way there is resolution."

"Was, you mean. Was resolution."

I smiled. "Yeah, that's what I meant. Was."

CHAPTER TWENTY

We woke late after our mountain sojourn, the sun high in the sky and the waves gently lapping at the beach outside our window. I got up and pulled the drapes, flooding the room with fresh light. A catamaran skipped across a light chop, the scent of spices and coconut lotion mixing on the air. Danielle tossed on a sarong over her bathing suit, and I put on a shirt with old wood-sided wagons and surfboards on it, over a pair of board shorts in the Miami Hurricanes colors.

We walked along the beach, picking at shells, looking at starfish in the clear water, watching small children splash in the shallows. After our walk we wandered up past the pool, where a crew of kids barely out of college had taken up post at the swim-up bar. We got a carafe of coffee and a tropical fruit bowl and sat in the sunshine. The buffet room behind us was rotating into lunch mode, trolleys of plates and silverware being pushed from the kitchen to the restaurant along a palm-shaded path. I was pouring a second cup of coffee when one of the doormen came to our table.

"Suh, you have a visitor," he said.

"Me?"

"Yah, suh."

"Who is it?"

"Mrs. Swan, suh."

Danielle and I exchanged glances and stood. We followed the doorman back into the lobby, the breeze wafting through, to the front of the resort, where Mrs. Swan stood. She was dressed in her Sunday best, a blue knee-length dress with a white belt around her thin waist and a wide-brimmed hat with a small bouquet on top. She held white gloves in her hand.

"Mrs. Swan. Is everything all right? Is Markus okay?" Danielle asked.

"Yes, tank you."

"What can we do for you?"

Mrs. Swan looked at me. "I got your note."

I nodded. "I see. Good. Let's sit." I looked around and saw some plush chairs arranged around a travel trunk that was playing the part of a coffee table. We sat, and I asked Mrs. Swan if she wanted anything to drink. She declined.

"I am sorry to bodda you on your holiday, especially after ev'ryting you've done."

"It's no bother at all."

"It's just you said to call you, but I got no phone."

I felt bad about making an error on such a basic assumption, but glad that Mrs. Swan was resourceful enough to make our meeting happen.

"Well, I'm glad you came."

She looked at Danielle and me and then at her gloves.

"Your note said sum'ting about Markus goin' to university."

"Yes, ma'am. You see, in the United States, we have many colleges, and they compete for everything. The best students, the most research funding, the best athletes. One way they attract the best student-athletes is to offer scholarships. That is, they pay for the tuition, and sometimes the accommodation, for students who also compete in athletics for the school."

"Dey pay for it?"

"That's right. Now, I don't want you to think that this will definitely happen, that a school will be interested. But there is a chance. I've seen him run. He may be good enough."

"So he run dare, or he run here. Wot da difference?"

"Well, the difference is that at a college, he will not only have state-of-the-art facilities and top coaching, but he will also be required to go to classes. And at the end of four years, he will come out with a college degree."

"Like at school."

"Yes, pretty much. But he'll be running against the best in the United States, and if he's good enough, the world. And if he is that good, he'll still be able to make it to the World Champs or the Olympics for Jamaica. Many

Olympic athletes are also students at US colleges. But if it happens that he isn't that good, that he can't make a living from running, he will still get a degree at the end."

"Dot is good."

"Yes, ma'am, it is. The question is, are his grades at school good enough to gain admission to a good college?"

"His report is good. Markus is a good student. He has As in all his classes, except home economics."

"Home economics?"

"Cooking class. It is not his gift."

"I understand. Mine either. But if his grades are strong, that will help."

"So what must we do?" she asked.

"I know some people at my old college. It's in Florida, so not too far away. I can speak to them and see if there is any chance."

"Dot would be good. Tank you."

"It's no problem. But there is one issue."

"Mista Richmond," she said. Her face scrunched up as she said it.

"That's right. I mentioned the idea to him last night, and he didn't seem keen at all."

"Markus runs for a university, dare be nuttin' in it for Mista Richmond."

"Right. That was my impression. He seems keen to focus on races that pay to win."

"Or pay not to win."

I nodded and thought about what she had told me about her husband being forced to throw cricket matches by Winston and how it ended up driving him away. She clearly saw Richmond as the lesser of two evils. But evil nevertheless.

"Well, for now, let's keep it to ourselves. I'll deal with Mr. Richmond if and when I have to."

She nodded, looked at her gloves, and then looked up at me. Her frown had returned.

"E'body wants sum'ting from my boy. Mista Winston, Mista Richmond, most e'body who you saw last night. My question is, suh, you do all dis for him. What do you want?"

It was a good question. I'd been watching everyone around Markus Swan with an eye to what was in it for them, what they wanted from him, and I hadn't stopped to consider my own motives. Of course, I thought my reasons pure, just as I was sure everyone else thought theirs to be. But Mrs. Swan's question gave me pause. Why was I helping them? Was it simply because I was there, and because I could? Was there more to it? Did I want something from the kid? Glory revisited, perhaps? Then I remembered my mentor, the late, great Lenny Cox. He had done more for me when I needed it than any other person besides my own mother, and he had never asked for anything in return, except to invite me to join his firm when I quit baseball. And then he had left the firm to me in his will. But during the in-between time, he had lived by and taught me one overriding life principle: pay it forward. It sounded like a hippie, tree-hugging kind of deal, to live like karma was your guiding light. But the thing was, Lenny had never spoken of it. He never once told me to pay it forward, never used the word *karma*. He just did it. He helped people who needed helping, just because he could. Maybe he did it to feel good, but I never really knew for sure. And in my book, if all the payment you asked for was to feel good inside, it was a price worth paying. Every time. I held Mrs. Swan's eyes and told her the only thing I could think of to say, regardless of whether she believed it or not.

"I'll tell you what I want, Mrs. Swan. To feel good about myself. When I was young, someone helped me and asked nothing in return. And now it's my turn. That's all I can tell you."

She watched me, and I saw her pupils move across every line and every wrinkle in my face. Then she nodded. She didn't smile, but she seemed comfortable.

"I'll speak to the college, and we'll take it from there, okay?"

She nodded again and stood, and we stood with her.

"Tank you, Mista Jones."

"You're welcome."

As we walked her to the lobby entrance, Danielle spoke. "How did you get here, ma'am?"

"I walked. It not be far."

"Well, let us get you a taxi home."

"No, I cannot accept dot."

I stopped before the valet desk. "Mr. Richmond paid me for looking out for Markus. I don't need his money. Let him pay for your ride home."

Mrs. Swan offered a small smile. "Why not?"

We put Mrs. Swan in a battered-looking minivan, and I handed the driver two twenties and told him to take her home. We stood under the portico and watched the van turn around and pull out through the security gate and out of view. Then Danielle turned to me.

"Do you think you can really make a scholarship happen?"

"That's not up to me. All I can do is connect the pieces—I can't make them fit."

We turned from the driveway of the resort but were stopped by the sound of a car coming to a skidding stop behind us. We turned to see a police-issue Suzuki Jimny. The door flew open and Corporal Lucia Tellis stepped out.

CHAPTER TWENTY-ONE

Lucia drove us back into MoBay with me coiled up in the back of the miniature SUV like a discarded garden hose. Clearly the bigger Vitara wasn't available to her during the day. Lucia had come up with the bright idea that no one had actually questioned Cornelius Winston, and she had decided she was the one to do it. Her plan was to wear a wire, on the off chance Winston said something incriminating, and she figured we could make sure the recording equipment was working. Plus, she thought we'd get a kick out of seeing the place where Winston was due to have lunch. She had a mischievous glint in her eye.

"Are you sure you want to do this?" I asked from the back seat. "It could bring some heat."

"He thinks he is untouchable, and as long as we are afraid to do our jobs and question him, he is going to continue believing that."

I raised my eyebrows at Danielle in the front, and she returned with a grin that said she liked the way Lucia went about things.

The Uxbridge Club simply didn't belong in Jamaica. It was a throwback to a colonial past that Winston and his ilk were trying to preserve. The irony that they would never be in the positions they were in if the British still ran the island had no place in the wood paneling and leather chairs of the Uxbridge Club. We pulled up to the tall iron gates, and Lucia showed her ID to the guard, who frowned and shrugged in one motion and then opened the gate. The club sat on lush grounds in a stately home that the tourist set would have given their last drop of sun lotion to visit. But that wasn't going to happen. The Uxbridge Club was an exclusive gentlemen's club, which meant something very different here from what it meant at home in Florida.

Lucia parked her police car to the side of the building. It was both in deference to the club not wanting a police vehicle sullying its circular driveway and because we didn't want the valet questioning why Danielle and I were there. We checked that Lucia's microphone was working and that the remote digital recorder was capturing her voice, and then she slid out and marched toward the front door. Danielle and I sat in the car, listening through one earbud each to Lucia's breathing as she mounted the stairs to the club. We heard someone question how he could help her, and clearly she had shown her police ID, because the voice then asked what her business was.

"I'm here to see Mr. Winston," she said.

"I'm not sure he's here, ma'am."

"He's here. So will you take me to him, or will I just wander through every room until I find him?"

"No, ma'am. I believe he's on the back patio. This way."

Danielle and I caught each other's look, and then we jumped out of the car and scampered along the side of the brick building. The palms were well tended but provided plenty of cover. We reached the end of the building and peered around. The back of the clubhouse featured an expansive wooden deck, with slowly rotating overhead fans moving breeze across white linen tablecloths and silver coffee carafes. All of the guests were men, and all wore jackets and ties. Plenty of frowns were directed toward Lucia as she followed a guy dressed like a butler across the deck. Perhaps it was the fact she was a woman; perhaps it was her police uniform. Perhaps both.

We saw the butler reach a table where Cornelius Winston was lunching with another man. We hurriedly stuffed the earbuds back in so we could hear the conversation.

"I'm sorry, suh," said the butler.

Winston frowned at the interruption, then glanced at Lucia, and his face dissolved into a smug smile.

"What is it?" he said.

Lucia stepped forward. "Corporal Lucia Tellis, Jamaican Constabulary Force, suh."

Winston raised his eyebrow to his lunch buddy. "My, the police are much more amenable to the eye now than in my day."

The lunch buddy had his back to us, so I couldn't see his reaction—but I was going with a smug grin, so I didn't like him already.

"What is it I can do for you, young lady?" asked Winston.

"I am investigating the assault of a young athlete, suh."

"You are? Well, good for you."

"Yes, suh. You are aware of the assault, of course."

I thought I saw the smug veneer crack a little on Winston's face.

"I'm afraid not. Why would I know anything, young lady?"

"It's Corporal, sir. And I assumed that being head of the Inter-Secondary Schools Sports Association, you would be concerned by an assault on one of your athletes."

"You assume that, do you? Well, I assure you I am concerned. But it seems to be a police matter, and I have the utmost confidence in your ability to do your job."

Danielle glanced at me. "Cheeky," she said. I nodded in return. I was focusing hard on Winston's face, but my attention was pulled away by a heavy hand slapping onto my shoulder. I turned to see a giant of a man holding a machete. He was sweating like a weightlifter, and his white shirt fell open to reveal a strong, ebony chest. He looked as if he'd just wandered off a sugarcane plantation from a hundred years ago.

"What are you doin'?" he asked, though it didn't really sound like a question. "You can't be here."

We pulled around the corner a touch so we wouldn't be seen from the patio and faced the big man. Danielle gave him a smile, which did nothing for his demeanor. I was more focused on the machete. I was trying to think of something to say when I heard voices in my earbud.

"Suh," said Lucia, "were you also not aware that two of your guests were run off the road and attacked coming home from your fundraiser the other night?"

"Of course I heard. It was a terrible occurrence, but since it happened on a public road, it really is none of my concern."

Danielle glanced back toward Lucia, and the big guy watched her do it; his eyes were drawn toward the patio. I thought about going for the machete, but even with him distracted it would be a tough get, and I didn't like the odds. The big unit looked back at me.

"What are you doin' here?" he demanded again.

Words escaped me as I canvassed the options that would make him lose the frown and the machete, not necessarily in that order. Danielle came up with something first.

"We're with the police," she said. It wasn't the direction I would have gone, but that was now irrelevant.

"Police?" said the big guy. Danielle nodded.

"I get da boss man." He went to move, then appeared to think about what we might do if he left us alone. He waved the machete, pointing us back toward the front of the building. We followed his order, keeping close to the wall and away from the machete. I heard Lucia tell Winston that the assault victims had confirmed they were followed from Rose Hall, so the assailants must have been at the Hall during the event. Winston gave a dismissive laugh and said there was no evidence of that. Then the big guy in front of me waved the machete just a little too close, and I leaned back, pulling the bud from my ear.

We reached the front of the building, and the big guy hesitated. It seemed that his remit at the club did not extend to public appearances in front of the patrons, and I wondered if he'd been threatened by a member of the club for nothing more than being a giant black man. He caught the eye of a valet, who looked us over, raised his eyebrows as his brain kicked into gear, and then ran inside. He returned a moment later with another man who was dressed in a fine-looking suit. He was a short fellow with a considerable girth, but the suit fit him well. He strode over to us, throwing a glance at Lucia's police car parked askew.

"What is going on?" he said with the frown that was becoming the popular response to our presence wherever we went.

"I found dem in da garden," said the big guy. "Dey say dey wit da police." He shook his head at the last part, sure that it was complete baloney. Danielle was in a sundress and I wore cargo shorts, so it was a fair assumption. The well-dressed fellow gave me a good looking over, like a school principal who knows you're up to no good but just hasn't caught you at it yet, but then his face opened up as if the penny had dropped, and he turned to the big guy. He spoke in rapid fire, possibly English but impossible to follow. The big guy nodded deeply, took two steps back, then turned and wandered away into the foliage from whence he had come. We watched him go and then turned back to the well-dressed man, clueless about what was happening. The man stepped close to me.

"You are Miami Jones."

Like they say, everybody dies famous in a small town. When you've played professional sports, even minor league ball like I had, more people know you than the average Joe. It was true—I'd even made the papers a few times with cases we had broken. But none of those things had happened in Jamaica, so I had no clue how this guy knew me.

"How do you . . .?"

"Mista Jones, you are protectin' young Markus. His *fadda* is my cousin."

"That so?"

"Yes, suh. Now what brings you to da Uxbridge Club?"

I gave him the abridged version, and his frown returned. "Mista Winston not a mon to be mussed wit, suh. I suggest you wait in da car, let da police do dare bidness."

I agreed and thanked him, and he bid us good day. Danielle and I clambered back into the police car and stuffed our earbuds back in. All we heard was static. I played with the receiver and wiggled the wires, then Danielle put her hand on mine to get my attention. I followed her gaze to see Corporal Tellis stepping down to the driveway. She marched back to us and got into the vehicle.

"Did you hear?" she asked.

"To a point," said Danielle. "We got interrupted."

"Interrupted?"

"Doesn't matter," I said. "You told him we knew we had been trailed from Rose Hall, and he said there was no evidence of that."

Lucia nodded. "Yes, he said that. And I told him that one of the victims was a visiting law enforcement officer who had been trained to notice such things."

"You overestimate PBSO training, methinks," I said.

Danielle slapped my arm. "I am well trained."

I rubbed my arm theatrically. "Don't I know it. So what happened then?"

"I told him based on that evidence, I would need a complete list of all guests and staff at the event. He didn't think that was such a great idea."

"I bet," said Danielle.

"So I suggested that noncooperation with the investigation wouldn't look very good for someone in his position. At that point he suggested that he would look into it and I would receive any information needed through the assistant commissioner."

"Ooh, namedropper," I said.

"Quite, and—" She was interrupted by the crackle of the police radio. She grabbed the handset and responded; then there was a burst of speech that between the static and the accent was completely beyond me. Lucia responded in the affirmative, replaced the handset, and then started the car.

"What was that?" asked Danielle.

Lucia smiled. "I've been called into headquarters. The assistant commissioner wants to talk to me."

"Your grapevine is like a superhighway," I said, flopping back into the rear seat as Lucia pulled around the large circular driveway and out toward the iron gates that opened like massive jaws as we approached.

Had the police headquarters had a better paint job it would have peeled. Such was the dressing-down that Assistant Commissioner Harrow gave Corporal Tellis. Danielle and I hung back and waited in the lobby, but Harrow's stern voice echoed down the stairs for all to hear. I noted a few other officers shaking their heads, mostly with wry grins on their faces, so I assumed it wasn't the first time. My guess was that it was Lucia's first time, though, and I was fully prepared for a browbeaten young officer to reappear on the stairs. I could see Danielle felt it too.

"It's not your fault," I said.

"I encouraged her."

"Exactly. She was headed in that direction anyway. And you know it's the right direction."

Danielle nodded softly but said nothing, so I let it lie. The yelling died away and the silence was worse. I had all sorts of visions of what was happening upstairs, from Harrow ripping the name patch from Lucia's uniform to him asking for her badge, and her gun, which I realized she didn't even carry. We waited for longer than was necessary for whatever Harrow might be doing, and I started to think she wasn't coming back. Then I saw her come down the steps, and Danielle and I both stood. Lucia didn't look browbeaten. She looked defiant. She saw us and as she approached, grinned and gave us a wink.

"Are you okay?" asked Danielle.

Lucia smiled. "Seems we're getting somewhere. Harrow told me I was hassling important people without reason and that I was lucky to not be suspended."

Danielle frowned. "What did you say? Nothing silly I hope?"

"I apologized and told him I was simply following up on an official complaint from the victims. Harrow said you had made no complaint, and I told him that in fact you had, at the front desk, to me. I told him I was unaware that he had been involved in the matter, and he backtracked and said he hadn't, but he wanted to see the complaint."

"That's a problem," said Danielle. "The complaint was never put in writing."

Lucia stepped to the duty desk, grabbed some papers, then came back. "That's why I need you to fill these forms out." She handed the papers to us. The top of the paper read *Police Report.*

Danielle smiled again. "Good girl." She took a pen from Lucia and began filling out the form.

"So what happened in the end?" I asked.

"The assistant commissioner warned me off the issue until he had personally had time to read the complaint. He asked me when my next leave day was, and I told him tomorrow. So he said I should go home early, and he'd speak to me when I was next in."

"Maybe that's a good idea," I said. "Laying low for a day or two might be the prudent move."

"Prudent my eye," she said, with a cheeky grin. "I've still got the ownership details of the van that ran you off the road. I'm off duty now, and I've got nothing better to do. What say we pay them a little visit at home?"

CHAPTER TWENTY-TWO

Danielle completed the police report on the drive. We wound away west from town, to a collection of fiberboard cottages that had seen better days when Victoria was queen. Lucia cross-checked a note she had scribbled down against the location, and although I didn't see any kind of street signage or house numbering, she turned off the engine.

"That's it there," she said, pointing to a shack that might have once been lime green but had turned closer to white by years of constant sun.

"We should come with you," said Danielle. She was checking the police report as she spoke, and then she passed it to me to cosign. I did so without bothering to read it, and then I gave it to Lucia.

"With these guys, I'm not going to say no to the backup," said Lucia.

We let Lucia take the lead. It was her turf, and she was still in uniform, so it all looked official. She banged her small fist on a thin aluminum door that reverberated like a drum. It took a second go to encourage a response from inside the house.

"Who is it?" came a voice that sounded half-asleep, or high.

"Mista Winston," I called.

There was a long pause, then the door cracked open. A face appeared but quickly recoiled from the sunlight. I didn't recognize the face but I didn't expect to. It had been dark when we were run off the road, and being attacked with cricket bats hadn't left much time to draw up sketches of the perps. But what I did recognize was Danielle's handiwork. The face in the doorway had a broken nose. There were black and purple welts creeping from under the plaster that covered his nose and half his face. Evidently he either didn't recognize us, or he couldn't see that far right now. Lucia stepped forward.

"Corporal Tellis, JCF. I'd like a word. Can I come in? Thanks."

She pushed the door open, and the guy stepped back, unsteady on his feet. We moved into a small room that might have been called a living room in another house, but in this case it was covered in mattresses. Several bodies lay snoring, splayed out in the heat. The heavy scent of ganja hung in the air.

"Whaddaya wan, mon?" said the guy with the busted face. Lucia paid him no mind. She moved slowly around the room and into a kitchen full of trash and unwashed steel pots. The countertops might have been laminate, but it was hard to say with the thick layer of cooking grease covering them.

Lucia checked the two other small rooms for any surprises and then looped back to us. I stopped by the kitchen doorway and looked over a guy who was propped up against the wall on a torn mattress. He had a bandage around his head that looked as if it had been wrapped by a first-grader. It wound around his head from side to side and then top to bottom. Dried blood caked one side of his head. It looked like someone had attempted to repair a broken jaw without a visit to a hospital. He was staring into the middle of the room but seeing something altogether different from the rest of us, in a universe I had yet to visit. No doubt it was the result of the ganja—and whatever else the guy was taking to dull the pain inflicted by Danielle when she'd cracked him in the chin with his own cricket bat. The net result was that the guy wasn't telling us anything.

I looked back at Lucia and shook my head, so she turned to the guy who had let us in. He was lucky. Danielle had only thrown a cricket bat at him, so he'd just received a busted nose. Whether that meant his dose of painkillers was less or he just had a higher tolerance, I didn't know, but it meant he was the only one with the power of speech, so we gathered around him.

"Wot, mon?" he said.

"Do you remember me?" I asked.

He wobbled his head, which I took to mean no.

"What happened to your face? Looks like someone threw a cricket bat at you," I said. I smiled and waited for his drug-fuzzed mind to play catch-up, and even then it took longer than was necessary. But the look on his face changed as it all came back to him, and he took an involuntary step backward, only to find himself face-to-face with Danielle. She smiled, and the guy lurched away from her, bent over, and threw up. It was nasty. Nausea always is, but the fact that his lunch landed on the unconscious body lying on the mattress at his feet made it worse. We waited for the guy to gather himself a touch, then Lucia stepped forward.

"Darrin? It is Darrin, right? I'm a police officer. We know you ran these people off the road and tried to assault them," she said.

The guy started shaking his head, but Lucia didn't wait for his denials.

"And we know Cornelius Winston hired you to do it."

"Nah, mon. I don know nobody like dot name."

"Yes, you do."

"Nah, I don know nobody."

"Really? Because he seemed to know you."

The guy looked at Lucia and blinked hard. From the waist up he wobbled as if his hips were over lubricated as he tried to process what she was saying.

"Yes, Darrin," continued Lucia. "Mr. Winston said he knew you when we confronted him about the assault. He called the assistant commissioner, who gave me orders to look into it," she lied.

"Nah, mon, he don do dot."

"Who don't do that?"

"Mista Winston."

"So you do know him?"

The guy blinked hard again. It was taking a lot of processing power just for him to stay upright. Blinking seemed to be the way he pumped electrical current into his brain.

"We do some gard'nin fo' Mista Winston. Dot's it. Dot's all."

"The van that ran them off the road is registered to you, Darrin," said Lucia.

Darrin shook his head and nearly fell over. I was pretty sure this interrogation wouldn't be worth a bean in court, but that wasn't the point.

"Me van got stolen."

"It wasn't stolen," I said, getting right into Darrin's face. His breath smelled like a peat bog. "You said I could take it, remember?"

"No, I nevah, mon. You just took it."

"So you were there."

Darrin blinked again, but nothing seemed to click inside, and he stayed silent.

"So just tell us," I said. "Tell us what Mr. Winston told you to do."

"Mista Winston tell us to stay inside da house, so we is stayin' inside da house."

"Is that all Mr. Winston told you?"

"Mista Winston tell us to stay in the da house until he come back." The effort of so much speech made Darrin unstable, and he looked as if he might throw up again, so I stepped back from him.

"Until he comes back?" asked Lucia. "Where did Mr. Winston go?"

Darrin wobbled in place, looked blankly at Lucia, and shrugged his shoulders. Lucia, Danielle, and I traded looks, and then we turned back to Darrin as he promptly crumpled like one of those Vegas casinos they blow up every now and then. His knees buckled beneath him, and he dropped straight down, crossing his legs and landing in a seated position on the mattress. Then he flopped onto his back and began to snore. He might have been faking it, but I didn't give him that much credit for coming up with the move in his state. I stepped by Danielle and put my fingers to Darrin's neck, checking his pulse.

"He's sleeping now," I said.

"Are you sure he's okay?" Danielle frowned.

"I'm sure he'll live. *Okay* is a matter of perspective."

We left him sleeping and walked back out into the sunshine. It was blindingly bright after the dull ambience of the ganja house, and we stood by Lucia's car for a moment.

"So we know for sure these guys are linked to Winston," said Lucia.

I nodded. "He said Winston told them to stay in the house until he got back."

"Got back from where, though?" asked Danielle. "Where is he?"

Lucia looked at us both. "That is the sixty-four million dollar question."

Lucia drove us back to the resort. Danielle told her to take the time off and chill, but neither of us believed she would. We wandered back out past the restaurant, the line forming for the lunch buffet. The waiters had cleaned away the coffee and fruit we had left by the pool, so I asked Danielle if she fancied some lunch. She declined.

"A swim?"

She shook her head. "I feel like going for a run," she said.

I couldn't think of an argument against the idea, so we got our gear and ran along the beach. The people lying on the loungers down on the sand looked at us like we were crazy. But a good run really makes you feel alive. Do it enough and your body rewards you. We'd really gotten back into our runs in the past few months, along the Florida coast where we lived, from City Beach to the State Park. It was long enough to work out the kinks, but not so far as to leave us in pain. The resort beach wasn't designed for running. It sat between two breakwaters, large rocky outcrops where no runner dared go. We ran to the end, then back, and then turned again. As we reached the part of the beach opposite our room, Danielle slowed.

"Okay?" I asked.

She wore Lycra running shorts and top, bare midriff showing the kind of abs that a hundred sit-ups a day earned. Her tanned skin was peppered with pink spots where the shotgun spray had hit her when she'd been shot. I noticed they were disappearing with time. I also noted that she wasn't puffing in the slightest.

"I feel like a hamster in a wheel," she said.

"We could go out of the resort. Run along the road. If you dare."

"I've got a better idea," she said.

She took my hand, and we marched up to our room. She pulled off my t-shirt, pushed me back onto the bed, and leaped on top of me.

She smiled, that half grin that did all kinds of things to me. "Let's work out the old-fashioned way," she said, planting a long, wet kiss on me.

I lay on the bed, listening to the sounds of water and the laughter from the swim-up bar. Sweat was being lifted from my brow by the constant beat of the ceiling fan. Danielle lay snoozing on my chest. After a good workout and an afternoon snooze, I could feel a twinge of hunger coming on. I wondered what had brought out Danielle's amorous side, whether seeing a young cop like Lucia hard at work had her thinking about her own role. I knew Danielle worked in mysterious ways and that I would never really understand her. But when I was the beneficiary of her mood, who was I to complain? My reverie was disturbed by the shrill sound of my phone.

Danielle stirred as it rang across the room, and I wished I had turned it off. I apologized as I dashed across the room to quiet it, and was about to kill it when I saw who the caller was. Instead I answered, standing there in my birthday suit.

"Miami Jones."

"Miami, it's Aaron Katz. I'm just calling back about your kid, the runner."

"Yeah, I figured. What's up?"

"I showed the video to our track coach, Allan Lombardi."

"Your track coach is called Lombardi?"

"Yeah, and his nickname is The Trophy, but he don't get it. He's not a football guy. Anyway, he thinks the kid's got some stuff."

"That so?"

"Aha. He was impressed by ten thirty-five in flats. Now, we might be able to do something for him for next academic year, but here's the thing. We would have to verify that time."

"Like in an official race?"

"Exactly."

"Aaron, when I was recruited by UM, I did an official school visit. The school flew me down from Connecticut. Is that something we can do?"

"There's a wrinkle with that. Lombardi has used all his official visit budget for this recruiting cycle. He spends a lot of time in Europe, and the money goes fast."

"Nice work if you can get it. So a visit is out."

"Well, no. A school-funded visit is out, but prospective athletes are always welcome to do an unofficial visit."

"What's the difference?" I asked.

"No difference. Just one we pay for, one we don't."

"But you'll host him."

"Absolutely. We can arrange class visits, a student chaperone. He can stay a night in dorms, and Coach Lombardi will show him the facilities."

"But he has to pay to get to Miami?"

"That's the only problem. Budgets are tight, and when they're gone, they're gone."

I looked across the room at the bed, where Danielle was sitting up, her arms wrapped around her knees, still naked and hair suitably mussed. She could read me like I was the pledge of allegiance. She gave me that half smile, and she nodded.

"Okay, Aaron. Let's say I can get him there. You can watch him run and make a call on it?"

"That's the other thing. NCAA rules disallow tryouts for non-students."

"They don't make it easy."

"No, they don't. Can you hold while I run this past Lombardi?"

"Sure."

Aaron put me on hold, and I heard an announcement about upcoming games in all sorts of sports and a booster rally that was being held at Mark Light Field. I had been to my share of those, and the thought sent me almost twenty years into the past. Then I was swept back by Aaron's voice.

"Miami, you there?"

"In the flesh." Literally.

"Okay, Lombardi says there is a regional track meet here in Miami over the weekend, and he can get the kid a wildcard entry if you can get him here."

"Great. I'll confirm with his mother. Danielle and I are flying back day after tomorrow, so I'll arrange for him to come with us. I can deliver him to campus on Friday morning. That work for you?"

"Perfect. The race is Saturday morning, so that will give Lombardi time to do the tour and for the kid to see the campus."

"All right. Well, I'll call to confirm after I speak to his mother later today, but assume it's a go."

"There's just one other thing I need to confirm, Miami. And this is just to make it official-like. You're not representing the kid, right?"

"You mean like an agent?"

"Exactly."

"No, Aaron. I was a student-athlete. I know the rules. No agents, no exceptions."

"So your role in this is . . .?"

"A friend of the family who's just trying to give the kid a chance to get into his alma mater."

"That's what I thought. I just needed to check. We can't afford more NCAA scrutiny."

"It's a clean deal, Aaron. I wouldn't sell you a bill of goods."

"I never thought that. So I'll see you Friday."

"You will. Thanks."

I hung up and looked at Danielle. Her impish smile was gone.

"No agents, no exceptions," she said.

"NCAA rules," I replied.

"So what is Desmond Richmond?"

"A benefactor."

"And the difference is?"

"A very thin line."

CHAPTER TWENTY-THREE

I got into some shorts and an old St. Lucie Mets t-shirt, and crawled across the bed and kissed Danielle. She returned it with interest, then bounced off the bed and headed for the shower. I had to talk with Mrs. Swan and Markus, preferably together, but I had to do it when Desmond Richmond wasn't around. I was also worried about Lucia. She was walking a tightrope, doing her job for sure, but potentially annoying some serious people in her small community at the same time. I knew from experience that you could only effect change if you were in a position to do so, and being fired or sent to the Jamaican equivalent of an Antarctic post would not serve her well.

I went out to the small balcony and watched a catamaran skipping across the deeper emerald water. An attendant from the resort was at the helm, taking couples and families for joy rides on the placid ocean. I supposed that allowing guests to take their own boats out might end up in recovery efforts off the coast of Cuba. The lunch crowd had retreated back to the beach and the poolside bar was standing room only. It was a squat building, concrete and hurricane-proof, except for the roof, which was palapa style and reminded me of Longboard Kelly's back home. Which made me think of Ron. Which made me go back inside to grab my phone and give him a call.

"Ron Bennett," he said.

"You don't have a special picture of me that comes up on screen when I call?" I asked.

"I'm looking at video of a Russian oil guy getting all kinds of nasty done to him by a couple of Latinas dressed as cheerleaders. I'm not looking at my phone."

"Business or pleasure?"

"All business, you know me. His wife is paying us two grand a day plus expenses to get the dirt on him."

"Sounds like you got it, but I didn't think Peeping Tom work was really your thing."

"Actually, I didn't get this. The hotel he was in runs a good little blackmail racket. They have HD cameras throughout the rooms. This thing is even edited."

"How'd you get it?"

"The guy who runs the hotel has a kid who wants to learn to sail, so I'm sorting him out at the yacht club."

"Of course you are."

"And what can I do for you?"

"I just wanted to tell you that you were right. The consulate was a bust. That guy didn't want to upset his little paradise friends."

"Yeah, that happens a lot, especially in the backwater offices where the reps are local residents rather than career foreign service. Those guys live there, so sometimes they aren't too keen on making waves."

"Not the greatest advertisement for the old US of A."

"No. The embassies try to keep them on a tight leash, but they can't be there day to day."

"Well, this day we struck out."

"Maybe not. I had a think about it after you called, and I remembered you told me the guy was after the top athletics job. What was his name?"

"Winston. Cornelius Winston."

"Right. Well, I remembered that my father used to know the guy who held a pretty top position in Jamaican athletics, so I googled him to see if he was still around."

"And?"

"And he is. Turns out he's the guy who holds the IOC slot right now."

"You don't say."

"I do. And he's about to retire. He must be worn out from all those first-class flights and five-star hotels and champagne."

"It would wear on you."

"No doubt. Anyway, I gave him a call."

"You are super resourceful, aren't you," I said.

"You have no idea. Turns out, not only did he remember me, but he also knew Cassandra's late husband."

"It's a small world up there at the top."

Ron's lady friend, Cassandra, was a rich widow in Palm Beach. Anyone with a lot of zeros on their bank account who wintered in South Florida knew the Lady Cassandra. She was a feisty old bird, and she made Ron happy, which made her all right in my book.

"So long story short," said Ron, "he is expecting your visit in Kingston."

"Kingston? Can I call him?"

"You can call his assistant. But he really insisted you come for tea. He's like that."

"He's also on the other side of the country."

"It's not LA to DC. It's like crossing Andorra."

I had no idea what crossing Andorra would entail, except perhaps ski gear, and I didn't think that was where the simile was supposed to go.

"All right, give me the number."

I jotted down the details and thanked Ron and told him I'd see him at Longboard's on the weekend. I was tossing around the percentages of making it to Kingston alive on the motorbike, when a better alternative popped into my head. I grabbed my phone and made another call.

"Lucia? It's Miami Jones."

"Miami? What's wrong?"

"Nothing wrong. I was just on a call from my partner in the States. Does the name Bradford Prestwich mean anything to you?"

"Of course. He's Jamaica's delegate to the International Olympic Committee. Why?"

"He's about to retire. Did you know that?"

"I'd heard rumors, nothing more. He is pretty old."

"So that's the job Winston wants."

"Yes, and if he knows Prestwich is about to retire, that might explain why he's so skittish. He needs all his ducks in a row, and he needs them now."

"Right. Well, Mr. Prestwich has invited us for tea."

"Doesn't he live in Kingston?"

"He does. And it's a good hundred miles away, right?"

"About a hundred eighty kilometers. And I wouldn't do it on a bike."

"Me either. So what are you doing tomorrow?"

"Looks like I'm having tea in the capital."

CHAPTER TWENTY-FOUR

It all felt a little too secret-agent, but I didn't want Desmond Richmond wandering in on our conversation. I rode the motorcycle to the workshop where I had bought the thing and asked the guy there if he could get in touch with Garfield. He told me Garfield was probably working, at a resort two along from the one Danielle and I were staying at.

I rode over to Garfield's resort and received the same strange looks from the doormen as I'd gotten the first time I pulled up to our hotel on the bike. I told them I was looking for Garfield, and they directed me to a sports bar on the second level of the main building. The sports bar was aptly named The Bat and Ball, which covered a multitude of sins. Inside it was dark and clubby, with a brass-ringed bar that reminded me of *Cheers*. Garfield stood behind the bar, polishing glasses and chatting to a handful of people who were watching what appeared to be a cricket match on the screen behind the bar. Garfield saw me walking in and offered his generous smile.

"Miami, what brings you to da Bat'n'Ball?"

"You, actually," I said, taking a seat at the bar. "Can I order a beer for cash?"

"Yah, mon. What's your poison?"

"What do you recommend?"

"You tried Balashi? It from Aruba."

"Hit me."

Garfield opened a bottle and poured its contents into a frosty glass, then placed it on a beer mat before me. I took a taste and gave him the thumbs-up, and he gave me his trademark smile.

"You come all dis way just for da best bartender in MoBay?"

"I did, actually. I need to have a chat with Markus and his mom about something, and I don't want Mr. Richmond or his people to know about it."

"Good stuff or bad stuff?"

"Good stuff. There's a chance we might be able to get Markus a college scholarship in the States, but Richmond isn't keen on the idea."

"No, I would tink not. If dare no coil in it fo' him, Mista Richmond no much interested in anyting. But dot is good news. I can arrange it."

"You can?"

"Yah, mon. Tonight. I will make a story, den I will bring dem to your hotel."

"That would be great."

"No problem, mon."

I stayed and enjoyed another beer and watched a bit of cricket with the other guests, who turned out to be from Germany and knew as much about it as I did. Garfield tried his best to explain, but when the batter hit the ball directly over his own head, over the top of the catcher, who Garfield called the wicketkeeper, and scored runs, I was lost. I bid Garfield a good afternoon, and he promised he would see me later.

Danielle and I took an early dinner at one of the non-buffet restaurants in the resort. Apparently one had to line up at the concierge desk at six in the morning to get a reservation for that evening in one of the prime restaurants, which I was told were the sushi and the Italian places. We made our way upstairs without any reservation to the Jamaican restaurant, which was mostly empty. Should I ever visit Rome, I won't be eating saltfish and ackee, so I didn't see the point of pasta in the Caribbean. We had a lovely view of the pool and the beach beyond, the water glowing as the sun set in the distance. We drank Red Stripe and dined on grilled snapper with locally grown vegetables, and for dessert light banana fritters with ice cream.

We were just finishing up when the young woman serving us came to the table and whispered that Garfield was in the lobby. I went down to meet them while Danielle signed for dinner, and we retreated back upstairs to our resort's equivalent of The Bat and Ball. This one was called *Winston's*, which caught everyone's attention, but we were relieved to see a large painting of Churchill on the wall inside. All the other guests were at the pool bar or at dinner, so we had the room to ourselves. We sat in a circle of club chairs: me, Danielle, Markus, and Mrs. Swan. Garfield made to leave and I told him to take a seat. He'd proven himself one of the good guys as far as I was concerned, and he seemed not the slightest bit interested in Markus's coattails.

"Thanks for coming," I told Mrs. Swan and Markus. Both of them wore curious frowns. Evidently Garfield had not told them exactly why I had called them there. The bartender brought a tray of ice waters over and gave Garfield a soft low five.

"Why are we here, Mista Jones?" said Mrs. Swan.

"Can I ask, did you mention to Markus what we spoke about previously?"

"No, suh. I did not want hope for sum'ting dot may never be."

"Well, there's a chance that it may be." I explained to Markus what I had told his mother about the college and the scholarship. Then I expanded on the story with the news that they had seen video of Markus running and were interested.

"I don need to go to America," said Markus. "I can run here, win here."

"I'm not suggesting you can't," I said. "But this would allow you to get a college degree and race as well."

"I go to school now 'cause I have to," he said, glancing at his mother and then quickly away. "Once I finish school, I can train more. I will get faster."

"College studies don't get in the way—they complement your athletics."

"How you know, mon? What do you know about it? You no runner."

"No, you're right. I'm not. But let me tell you what I am. I have my own business. I have staff who work with me. I get to set my own hours, I choose my clients, and I have plenty of time to relax with my friends and family." On the last word I smiled at Danielle. "But I wouldn't have any of that if I hadn't gone to college. When I was your age, I didn't want any of that. I was an athlete. I played American football and baseball. I got recruited by the University of Miami to play both those sports, and I went to college on the same sort of scholarship I'm talking about for you. Without that scholarship, I probably wouldn't have been able to go to college either. But here's the thing." I leaned in toward Markus and took his eye. "I got to play two sports, and in one of them, baseball, I got drafted and played professionally. College didn't get in the way of my sport; college made that happen. I had the best coaches, great facilities, and we competed against other great teams. All that made me better. And I got to go to the big leagues because of it."

I leaned back and sipped some water. "And I had a good sports career. But you know the thing about athletics? It ends. It ends young. You don't stay a pro athlete your whole life. One day it's over. Younger guys come through, faster guys. Your legs get old, and they get heavy, and you slow down."

"I'm not gonna do dot. Become some big fatty," said Markus. His mother slapped the back of his head.

"I'm not saying that. But to be at the top, you have to perform at a level that can't be sustained forever. Think about it. How many sprinters are there over thirty? Not many. How many win big races over thirty? Not many, if any. And at thirty, you're hopefully only one-third of the way through your life. There's a lot of time left. Even if you become Usain Bolt, and win big and get rich, you still have a lot of life left. And let's be honest, most guys don't become Usain Bolt. Most guys don't reach those heights. I was one of those guys. I did well, played pro sports, and then it ended. I wasn't rich. But I did have a college degree. And that degree got me into graduate school toward the end of my baseball career, and that got me this career. The second part of my life."

Markus sat back in his club chair and frowned. He wasn't convinced, and I didn't blame him for that. He wanted to run, to use the wonderful body he had to do the thing he did best. He felt indestructible, unbeatable. Just as a boy his age should. I wouldn't have listened to me either. So I changed tack.

"How would you like to run on state-of-the-art training tracks every day? Run in competitions against the best up-and-coming athletes every week. Lift weights in brand-new gyms that offer fresh towels you never have to wash. And have them pay for it all?"

"But I heard you can't race in da Diamond League if you is a student," said Markus.

"Not so. You can race anywhere you qualify. Now it is true that you cannot accept prize money as long as you are a student. US college athletics are strictly amateur, and they enforce that, believe me. But how many races do nineteen- or twenty-year-olds actually win at that level? Your body is still developing. A sprinter doesn't hit peak form until his midtwenties."

Markus lost the frown some. I could see I was hitting home, at least a little.

"Let me ask you something," I said. "How many Olympic gold medals has Jamaica won to date?"

"Plenty," said Markus.

"Seventeen, all time, as of the last Olympics. Do you know how many golds were won by athletes who were either studying at or had graduated from a US college at the last Olympics?"

Markus shook his head.

"One hundred thirty six. That's golds only, and just the last Olympics." I had to thank the internet for my new knowledge on the subject. I couldn't verify the figures, but I was confident there was some truth to them, and they made my point well.

Markus nodded slowly to himself, and I left him to consider those facts. I turned to Mrs. Swan.

"The University of Miami wants to meet with Markus this weekend. There is a race, a regional event, lots of runners from Florida and the South, and they can get Markus an entry. He can tour the campus, meet other student-athletes, see if he likes it."

"We don have da money to go to America," she said.

"Don't worry about that. I can take care of that."

Mrs. Swan shook her head. "No, we don take charity."

"It's not charity, Mrs. Swan. Mr. Richmond paid me for watching over Markus, and I don't need his money. Let's call it the down payment that your husband never got."

She nodded to herself, letting that sink in. I knew she was a proud woman who had brought up a son alone. A son who had turned out to be a good kid, thanks to her. But I could see that she was just looking for an excuse to put her pride aside so her son could have a better opportunity.

"Look, the plan is this. Markus flies over to the States with us, day after tomorrow. He meets the coaches, tours the facilities. They'll look after him. He'll stay on campus, get a feel for it. Then on Saturday, he'll race. If he runs a good enough time, the university may offer him a scholarship that will cover the cost of his education."

"What is a good enough time?" asked Garfield.

"If he can run the sorts of times I've seen him do at training, I think that will impress them."

Markus snorted. "I can do dot. Easy. I got my new shoes. I can go faster."

"You got new shoes?" I asked.

"Sure."

"From where?"

"Mista Richmond."

I took a deep breath, in through the nose, out through the mouth. I wasn't sure how this part was going to go down.

"You can't take those shoes. You need to leave them here."

"Huh? What you talkin' about?"

"College rules don't allow you to get paid or accept gifts that might be considered sponsorship. And they don't allow you to have an agent."

"What's an agent?" asked Mrs. Swan.

"An agent is anyone who represents an athlete. Anyone who gets you free stuff or money or does deals for you."

"Mista Richmond got all my shoes," said Markus.

"Has he ever given you any money or offered your services to anyone, like a business?"

"No. Just da shoes."

"Okay, so if need be, we can argue that it is race equipment provided as a gift. That would be permissible. But beyond that, you need to cease any relationship with him."

"Cease? Whaddaya mean?" Markus's frown returned. "He helped me, no one else did. Now you say cease?"

"You can't be represented by anyone, and that is what he seems to want. Markus, if this doesn't work out, you can go back and work with him. But if you get an offer from the college, that's it. You can't work with him anymore. So it's best he doesn't know."

"How we do dot?" asked Mrs. Swan. "How we get off da island witout him knowin'?"

I shrugged. "We just go."

CHAPTER TWENTY-FIVE

We were standing at the entrance to the resort when the dark green Range Rover Sport pulled in the next morning, but we paid it no attention until Corporal Lucia Tellis stepped out of it. She smiled and beckoned us over. Inside the car smelled like new. There were swathes of beige leather and a digital touchscreen navigation system.

I nodded and gave my impressed face. "Cops do all right in Jamaica, don't they?"

"It's a drug impound. It's going to go to auction at some point, but for now it was just sitting in the yard. So I borrowed it."

"You're not going to get in trouble?" asked Danielle.

"No. The officer in charge of the impound is married to my cousin."

I was liking Lucia more and more. She took us out of the resort and headed east along the coast road around

Falmouth. We cruised alternately along the water and then inland slightly, always hugging the coast. When we reached Steer Town, where the road broke off to Ocho Rios, Lucia cut south across the island toward Spanish Town and on to Kingston. The capital sat on the south coast, and we came in past Calabar High School, which Lucia explained was one of the top schools competing each year in the Champs. We drove past the Canadian embassy, and then Lucia cut into a leafy area called Jack's Hill that offered expansive views of the city below, out across Port Royal to the blue Caribbean. Even in Jamaica these homes had to have been in the million-dollar-plus bracket.

Lucia pulled the Range Rover to a stop before a massive set of wrought iron gates flanked by ten-foot-high whitewashed walls. She punched an intercom and gave our names, and the gates opened. The house was some kind of colonial style, and reminded me of a Southern plantation. It had an expansive yard of palms and oaks, and a circular driveway where we were met by a guy in a butler uniform whom I belatedly realized was indeed a butler. We got out and stretched the bones from our three-hour journey, and the butler let us know that Mr. Prestwich was waiting for us. The house was no less grand inside, lots of old wood that smelled musty and if not kept up constantly, seemed only months away from disrepair. We were led through the home to a rear patio that had been designed to make the most of the cooling breezes that came off the hill above.

An old man sat at a round wooden table. He wore a pink button-up shirt and matching tie and a dark blue blazer. He had a head of thick hair as white as the proverbial snow and deep blue eyes. He stood as we approached, a task that required considerable effort.

"Suh, Mista Jones, and party," said the butler.

I raised my eyebrows to Danielle at the *and party*, but I liked it and resolved to use it again whenever appropriate.

"Bradford Prestwich," said the old man with a smile, shaking my hand. I introduced Danielle and Lucia, and Prestwich kissed the back of each of their hands, then offered us a seat at the table.

"I'm so glad *dot* you could drop by," he said. I was surprised by his accent. It was the same as Cornelius Winston's, the singsong patois overlaid by years of formal education. For whatever reason, I had assumed the accent belonged to black Jamaicans—rather than it being a regional thing like most accents—but was proved wrong by this white man who looked like an English gent and sounded like Mrs. Swan.

"It's our pleasure," I said.

"So you know young Ron?"

I smiled at the thought of anyone referring to my silver-maned partner-in-crime as young.

"I do. We work together. He sends his regards. He mentioned you knew his father."

"That I did. When he was *deputy chef de mission* at da US embassy. A good mon."

I nodded. I didn't know Ron's dad, so I didn't have much to add. The butler came back out with a tray of cookies and biscuits, or as the butler referred to them, biscuits and scones. He then pulled a carafe out and asked us if we would like coffee, to which we all said yes.

"So Ron tells me you are the IOC delegate for Jamaica," I said, sipping the dark roast.

"Yes, suh. I am. It has been my life's work to help put Jamaica's fine sports men and women in da spotlight."

"You certainly have quite the athletics culture," said Danielle.

"Thank you, ma'am."

He buttered part of a scone and took a bite, and it crumbled onto his shirt.

"So what is it I can help you young people with today?"

I put my coffee down. "Sir, I understand you are soon to retire from your position."

He smiled an old man's smile. "I have made no formal announcement, but I suppose it is already old news. I am not a young mon, and all da travel takes a toll."

I thought of the first-class flights and five-star hotels, but kept the thought to myself. "And I am sure there are a number of suitors to such a prestigious position."

Prestwich nodded, his body movements slow and purposeful. "Of course. I am under no illusion that it is da pinnacle for a sports administrator in our country. What would be your point, young mon?"

It had been a good while since anyone had called me *young man*, so I smiled. "What would a potential candidate need in order to be considered for such a job?"

Prestwich buttered some more of his scone and appeared to think the question through as he did. He bit into the scone, and again I watched crumbs fall.

"I suppose one would require a strong background in sports administration, an understanding of da complexities of da international sporting and political arenas."

"And votes?" said Lucia. She was certainly ready to get straight to the point.

"Yes, and of course votes."

"How would they get those votes?" I asked.

"Well, one develops a network, I suppose, over time. Dare are competing needs, competing sports. One would need to become conversant in da issues, and show solutions to da problems."

"Like a politician?"

"Yes, I suppose. But perhaps a tad more endearing." He grinned the way old men do, as much with the eyes as the mouth. He was right; he was endearing. He was also the product of another time, a different generation. I wasn't convinced that endearing was the key ingredient anymore.

"What about results? Wins? Does that count?"

"Yes, of course. It shows dot one can run an effective program dot produces results. It's not da be-all and end-all, but it is important, yes."

"So who do you think is in line for the role after you?" I asked.

"I couldn't comment on dot—it wouldn't be proper."

"Smart money seems to be on Cornelius Winston."

Prestwich put his scone down on his plate and tapped his papery lips with a cloth napkin.

"Mr. Winston has done a fine job with junior athletics, yes. It is quite a step to da IOC, however."

"How so?"

"The Olympics is more dan track and field, Mr. Jones. Granted, dis is da most important part, in my opinion, but dare are many, many sports. An IOC representative needs support across a breadth of sports, not just track."

"And how would he get that support?"

"Years of work, I would say."

Lucia put her coffee down and leaned into the table. "Mr. Prestwich, suh, would it be fair to say that if one brought money into those other sports that this would trump other considerations that those sports had?"

"Money is not everything, young lady."

"Of course not. But if I were running for your post, and I could, say, offer money to those sports to improve their facilities or visibility?"

Lucia's line of questioning sparked me, so I jumped in. "Take tennis, for example," I said. "Not the highest-profile sport in Jamaica. But if I could bring in money to build new indoor courts that could be used in the height of summer, day and night, might that encourage the tennis folks to support a certain IOC candidate?"

"All right, I'll play. Yes, it might engender such support. But it is not so easy as you think. Money does not grow on trees, and promises without validation win over no one. Even Mr. Winston cannot make money appear from nowhere."

Lucia's phone buzzed, and she excused herself from the table and strode along the patio with the handset to her ear. We took the interruption to drink some coffee. I followed my host's lead and tried a scone, which was lighter than a southern biscuit, buttery and delicious.

"Mr. Prestwich, are you familiar with Desmond Richmond?"

"Da bobsled Olympian?"

I nodded. The man knew his athletes. "That's the one."

"I haven't heard much in years. He moved to da United States, did he not?"

"He did. But he's involved in athletics now, in Montego Bay."

"Dot's news to me, young mon."

"Is he in the picture to take on your role?"

"I don't see it. He might one day. Certainly as an Olympian, he has da profile. But I am not familiar with any of his administrative work. He would need a higher profile in sports administration to realistically take on dis role."

I nodded as Lucia came striding back to the table. She dropped into her seat. "Mr. Prestwich, I wonder if you could help me with something. Is there a sporting event going on in the next few days in the United States?"

"Young lady, I don't mean to sound facetious, but dare are sporting events every day in da United States. Even on Christmas."

"Yes, of course. I'm sorry—I meant an event that might be of interest to you?"

"To me? No, I don't believe so. Why do you ask?"

"Mr. Winston just flew out to the United States. I wondered why he would be doing that."

Prestwich shook his old head. "I have no idea. Dare's nothing going on in da United . . ." He didn't finish his thought, or at least he kept it to himself and stared up at the mountain above us. The morning sun had burned off the cloud, and the green was contrasted with the bright blue sky.

"What is it, suh?" said Lucia.

"Well, it's probably nothing. But Mr. Jones talking about tennis gave me a thought. Dare is no significant sporting event right now in America, but dare might be sum'ting else."

"What do you mean?" Lucia frowned and edged forward on her seat, as if she could feel her wheels biting the dirt and getting some traction.

"The Americans are bidding for da next athletics world championships."

"Do you vote on that, Mr. Prestwich?" I asked.

He shook his head. "No, son. I don't. Dot's the International Association of Athletic Federations, the IAAF. I don't sit on dot association."

"Who does?"

Prestwich looked at me, and his eyes danced as if his brain was processing information like a supercomputer.

"Da seat is vacant."

"Vacant?" Lucia almost spat the words out. "How is it vacant?"

"Da past chair of Jamaican Athletics took a job in Europe dot prevented him from undertaking his duties here at home."

"Could a person hold both that position and yours at the IOC?"

"I see no reason why not."

"Could Winston really be making a play for both roles?" asked Danielle.

Prestwich glanced at Danielle but didn't answer her question. He turned to me. "Why did you bring up da tennis association?"

"I met the president of Tennis Jamaica at Winston's fundraiser at Rose Hall. He was at our table, but he didn't say much, other than he had driven all the way from Kingston. It made me think why he would do that."

Prestwich rubbed his chin with a hand that looked polished to a shine. "I told you money doesn't grow on trees, and I'm right. It does not. But if Mr. Winston has contacts in da US, den maybe . . . you see, we try to make sure da best locations host events and dat dare is a spread across da world. Not everything in Europe or da Americas, for example. But in some quarters, dare is more to it. Some folks partake in a little quid pro quo. In return for a vote on, say, da awarding of a world championship or an Olympics, one might offer development grants."

"What does that mean?" I asked.

"Development grants are what they say on da jar. Grants from rich associations to poorer associations to help build dare sporting infrastructure."

"Like the US helping Jamaica build new tennis courts?"

"Perhaps, but unlikely. See, for such grants to be kosher, dey must be from one sporting association to da same sport in another country. So USTA could help Tennis Jamaica, but da US athletics association could not. That would not pass muster."

"And Winston doesn't even have the authority to make such a deal," said Danielle. "He doesn't have the IAAF job yet."

We sat in silence, drinking coffee and mulling over the scenarios but not coming up with anything concrete. I noticed Prestwich was starting to flag, his eyes growing droopy. His butler came out and told us that it was time for Prestwich's morning calls, which I took as code for nap time, and I wondered if the old guy was in failing health, or whether his engine was just running low from too many years on the planet. We made our excuses and thanked him for his time, and he invited us for coffee any time we found ourselves in Kingston.

Lucia guided the Range Rover out of the gate and followed the signs toward Spanish Town. We drove in silence, but Lucia kept glancing at me in the rearview mirror.

"What are you thinking?" she finally said to me.

I noted Danielle suppressing a giggle at the query. It wasn't my favorite question. It was, as often as not, a trap. In this case I figured it wasn't, but I still didn't know how to answer it.

"Nothing coherent," I said. "I can't make sense of it."

Danielle half turned in the front passenger seat to face both me and Lucia. "Let's recap. What we know is that Winston holds an important but relatively low-level role as chair of the school athletics. From the Rose Hall party we know he's connected—to the constabulary, other sports associations, and basically anyone important in MoBay and beyond. We can connect him to the thugs that attacked Markus and also to the ones that ran us off the road," she said, looking at me. "And we know he's gone to the US." She looked at Lucia. "We do know that, right?"

Lucia nodded. "Yes, we know that. I have a friend who works in customs at Sangster Airport. She was the one that called me earlier. She said Winston just left on a flight to the US."

"To where? Do you know?" I asked.

Lucia glanced in the rearview mirror. "Miami."

"Interesting," said Danielle. "All right, that's what we know. Now, what we assume. We assume Winston wants this IOC job to be vacated by Mr. Prestwich, and we can add to that the vacant position with the IAAF."

"Could be one or the other, or both," I said.

"Right. He might go for the one-two punch, athletics then Olympics, but then he might just try for the brass ring. We also assume that he wants any other pretenders to the throne out of the way. This includes Richmond, and his athletes—namely Markus."

"But how do those dots connect?" said Lucia.

"That's what we need to figure out," said Danielle.

"Well, let's do that," said Lucia.

We spent the next three hours playing it out. We came up with a thousand possibles, but no definites. As we got just outside of MoBay, Lucia drew a line under the conversation.

"Okay, I think we need to look ahead now. What's the next step?"

"For us? We leave tomorrow," I said. "I'll take Markus to UM so he can visit, try to do that without Desmond Richmond getting wind of it, and see if we can figure out why Winston has gone to the US. Did your friend say whether he was going onward from there?"

"No, just Miami. No ongoing ticket."

"But he could have had a domestic ticket she wouldn't know about?"

"He could, yes. But that seems unnecessary, don't you think?"

"I do, but I don't understand going to Miami. As a hub to somewhere else perhaps, but there's nothing for him there."

"Bad assumption," said Danielle. "You don't know what's there."

"True, but US athletics are where? New York City, maybe?"

Danielle tapped away at her phone and turned to me. "USA Track and Field is based in Indianapolis."

"Okay, I wouldn't have guessed that in a thousand years. But it's not Miami."

"Maybe Miami is not where, but who?" Danielle scrunched her forehead, which was still as smooth as a putting green.

"Or what," added Lucia.

That got me thinking. I sat back in my seat, dialed my phone, and waited for the officious voice at the other end.

"Prestwich residence."

"This is Miami Jones. Is Mr. Prestwich up? I mean busy?"

"One moment, suh."

A short wait and Prestwich came on the line.

"What can I do for you, young mon? Did you forget your baseball cap?" I heard the mirth in his voice, like he'd just laid a real zinger on me. I smiled.

"No, sir. I just had a quick follow-up question. You said that the US was bidding for the athletic world championships."

"Yes, although that's not what dey really want."

"What do they really want?"

"Why, da Olympics, my boy. A well-run world champs is da perfect basis for an Olympic bid."

"So the US Olympic Committee supports the athletic world champs bid."

"One hundred percent."

"So tell me, where? Where are they proposing to have these world championships and Olympics?"

"My boy, I thought we covered dot. I thought dot was da point of Corporal Tellis's questions. Dot city would be Miami."

CHAPTER TWENTY-SIX

Markus was taking the day off school. He didn't have training that morning, so Danielle and I packed our bags, grabbed a quick coffee, and met Garfield in the resort lobby. He was in a ubiquitous minivan driven by a thin guy with a red, yellow, and black Rasta hat the size of a wasps' nest. We tossed our bags in the back and drove to the Swans'. Markus was in the kitchen with a small duffel.

"Shoes?" I said. He held up a ratty-looking pair of worn-out Nikes. The new ones were staying in Jamaica.

"Ready?" I asked.

He looked serious, perhaps nervous. I didn't blame him for that. He was about to get on a plane to another country with people he hardly knew who were offering a dream almost too good to be true. If it were me, I'd be waiting for the catch. But Markus grabbed his bag, kissed his mother, and walked out the door. Mrs. Swan gave me her best school-ma'am look, firm and serious.

"You look afta me boy," she said.

I nodded, and Danielle gave her a hug that she seemed to need. We got in the van and headed to Sangster Airport. It's not the busiest airport, but it was still chaotic, minivans and coaches jostling like cattle in the parking lot, people with way too much luggage fighting their way to the front of whatever line they were in. Garfield ignored all direction and pulled the minivan to the curb right by the door to the terminal. We got out, and I shook Garfield's hand and thanked him for all his help.

He smiled. "No problem, mon."

As I let go of his hand, I grabbed his wrist and opened his palm, then I dropped the keys to the motorcycle into his hand.

"You want me to sell it fo' you?"

I shook my head. "It's yours now. They're expecting you to collect it at the resort. It's not a fast car, but a man like you needs some wheels."

He beamed and gave me a high five. We said our final goodbyes, Garfield and Markus slapped low fives, and then we wheeled our luggage inside. I tapped my pockets for tickets and passports. Then I stopped dead. I had bought Markus a ticket with Richmond's money, and as we lined up to check in, it occurred way too late that the boy would need a passport to get into the US.

"Oh, man. You need a passport. I completely forgot."

Markus smiled and held up a blue book with the words *Caribbean Community* at the top, a coat of arms, and *Jamaica Passport* at the bottom.

"We need it when I run for Jamaica in interisland race meets, mon."

"You're way ahead of me."

"I tol' ya, mon. I'm dead fast."

We got our tickets and grabbed a sandwich each for breakfast; then our flight boarded, and we did that sad shuffle across the tarmac to the plane, folks getting the last rays of sunshine before climbing into a tin tube that would deliver them back to whatever frostbitten part of the world they came from. For us, it was business as usual. We would leave the sun in MoBay and find it waiting for us in Fort Lauderdale.

There was another problem with my plan. Danielle and I had left my car in the long-term lot at FLL, but it was a Porsche Boxster, designed for two people and their pet hamster and no more. Unlike how it was for most folks, our luggage size had not been dictated by the airline but rather by what the little car could hold on the ride down. But three doesn't go into two in a stick shift, so I had called Ron. He stood by the carousel as we exited. He looked the same as he had when we left—thick silver hair, tanned with blotches of removed skin cancers giving his face character, and gleaming blue eyes full of life. He was wearing blue trousers and a red Helly Hansen polo shirt. I had only been gone a week, but he was still a sight for sore eyes, whatever that meant.

I introduced Markus, and Ron shook his hand like an old friend and took the boy's bag. Despite being a good forty-five years older than Markus, Ron's view was that guests don't carry their own luggage. Folks in Florida are like that. I fished out my keys, and Danielle took them from me with a smile. She'd drive the Boxster. I didn't see her leave the lot, but I knew the top would be down before she even pulled out. Markus and I and the luggage got in Ron's old Camry, and we chugged up I-95 while I gave Ron the rundown on our adventures in Jamaica. We got back to Riviera Beach by midafternoon, and Ron dropped us off at my house on Singer Island and headed back to the office. He told me not to come in until Monday, and I told him I did my best work away from my desk.

I showed Markus the spare bedroom, and he wandered around my sparsely furnished home. The kitchen was orange Formica, and the living room had a deep shag rug and wood paneling that led out to a paved patio overlooking the Intracoastal Waterway. Singer Island, like most places around the Palm Beaches, had seen all the waterfront properties razed to the ground and rebuilt as grotesque minimansions that required three air-conditioning units on the roof to keep cool. My place was a seventies original, just like me, and I was okay with that. My neighbors, one a faux-Tuscan villa and the other a massive Greek wedding cake, didn't agree. But there's plenty of proof in South Florida real estate that money doesn't equal class.

I asked Markus if he was hungry, and he said no. I told him we would probably go out for dinner since we didn't have much in the house, and he said he was fine with that. He went and unpacked his things, which would have taken all of one minute, so after ten minutes I went to check on him. I found him with a medal in his hand, commemorating University of Miami's win in the College World Series baseball in my senior year. The spare room was my repository of sports paraphernalia. There were two CWS medals, a framed Oakland A's jersey that never got dirty, trophies from high school and college, an old Hurricanes football helmet, and a poster of me pitching on the mound for the Modesto A's. Lots of guys have rooms full of memories—they called them their dens or man caves. The place they go to watch the big game or drink a bourbon alone and reminisce about the glory days. But this wasn't that kind of room. I watched big games at Longboard Kelly's or one of the sports bars on City Beach, and I didn't drink bourbon. It wasn't that I was hiding the stuff away, it just wasn't who I was now. Nothing in the room—not the posters, not the trophies, not the old uniforms—could beat the memories I had stored in my head.

"You won all these?" Markus put down the medal and looked up at a framed photo of me in Oakland garb, my official team photo, taken at the Coliseum before I left to join the team for twenty-nine days.

"I did," I said.

"You wasn't kiddin'," he said. "You went pro."

"Yeah, it wasn't a story. I played in college, like I said. Baseball and football. And I still had time to graduate."

"What was dot like, playin' professional?"

"It was hard work. Honestly, the toughest thing I've ever done. And the pro part was just the pinnacle of a lifetime playing. For fifteen years, most days I hurt. Somewhere. I trained hard, I played hard. It was tiring, mentally and physically. I'll never do anything harder, not that I can think of."

Markus frowned at the photo, and then at me.

"What was it like, playin' in fronta those big crowds?"

"I never really played in front of big crowds."

"But Oakland? Dot's major league, ain't it?"

"Yeah, it is. I was a backup for one of the starters who was injured. I was with the team for a month. But the guy I was backing up got fit, and then the season ended and I got traded."

Markus bowed his head. "Sorry, mon."

"Don't be. This is what I'm saying. It was rough at the time, I'll admit. But eventually I realized that it is what it is. I gave it my all, and that was as far as that adventure was meant to go. I was lucky to meet a guy who kind of took me under his wing and helped me find a new adventure." I looked up at the poster, and then around the room, and I realized I didn't have a photo of Lenny Cox in here. I thought about my former mentor often, more often than I thought about the baseball career, so I didn't need a picture to remind me of everything he did for me. I looked at Markus and wondered if there was a little bit of Lenny in me. The idea made me smile. I looked back to the baseball poster that had captured Markus's attention.

"But it was a great time in my life. My body worked the way it should, and I pushed it to the max. And when I did the right thing by it, it saw me through. I had the best teammates, and my fair share of success. Good times."

Markus moved to a photo of the team that won the College World Series in my sophomore year. We all looked so young. Faces without lines, foreheads covered with hair, limbs yet to fully flesh out into muscle.

"But they end, you know." I laughed to myself. "No, you don't know. That's okay. I didn't either. And you shouldn't worry about it. Time will catch up with you soon enough. Doesn't warrant worrying about. Just enjoy what you're doing, and give it everything you've got, whatever it is."

"I love to run." He smiled and nodded to himself, and I could see he meant it literally. Not like *I love ice cream* or *I love that TV show*. He loved to run. It was why he was put on this earth, if you believed that kind of thing. His raison d'être.

"So Saturday, you do that. Run. Don't worry about it. Just do what you do."

"My mudda really wants dis, don she?"

I nodded. "Your mother wants you to have a better life than she had. That's all. She doesn't care if that's running or mixing drinks in a bar like Garfield. She just wants you to be happy and have a good life. And this is the best of both worlds. You get to run, you get the best training, and you get to study toward something that might be good later. Trust me, after college, you'll never have so much free time ever again. College isn't a chore; it's the best opportunity you'll ever have to chase your dreams. Whatever they are."

I felt myself laying it on thick, like I was a college recruiter, or some rich kid's father, demanding they understand that the Ivy League is the only good option they have. I patted Markus on the shoulders and walked out. He followed me and stood in the living room. I went into the kitchen and heard the Boxster pull into the drive.

"Dis is a normal American house?" asked Markus.

"I guess. Pretty average."

"Where's da TV?"

I smiled. "I don't have a television."

Markus turned and gave me a look of disbelief. "I thought everyone had a TV in America."

"Yeah, pretty much everyone but me."

"Are you poor?"

I could tell it was an honest question and that he didn't mean anything by it.

"No, I'm not poor. I've just got better things to do."

Markus watched me, looking to see if I was pulling his leg. Satisfied that I was on the level, he nodded as if this was an acceptable answer, and he turned back to look through the sliding door out to the patio.

Danielle came in through the front door and gave me a wink. I don't know where she had gotten to in the

Boxster, but she should have beaten us home, not been an hour behind.

"Nice drive?"

She nodded. "Just got some fresh air. How are you guys doing?"

"All good."

She came into the kitchen and kissed me. "What's the plan for dinner?"

"I figured we'd go to Longboard's."

"We should go early. He's got a big day tomorrow."

So we went early. The colored party lights were strung up in the back courtyard as usual, but with the sun still up, they hadn't yet come on. I watched Markus take it in. The tables with beer logo umbrellas, the palapa shade over the outdoor bar, the surfboard with a shark bite taken out of it hanging on the back wall. There was no view, and that was just how I liked it. Views are for tourists. All the view I needed was Muriel, standing behind the bar in her tank top, shoulders back so her breasts thrust at the seams, as if making a break for it. She nodded as we walked in and started pouring a beer. The stools under the palapa had indentations that matched Ron's and my butts, but with Markus in tow, we decide to take a table under an old Miller High Life shade. I went to the bar.

"Long time no see," said Muriel, handing me a vodka tonic for Danielle.

"Back at ya."

"How's Jamaica?"

"Like Florida, without the freeways."

"Looks like you brought some of it back with you," she said, nodding at Markus.

"Yeah, kid's a runner. He's gonna visit UM tomorrow."

"Nice. Does the runner want a drink?"

"Do you have cola?"

"This is a bar."

"It's Mick's bar, which means you do beer and vodka tonics. That's all I know for sure."

"Ever heard of rum and cola?" She squirted a cola from the post mix gun and handed me the glass. "*Sans* rum," she said.

I took the drinks back, and we sat for a while and chatted about the differences between Florida and Jamaica. I said there weren't as many uncompleted homes in Florida, but then I thought about it again and conceded I might be wrong on that. Markus said there were a lot of white folks. I told him that was the Palm Beaches.

"Just wait until we get you to Miami."

CHAPTER TWENTY-SEVEN

When you grow up in New England, go to college in South Florida, and play ball in California, you realize that the United States is not some homogenous mass of people. They might share a currency, a love of football, and an inherent distrust in government, but the towns across the nation have little else in common. Take NFL towns. Seattle, Green Bay, and Jacksonville share almost no common traits: not size, not population, not favorite foods or even political leanings. But they are all as American as apple pie, in their own way.

So it is with Miami. There's no city in the US like it, and within it, not a campus like University of Miami. The U campus found itself adjacent to an area that had become the biggest Cuban community in the world outside of Havana. The campus was tropical, a sporadic mix of buildings, from sixties whitewashed structures with coral inlay to the space-age architecture of the new student activities center. There were palms of staggering variety and long-leafed grasses that were like small ferns. The Latino and Cuban restaurants and cafes lined Route 1, separating the tony houses by the coast from the student community on the other side of Ponce De Leon Boulevard.

I parked the Boxster in the small lot by the tennis courts off San Amaro Drive, and I led the way into the Hecht Athletic Center. It was déjà vu all over again for me. I'd spent some of my best years in and around this building: sweating in the gym, throwing up in the heat on the training fields behind it, and pitching our way to the College World Series on Mark Light Field further on. We strode in like we belonged, even with Markus wide-eyed at the size of the college and its facilities. We went straight to the office of the athletic director, and I told the assistant who we were. Aaron Katz came out to meet us. He was tall and lean and looked like a runner himself, but he wasn't. He had been a champion tennis player in his undergraduate days at Stanford. Now he was a damned good administrator, brought in after the school had suffered through NCAA sanctions brought about as a result of improper benefits provided to student-athletes by school boosters. The events had taken place after my time there, but even in my time, I had seen some things happen between players and boosters that were more than questionable, but those things were going with me to the grave. Aaron ran a good show and was getting things back on track.

And the track was where we went. Aaron shook hands with Markus and welcomed him to the school, took copies of his school report cards, and then took us straight outside and around to the ambitiously named Cobb Stadium. It was really a running track with a small set of bleachers. There was a grass soccer field in the middle and equipment set up at both ends for things like high jump and pole vault. Some kids were running drills, and a muscular guy with a whistle was directing the traffic in a booming voice. Aaron took us to the big guy.

"Allan, this is the guy I was telling you about. Miami Jones, Allan Lombardi."

The big guy shook my hand hard. I wasn't sure where the Lombardi had entered the family, but he looked about as Italian as Swiss cheese. He was dark and heavy, skin the color of coal and eyes with a hint of yellow, like he had stayed up too late for the past twenty years. I gestured to Markus.

"This is Markus Swan. Markus, meet Coach Lombardi."

"Good to meet you, son," said Coach. Even his regular talking voice hit me in the chest.

"Suh," said Markus.

"I'm not your sir, son. Call me Coach."

"Yah, mon. I mean Coach."

"Mr. Katz tells me you like to run."

"No, suh. Coach."

"You don't like to run?"

"No, Coach. I *love* to run."

Lombardi gave a snarl that might have been an attempt at a smile. "Good answer. Get your spikes on, and let's have a run."

Markus smiled. "Yah, Coach." He jogged to the grass, dropped his duffel, and sat down and slipped on his old running shoes.

"You got spikes, son?"

"No, Coach. Dis all da shoes I got." Markus glanced at me.

"All right, we can work with that," said Lombardi. "Let's go." He turned to me. "We'll take it from here. One of my guys will take him on a tour this morning, and then I got a student set up to show him, you know, the other side. He'll stay on campus. You got any problems, call me."

"You'll get him to the race tomorrow?"

"We will."

"Then I'll see you there."

I wished Markus all the best and told him not to worry about what anyone else was doing or saying, and just run.

"Don worry, Mista Jones. Dees boys din't invent smack talk." He smiled like he was in his element, and I hoped his insides were as confident as the veneer he was projecting.

"Just remember, they're not looking for perfect—they're looking for talent they can train. You're a smart kid, and your mother brought you up right, so show them that and you'll be just fine."

I walked back to the parking lot with Aaron, and I told him to call if there were any problems. I got in the Porsche and headed to the marina to see a man about a dog.

CHAPTER TWENTY-EIGHT

The marina at Miami Beach is home to some of the biggest boats ever built for nonmilitary and nonfreight purposes. Dot-commers, media moguls, sport stars, drug runners, and heads of state all held their megayachts in Miami Beach. I stopped by the office and found a young kid taking orders from a Russian customer who was barking like a drill sergeant. I nodded to the kid, and he saw me, left the Russian ranting to himself, and came over. It didn't seem to improve the mood of his customer, but he tossed me a key card attached to a float and told me to go to B14. I left and wandered out into the sunshine. The marina sat on the Intracoastal side across from South Beach, tucked in behind the island from the hurricane winds that came through as and when they chose. I found Lucas polishing the glass on the sliding door of a speedboat shaped like a spear.

"I need to see a man about a dog," I called.

Lucas didn't look up. "A mongrel for a mongrel, eh?" he returned in his broad Australian accent. He finished polishing the window until it was practically invisible and then turned, rubbing his hands with the rag. Lucas didn't just manage a marina. He had been close to my mentor, Lenny Cox. The two of them had met when they were both doing goodness knows what for their governments, in places like Iraq and Afghanistan and who knows where else. Now he lived the quiet life by the water, except, it seemed, when I came calling.

"How are you, mate?" He leaned over the transom and shook my hand.

"Not as good as you. Nice boat."

"Yeah, she's a beaut. Owned by that Mexican fella who's got all them Spanish language TV stations."

"Nice. Looks big enough to cruise down to Cuba," I said with a wink.

"Nah, you'd want something like that Magnum Marine 80 down there. This thing would light up the radar."

"You'd know."

"Yeah. Listen, this fella's comin' down soon, and I'd like to make her sparklin' for him. You okay to catch up for lunch? Monty's, in an hour?"

"See you then."

I took a walk back along the marina out onto the promenade and through South Point Park, where a group of athletic-looking folks in Lycra were doing lunges and spider crawls on the lawn. I strolled around them and over the sand hills covered in wispy grasses, and sat on the beach. I was south of South Beach, past all the action, the clubs and bars and art deco hotels. This part of the coast felt more like Cape Cod, a cooling breeze and foaming waves breaking on the beach. The main difference was the towering hotel and apartment complexes standing over the beach at the southern point. I sat for a while, not thinking about anything for a change, watching a flock of gulls play tag with the ebbing and flowing ocean, breathing in some good sea air, and then I stood and brushed off and wandered back along the promenade until I got back to Monty's.

I asked the girl at the desk if Lucas had arrived, and she said no but directed me to a vacant stool at the bar by the pool. Monty's was a little too spring break for me, with the view and the pool, but it was during term, and many of the snowbirds were already making the trek back to New England or Michigan or Quebec, so the crowd was light and the vibe was easy. I ordered a Sam Adams and was two sips in when Lucas arrived. He flopped down on the stool next to me and pointed at my beer to order one of his own.

"What's news?" he asked, sipping his beer.

"Just got back from Jamaica."

"Don't say."

"Yeah. Good place, you'd like it."

"I'm all right here, mate. So what brings you to the big smoke?"

"I met a kid in Jamaica. Good kid, fast runner. Brought him over to meet some folks at the university. He might have a shot at a scholarship."

"Nice."

I nodded and sipped my beer. I gave Lucas the short version of goings-on with Winston and Richmond and Prestwich and the whole sports administrator boondoggle thing. In his line of work, Lucas dealt with a lot of rich and famous people and heard a lot of things. I wondered if he knew anything about the proposed Miami Olympic bid.

"I've heard rumblings, sure. I think the whole show's a waste of time, but not all folks agree. Some important people are going on about how it will make Miami an international capital. Like they've never walked around town and listened to all the languages chattering around them."

"Where's the bid money coming from?"

"The usual places, mate. The state will be kicking a bit in, and the city of Miami. The tourism guys. Then there's private sources, companies who wanna get their pound of flesh out of the whole shebang."

"How would they handle the money, do you think?"

"Crikey, mate, how do you reckon? You know there'll be two sets of books. One for all the official stuff, and then the payola."

"You know anyone who might be involved in the latter?"

"Is this Miami, or is this Miami?" He pointed out to the docks. "Look at all those boats. Now, I'm not saying it's all ill-gotten gains, but it ain't a church bake sale either. This is one of the drug capitals of the world. You know that better than most."

I did know better than most. I had been involved in a case with a drug cartel in Miami that nearly ended badly, and I resolved it with Lucas's help—and with considerable prejudice.

Lucas continued. "Those boys know how to move cash. So I'd be looking at your end points, and whether they have any links to anyone who might know a good deal about money laundering."

I wondered about that for a moment. Winston's best connection to the US was through athletes he had sent here, and the best connection they would have to South Florida would be through the Jamaican community in Lauderhill. I was tossing around whether I knew anyone in that community who might know something about moving money and had decided that I did, when my phone rang. I picked it out of my pocket and looked at the screen.

"Hey, Aaron, how's the tour going?"

"Not good, my friend, not good."

"Why? What's happening?"

"Your boy's doing okay. But I got a guy turned up here claiming to be the kid's agent."

"His agent?"

"Yes. And I told you, I can't have any NCAA issues. If the kid has an agent, he's out. I need him off the campus today."

I skidded into the parking lot by the tennis courts again and jogged into the Hecht Athletic Center. Aaron Katz was in his office, and his assistant sent me right in.

"What are you doing to me, Miami?" said Aaron.

"This is all bogus. Tell me what happened."

"The kid is off on a tour with some students, and this guy turns up at my office wanting to know where Markus is and claiming to be his representative."

"Who was it? What was his name?"

"Desmond Richmond," he said.

The look on my face must have betrayed me because Aaron shook his head.

"You know him, don't you?" He wasn't happy. "What have you got me into, Miami?"

I took a deep breath, in through the nose, out through the mouth. The same technique I had used throughout my baseball career, on the mound, before every pitch. I felt instantly calmer. I hadn't expected Richmond to turn up at all, let alone this quickly, but I had taken steps. I just hoped they were enough.

"Look, Aaron, this guy is not who he claims to be. He's trying to use these young athletes for his own purposes, positioning himself for some kind of play as a sports administrator."

"Miami, I hear you. But I don't care. I'm sorry, but I can't afford to care. I've got hundreds of student-athletes here with us right now, who will all be adversely affected by the NCAA getting any whiff of wrongdoing. And the word *agent* is a big red flag. You know that."

"Aaron, this guy is not an agent. There is no written agreement between Markus Swan and this guy."

"You know as well as I do, an agreement doesn't have to be written. Any implication that he is acting on the kid's behalf can be considered agency. And this guy says he handled a deal with Nike to supply Markus with equipment. That's an agent, and that's unacceptable. I don't make the rules, but I sure have to follow them."

"He said that? He said he had a deal with Nike?"

"He did."

I thought about the new shoes Richmond had brought to Montego Bay with him. They were certainly Nikes, but he never said how he acquired them. A deal with a big company like Nike seemed to be the sort of thing he would have wanted everyone in Jamaica to know about. But right now I needed time to find out, to put Richmond back in his hole, and to keep Markus on campus.

"Aaron, you saw the kid's shoes this morning. They were as old as Methuselah. Do you think if this guy had a Nike contract his athlete would be running for a scholarship in those old things?"

I saw Aaron's face soften a bit. "I have people looking for Markus now. I'm going to ask you to take him off campus as soon as we find him."

"Come on, Aaron. Give him a chance. He hasn't done anything wrong. He's just trying to run his way out of poverty. You know how that is. Lots of student-athletes here battle that, in football, baseball, all sports. And lots of them have to contend with people trying to ride their coattails. That's what this clown is trying to do."

Aaron looked at me and sighed but didn't speak.

"Just give me until tomorrow. Let Markus run. You're still not on the hook for anything. If you're not happy tomorrow, then fine, it's over, no hard feelings."

"What if this guy Richmond can prove a commercial relationship with Markus? All he needs is to show he gave any of this Nike stuff to the kid, and it's done."

"He can't prove what isn't true," I said, although I wasn't sure yet that he couldn't. "And this Nike deal doesn't smell right. You know folks at Nike. Why don't you call them?"

He nodded. "Okay, I will. But that might not work out for you. Or Markus. He's got running shorts, a track top. All Nike."

"What if I can show that all that stuff was supplied by his association for running competitions?"

"That would be acceptable. Is that the case?"

I looked at Aaron. I wanted to tell him it was. But I really didn't know. "Richmond's not his agent. You give

Markus until tomorrow, and I'll make sure you have enough proof to satisfy anyone."

He sat down in his chair and let out a long breath. "All right. Until tomorrow. But I will be calling the people at Nike."

"Good," I said. I hoped it would be.

CHAPTER TWENTY-NINE

I drove straight to Lauderhill. I had no idea exactly where Richmond bunkered down, but I had no doubt it would be somewhere near Lauderhill, and I also had no doubt he would be a known commodity in that community. As I drove I thought over what Aaron Katz had told me. I was fairly confident Richmond would find it hard to prove he was Markus's agent, but I wasn't quite so sure how I would be able to prove that he wasn't. What I needed was for Richmond to prove that point for me.

I stopped at a liquor and cigar store in a strip mall just off the turnpike, where I bought a bottle of water and a Powerball ticket and asked the old guy behind the counter where I could find Desmond Richmond. He frowned as though I had asked if he knew Johnny Depp, so I slipped an extra twenty into his palm when he handed me the lottery ticket, and his memory came good. He directed me up Route 7 to a rundown mall area known as the Sixteenth Street Shopping Center. This was no Westfield. It was like two low-rent strip malls had decided to mate. Rows of buildings with the design and charm of concrete shoe boxes, with stores for furniture and industrial uniforms and adult videos. The most common signage was *For Lease*, and the further I got into the area, the more boarded up the stores were.

I drove around in a circuit until I found the establishment I wanted. A printing shop, specializing in t-shirts, mugs, and Bob Marley posters done like Andy Warhol. It was in a strip of sickly green shops, one long building of about five storefronts, but only one appeared to be open for business. The rest were shuttered as if preparing in advance for the next hurricane. I parked in a lot that was plenty of acres but not many cars and walked over to the store. A little bell dinged as I entered. Sometimes the old-style security is the best. A dark man in a yellow t-shirt printed with the eyes and smile of a happy face looked up from a newspaper. He didn't speak and he didn't smile. But he didn't frown either, so I took that as a good sign.

"Looking for Mr. Richmond," I said.

Now he frowned. "Not shah I know dot name," he said, like he'd just gotten off the boat from Jamaica.

"Yeah, you do. He used to be one of those guys who wore rubber suits and shot down ski runs like it was actually a sport, as opposed to gravity."

"I think you mean bobsled," said the familiar voice from the doorway that led to a room in the back of the store.

"Mr. Richmond," I said.

"Did you compete at the Olympics?"

"No, I played real sport," I said, looking at a t-shirt with a photo of a wedding couple on it. I only had two questions about it. Who, and why?

"Ah, yes, baseball. A poor man's cricket."

"Yeah, I know Derek Jeter sure hurts for a penny."

Richmond stepped into the store but stayed behind the counter. I didn't feel good about that all of a sudden. A lot of deadly weapons get pulled from behind counters in strip malls like this one.

"Why did you steal my boy away?" He placed his fingers on the counter, splayed like a cage.

"Your boy? I didn't know you had kids."

"Oh, I have many kids. All of them run for me."

"Not all of them. Not anymore."

He grinned. He had a hard face, like life had been rough, but it had a roguish charm to it. "Do you really think you can steal my boy and I would do nothing?"

"First of all, he's Mrs. Swan's boy, not yours. Second, I didn't steal him. He came of his own volition and with his mother's permission. And third, whether he stays or goes isn't up to me. It's up to him."

Richmond shook his head. "You are right, it is not up to you. But you're wrong, it is not up to him."

"What is your problem with Markus going to college, anyway? You don't want him to get an education?"

"He don't need an education. He needs to run. And he needs to run for me."

"He can run at college."

"You really aren't that naive, are you, Mr. Jones? I know how it works here. If he is at college, he cannot run professionally. He cannot run for prize money. And if he cannot run for prize money, what good is he?"

"He's no good to you. So why not let him go?"

Richmond turned and ran his hand across a collection of t-shirts hanging on the wall behind him. He stopped at one grotesque item that read, *Jamaica? No, she wanted to!* He grinned again and spoke.

"If you let one sheep out of the yard, the other sheep start getting ideas," he said. "If Markus doesn't run for me, he doesn't run."

"You're crazy. You think the school is going to believe you're his agent? You don't have a contract."

"Mr. Jones, I have been around this merry-go-round once or twice. I know I don't have a written contract. I don't have one, because right now, I don't want one. I don't want some loser who couldn't make it trying to leech off me because he thinks we have a legal agreement." He turned from the t-shirts and looked at me. "I negotiate for merchandise, like shoes, with major advertisers, like Nike. I supply those shoes to my athletes. By NCAA rules, that makes me a manager. So I sign them up without ever putting a pen in their hands. They go pro, or they go home."

"Markus doesn't have your shoes. He didn't bring them. So you supplied nothing."

Richmond gave a deep *ha*. "You don't even believe that makes any difference yourself." He looked out the window at the graying sky, matching the cracked asphalt in the parking lot. The guy in the happy face shirt kept reading the paper as if he didn't speak our language.

"I don't care what Markus is doing at the university, Mr. Jones. But I know he isn't studying there. And if you are truly concerned for him, you will deliver him to the airport tomorrow so he can go home and resume his training." He stared me in the eye. "Before he gets himself hurt."

Richmond stood upright and rolled his neck around like he was stretching, and then he turned slowly and walked through the door to the back room without a word. I watched the doorway for a moment, expecting something to happen, maybe a gunshot, or confetti. But nothing happened, so I turned to the smiley face guy, who had finally looked up from his paper and was watching me like a zoologist watches a turtle: with a mix of professional interest and inherent boredom. I looked at his t-shirt once more, and I smiled.

"Have a nice day," I said, and I walked out.

CHAPTER THIRTY

The days were getting longer, but daylight savings was yet to kick in, so the light was fading by the time I reached West Palm. My interaction with Richmond hadn't completely shaken me, but it had sapped my confidence some. And the perfect antidote to a lack of confidence was a few hours with good company. I pulled the Boxster into the lot behind Longboard Kelly's and moseyed into the courtyard. The party lights had come on, their colors playing off the tables and the beer taps, giving the place a festive feel. Some of the regulars were in. Quitting time was not quite upon us, but it was also a flexible notion in South Florida. I headed to my stool under the palapa, and Muriel had a beer waiting for me by the time I got there.

"Nickel for your thoughts," she said.

"Cost of living's high, and goin' up," I sang back.

"You are in a mood."

I took a long pull on my beer and wiped foam from my mouth. "I am. I've got a big day tomorrow, so don't let me get too out of control, will you?"

"You asking a bartender to not sell you beer?"

"At a point."

"You got it, sweetie." She thrust her tank-top-clad bosom at me and turned away to a customer in the indoor bar. I took out my phone and punched in a text message and sent it to Ron. It was just one word, like a code or Batman's spotlight in the sky, summoning him to the scene. *Longboard's*. Ron appeared seven minutes later. Muriel had a beer ready for him too. She was good like that.

"How's business?" I asked.

"All good. Closed my case with the Brazilian woman, and she wired the money this afternoon. She seemed happy with the results."

"Was that her husband's money?"

"Only half of it, now. How about you? How did your kid like the campus?"

I shrugged. "Fine, I guess. Who can tell what a teenage boy is thinking?"

I told Ron my sorry tale of how Desmond Richmond had turned up claiming to be Markus's agent, and how, despite my best efforts, that could muddy the waters enough for UM to pass on him.

"That would be too bad," said Ron.

I nodded and drank my beer.

"So, I'm no expert on these rules," said Ron, "but you say a student-athlete can't have someone represent them to an external organization or professional team in return for money or services."

"That pretty much sums it up."

"So who did Richmond represent Markus to?"

"Nike, so he says."

"Nike? That's pretty big cheese."

"It is. It really doesn't get much bigger."

"But did that really happen?"

It was a good question. Aaron Katz said he was going to call his contacts at Nike, and then we'd probably know. "My gut says no."

"Okay, let's work with that. If Richmond didn't get the shoes from Nike, where did he get them from?"

I frowned and took a drink and frowned more. My forehead must have looked like a potato patch. "He's a hustler," I said. "He could have gotten them anywhere. He could have bought them."

"Does his storefront make you think he bought them?"

"It does not. So maybe he has a stock of shoes."

"And he happened to have Markus's size. Does he run a shoe store?"

"No, he doesn't. Not in the traditional sense." That got me thinking.

"What about the other stuff Markus has? The shorts, the tracksuit?" Ron took a sip and continued. "You played high school sports. Where did you get your equipment?"

"From the team."

"Did the kid run for any teams?"

I started nodding, and the synapses starting firing in my brain. "He did. He told me in the airport. He had a passport because he needed it to visit other islands in the Caribbean. It's not one big country, of course. They're all separate nations. So he needed a passport when he represented Jamaica at age-level competitions." I slipped off my stool and grabbed my phone. "Excuse me a moment, Ron. I've got a call to make."

Ron smiled and turned to the bar taps. I walked to the back of the courtyard, near the surfboard with the bite out of it, where the reception was always best. I called a number in my recent calls.

"Corporal Tellis," said the voice on the other end.

"Lucia, this is Miami Jones."

"Miami, good to hear you. Did you get back alright? How's Markus?"

I gave her the two-minute tour version of the day, and then I got to the point.

"I need to get in touch with Cornelius Winston."

"You what? I thought he was the problem."

"The Russians were the solution to the Second World War in Europe, even if they were the problem in every other way. Sometimes you've got to use what you have."

"That little plan resulted in the Cold War," she countered. "Are you sure about this?"

"No. But I don't have time to wait. I've given Markus a glimpse of what is possible, and tomorrow the college is going to rip the rug out from under him. I can't let that happen."

"Give me half an hour to see what I can find."

"Thanks, Lucia."

I hung up and returned to the bar. In my absence, Danielle had joined Ron, just off shift and freshly showered. She wore a gray athletic top and jeans that made me want to go for a run on a tiny Jamaican resort beach. She gave me a kiss and sipped her vodka tonic.

She smiled. "Calling your girlfriend?"

"Lucia," I said.

"I knew you had a thing for her." She gave me the half grin that made me miss a beat.

"She is a cutie, and smart as a whip. But she ain't you."

Danielle looked at Ron. "It's like living with Keats."

"Hey, I'm just a gumshoe."

"With a master's degree," said Ron.

"Not in English lit."

"Fair point."

Ron ordered another round, and Danielle recounted her day. Cop shows always look so exciting, but a lot of law enforcement isn't about enforcing the law. It's about data entry. Danielle's office on Gun Club Road looked like a brokerage firm. The main difference was that brokers' tedium was rarely punctuated by being shot at. My phone rang, and I sprang off my stool and went back to the rear of the courtyard.

"Lucia?"

"Miami. Here's what I've got. Don't ask how I got it."

I liked her style. "Ask no questions, tell no lies, Corporal."

"Exactly. This is Winston's message service. Apparently he checks it several times a day when abroad. I hope it will do."

"It's as good as we're going to get on short notice."

She gave me the number and wished me luck.

"Thanks, Lucia. Good work."

"What are you going to tell him?"

"You don't want to know. I'll let you know how Markus gets on."

"Thanks. Regards to Danielle."

I didn't return to the bar. I had put the number in my phone as Lucia read it out, so I just hit the little phone icon and was connected. An English woman's voice came on the line. It was damned sexy and would have sold a lot of magazine subscriptions.

"You have reached the message bank for . . ." I lost the lovely Englishwoman and got an aged baritone instead: "Cornelius Winston." Then the woman was back. "Please leave a message and return number, and your call will be returned promptly." There was a period of electronic silence, which really isn't silence at all, and then a beep.

"Mr. Winston. This is Miami Jones. I have an offer for you. If you want to scupper Desmond Richmond's play on Markus Swan and bring Markus back into the Jamaica athletics fold, I need a favor from you. Richmond claims to be Markus's manager. I need a letter, on official letterhead, saying that Markus was provided all his race equipment as part of team kit when representing Jamaica. If you can provide such a letter, Markus will be done with Richmond. Here's my email address." I gave my details and said he was welcome to call if he had any questions. I knew he wouldn't call. He would do or not do. There was no chatting necessary.

I went back to the bar and finished my beer, and then Muriel asked if I wanted another. I looked at Danielle. "How about a Jamaican-style workout?"

She blushed, which is quite a feat with a law enforcement officer, and slapped my arm. "He'll have one more. Me too, thanks, Muriel. And some smoked fish dip."

It was worth a shot. But Mick's smoked fish dip was a good second. He made it from scratch, from whatever big fish came in at the docks. When snowbirds leave South Florida for their northern nests, it's one of the things they miss most. I had no such problem.

I looked at Ron. I looked at Danielle. Then I picked up my cold beer and turned and looked at the twilight falling across the clear sky like a curtain, palm trees swaying gently in silhouette. I smiled. I wasn't going anywhere.

CHAPTER THIRTY-ONE

There was pressure in the air when I woke the next morning. I left Danielle sleeping and padded out to the patio. The sky was clear, morning just etching the scene blue, but I could smell it in the air. Miles offshore, somewhere near the Bahamas, clouds were gathering. I shivered despite the mild morning, and sauntered back inside to put on coffee.

The track meet was at Curtis Park in Miami. The track was in pristine condition and looked like it had recently been relaid. The lane markings were freshly painted white, and the grass in the infield was a deep green. It reminded me of the first time I had come to Florida. It was a high school baseball tourney in Orlando, and I couldn't remember any of the results, but the brightness of the sun and sharpness of the colors stayed with me. This was that kind of day. The deep blue sky set off the greens of the palms that surrounded the track like a leafy amphitheater. We sat in the bleachers like nervous parents. Danielle cheered when Markus was called onto the track, and he nodded in her direction, which was as demonstrative as he was going to get. His face was all business. He was about to do what he did best. We had seen him briefly before the race, just long enough to ask how the visit was going, and he said cool, which I took as high praise indeed.

He was wearing his old shoes and a green, yellow and black top. There were blocks at the start of the hundred meters, and I hoped they weren't a distraction to him. I worried too much. The gun cracked, and Markus took off slow as usual, but by halfway he had everyone's measure. He hit the finish line easing up, first by a couple of lengths. I didn't know the time but it was an impressive run, if the field was any good. There was electronic timing, which made times official, but no screen to display them. We waited for a long minute until the announcer called out the results. Markus had run a ten thirty. Not faster than he did on dirt in Jamaica, but good enough. I hoped. I saw Coach Lombardi sitting by himself at the top corner of the stand, and I weaved my way up the bleachers to him.

"What did you think, Coach?"

Lombardi looked at the track like he was replaying the race, and then back at me. "He can't start, his reaction time is like my grandmamma, and I don't like showboating at the finish." None of that sounded good to me. Then the coach smiled. "He's wearing the most beat-up pair of street shoes I ever seen. With proper training and a pair of spikes? Hell, he could break ten."

"So you want him?"

His smiled dissolved. "You need to take care of business. Yeah, I want him. But Aaron's freaking out."

"Let me take care of Aaron."

It was no surprise that Desmond Richmond had appeared at the event to claim his property. He was watching me as I found Aaron Katz standing on the grass beside the bleachers.

"Good run," I said.

"Boy's quick," said Katz. "You gonna help me out?"

"I believe I am."

Desmond Richmond sauntered over to us. "My boy runs fast, don't he," he said.

"He's not your boy," I returned.

"We going to have this conversation again?" Richmond offered a smile, the kind most often seen on the mouths of sharks.

"We are. You don't represent Markus; you just want to ride his coattails. Well, I'm cutting them off."

"You think you his manager now?"

I shook my head. "I'm just a family friend. But you? You're nothing."

"I represented the boy to Nike. How do think he got all that gear? So according to NCAA rules, he's mine."

Katz looked at me and frowned. I pulled some papers from my pocket and unfolded them. I handed the top one to Katz.

"This is a letter from the Jamaican Inter-Secondary Schools Sports Association, signed by the president of said organization, confirming that all of Markus's equipment was supplied as team kit for competition purposes, when he represented Jamaica at age level."

Aaron read the letter, and a small grin tugged on his lips. Richmond held out his hand, and Katz passed him the letter. Richmond's frown deepened as he read it. A snarl appeared when he saw the signature of Cornelius Winston at the bottom. Winston had come through big-time. I had received the letter attached to an email that morning. Along with another attachment, which I had printed and now passed to Katz.

"This is a copy of the race program for an interisland race meet. You can see Markus Swan listed as an athlete, representing Jamaica. And on the next page, you'll see the name of Desmond Richmond, listed as a trainer. Not a manager. Not an agent. A trainer."

That Winston had provided the second document proved, if it was required, that he saw Richmond as competition and wanted him gone. He mentioned in his email that interisland All-Schools also had rules against agents, and the only way Richmond could attend was to claim to be a trainer or coach. Doing so had backfired on him. He snatched the papers from Katz and read them over, then snarled again.

"This don't prove nuttin'," he said, his Jamaican accent getting thicker with his anger.

"Actually, the NCAA loves a paper trail above all else," said Katz. "Do you have any paper to contradict this information? A contract with Markus, perhaps?"

"I don need no contract," spat Richmond. "I got him Nikes!"

"Yes, on that," said Katz. "I called the executive vice president of global sports marketing at Nike. She and I went to college together. I asked her about you. She had never heard of you, and she checked with her team. Seems no one knew your name."

"Dot ain't so," said Richmond.

"Well, either way, she told me that Nike doesn't give individual sponsorships to high school prep athletes. They know that runs afoul of NCAA rules. They sponsor the teams, the schools where the athletes go, but not the individuals. She claims that a deal like you specify would not happen."

Richmond looked at me, and for a moment I thought he might take a swing, as the veins in his neck pulsed. But he took a breath and gathered himself. He handed the papers back to Katz and made to leave.

"Little battles don't win wars," he said, and then he walked away toward the parking lot. Aaron and I watched him walk, and as we did, I spoke.

"Who said that? Little battles don't win wars?"

Katz turned to me. "No one. No one who won anything, anyway. Little battles are exactly what win wars."

I nodded. "So about Markus."

"When is he going home?"

"Monday morning."

"He can stay on campus again tonight, but you'll have to get him tomorrow. There's a two-day limit to visits. Rules are rules. But I'll have an offer letter for him to take home to his mother before he leaves."

I shook hands with Aaron and walked back to Danielle, who was waiting at the bottom of the bleachers.

"How'd it go?" She looked like a nervous mother.

"He's in." I smiled, and she gave me a hug.

"What about Richmond?"

"He's done. He'll probably start getting written contracts with kids in the future, and we can't stop that, other than to spread the word about him. But Markus doesn't have to worry about him anymore."

"That's so great," she said. "Let's go tell Markus."

CHAPTER THIRTY-TWO

Markus called his mother with the news. He tried to act all casual, but the way he held my phone to his ear with a white-knuckled grip told me that he was pumped. Evidently the campus had made an impression, and the students who had shown him around had painted the best possible picture. It wouldn't be all smooth sailing. He'd miss home, he'd find the studies harder than anything he'd done before, and from the look of Coach Lombardi, he'd learn what it meant to lose your breakfast on the practice fields. But he'd love it too, and he'd train better than he ever had, and he'd run and run and run. I told Mrs. Swan that we would put Markus on the flight on Monday morning, and she said Garfield would be there to collect him.

We had driven Ron's Camry down to the meet so we could fit Markus in the car, and we offered a ride to two other student-athletes from Jamaica who had befriended

Markus. Danielle frowned as the boys got in the back of the car.

"Makes you wonder about the practicality of the Porsche, doesn't it?"

I shrugged. "If you buy a Boxster with any kind of practicality in mind, you're out of your mind."

"Still. Can't even fit a third person in it."

"What third person?"

She shrugged back at me. "No one. Just generally."

I didn't know where that train of thought was headed, so I left her alone with it. We got on South Dixie Highway and crawled through the Saturday morning traffic down to the campus. We parked and walked together back to the on-campus digs. It brought back some memories: snoring roommates, socks on doorknobs, and lots of good times that we thought would never end. Danielle and I sat in the sunshine while the three students took showers.

"You miss it?" She was looking at me.

I glanced around at the thick grass and the palm trees. If Florida was my heart, this place was the valve.

"No," I said. "'Miss it' is the wrong phrase. I did it, it helped make me who I am, what my life has been, and I'm happy for all that. So I'm glad I came here. It's part of who I am, and maybe, in a way, I'm part of who it is." Danielle nodded but didn't take her eyes off me, like she was studying a perp to see if he was telling the truth. "Besides, life's pretty darn good now." I put my hand over hers and gave a little squeeze, which she returned.

We bought the three students burritos for lunch at a place called Lime. Markus asked if it was okay for him to stay on campus again, and I said that was the plan.

"Just don't be stupid, is all," I said. "No alcohol or anything dumb like that. They've made you an offer, but they're still evaluating you. They want you on campus to see if you act like an ass. Don't kid yourself that they won't pull the offer quicker than you can run a hundred yards, if you mess up. You got me?"

Markus smiled. "Yah, mon. I got yah."

"We'll drop by tomorrow to collect you, okay?"

"Yah. Oh, dare's a few guys goin' to da cricket tomorrow. You okay to pick me up dare?"

"At the cricket? In Miami?"

"Yah, mon. West Indies are playing New Zealand."

"You sure that's not rugby?"

"Nah, mon." He turned to one of the other students. "Where da cricket at?"

The kid looked at me. "Broward Stadium. Lauderhill. You know it?"

I did. I had driven past it the previous day. It was in the heart of Lauderhill, otherwise known as Little Jamaica, and was a decent three-iron from Desmond Richmond's grotty storefront. I didn't feel good about Markus being in the same country as Richmond, let alone the same zip code, even if Richmond was moving on to other cattle.

"Okay," I said. "Perhaps we'll come and check out the game. I've never seen a cricket game live."

"Cricket match," said the kid.

"Yeah, whatever."

We walked the three young men back to the residence, and Danielle gave Markus a hug, which embarrassed the hell out of him. As she did, the kid who had told me about the cricket pulled me aside.

"I saw you talkin' wit Mista Richmond," he said.

"Yeah, he was giving Markus some trouble. Not anymore."

"He bod news, mon. Bod news."

I glanced at Markus, blushing through his ebony skin, and back at the kid. "You think Markus might be in danger?"

He shook his head. "Not here. Mista Richmond into all sorts of bod stuff here, stuff he don want to bring attention to. But back home, in MoBay?" The kid nodded. "Trouble."

I thanked him and gave Markus a handshake and sent them on their way. Danielle and I returned to the car, and I sat without starting it for a moment.

"You okay?" she asked.

"That kid just mentioned that Richmond might look to cause Markus some trouble back in Jamaica."

"What kind of trouble?"

"The bad kind."

"We can call Lucia. She'll keep an eye on him."

I nodded. I would do that. I'd call Lucia.

Danielle leaned her head back against the headrest. "You have another idea, don't you?"

"You know, even if Markus makes it back here to Miami, Richmond is always going to be just there in Lauderhill."

"So what are you thinking?"

"I'm thinking he's a bad dude."

"And?"

"And if he's up to no good in Jamaica, the chances are he's up to no good here, too."

"And you want to know what kind of no good he's up to," she said.

I nodded.

Danielle nodded. "Me too."

CHAPTER THIRTY-THREE

We drove back up I-95, enjoying the sunshine, but with the top down, talking was out. We headed straight back to West Palm and parked on Clematis Street. We wandered down to E.R. Bradley's Saloon on South Flagler, where Ron sat with an icy beer mug, a plate of conch fritters, and a smile that could power a small town. He had been sitting at Lady Cassandra's apartment, reading the paper and bored out of his mind while Cassandra lunched with some pals at The Breakers. Ron was more than happy to cross the bridge and meet us when I called him from Miami, and it appeared he had wasted no time in getting there.

Bradley's is an all-outdoor establishment, sitting under canopies that looked as if they were erected by the Army Corps of Engineers. In the summer Bradley's bakes, and the servers can't bring ice water fast enough. But in season, it is a pleasure to watch the traffic along South Flagler Drive and the Intracoastal Waterway beyond. Ron sat under a fan that gently moved the air around, watching clouds the color of aluminum mingle on the horizon over the barrier island of Palm Beach.

The lunch burrito weighed heavily on me, so I eschewed more food in favor of an iced tea, and Danielle got a daiquiri. We sipped our drinks, watching the scene for a while. I was lost in thought about Markus. I feared Desmond Richmond was the kind of guy who was like a starfish. You cut him in half and he grows into two new starfish. I wasn't sure if pushing him on Markus would end up coming back on the kid, but I was growing more confident that it would live to haunt young Jamaican kids in the future as Richmond worked to ensure his position was more ironclad. There was also the possibility—or if Markus's new college buddy was on the money, the likelihood—that Richmond might make an example of him.

"You're worried about Markus," said Danielle.

I nodded. "I don't like the thought of Richmond, here or there."

"What is his business here?" asked Ron.

"I don't really know, and that's the problem. He's got the storefront in Lauderhill. Custom printing. T-shirts, mugs, that sort of thing. But that place is a dump. There's no way that place is funding any kind of lifestyle."

"What else do you know about him?"

"He was a backup in the bobsled, parlayed that minor fame into a green card and some kind of mini empire. Everyone back in MoBay treated him like he was a big deal. But all I've seen is a low-rent printing shop."

"And running shoes," said Danielle.

"Yeah. Running shoes."

"So how do we find out what he's into?" asked Ron.

I let out a long breath. When I had been lunching with Lucas in Miami Beach, it had occurred to me that if I wanted to know who Cornelius Winston's links were in the US, I knew someone who would know that. Someone with connections in all the dark corners in Lauderhill. And if that someone knew about Winston, then a buck got you ten that he knew about Desmond Richmond.

Danielle was watching me, reading my mind, or something close to it. "You haven't practiced your saxophone lately."

I shook my head.

"You need to call Buzz Weeks," she said.

I nodded.

"Buzz will know," she said.

I shook my head again. "No, he won't. But he knows someone who will." I pulled out my phone and called Buzz.

Buzz Weeks was a saxophone player who played world-class halls around the world but called South Florida home. I had met him through a mutual friend, and he had not only helped me with a previous case but had also taken on the task of giving me lessons on the saxophone that I had been gifted by the same mutual friend.

"Buzz, it's Miami Jones."

"Miami, long time no hear."

"It's been a while. Where've you been?"

"New York. Fun town, but cold, brother. You still playing your horn?"

"Now and then. I think I've got 'Take the A-train' nailed."

"Good to hear. That's a great tune. One of the Duke's best. So, what can I do you for?"

"I have a favor to ask."

"Shoot."

"I need to speak to Cool-aid."

There was silence on the phone, not even breathing.

"Buzz, you there?"

"Yeah, brother. You sure about that? I nearly lost my lunch last time you met with him."

"Me too. But yes, I do need to meet him. Can you arrange it?"

"If you're sure. Come to Ted's tonight. He'll be there."

"You playing?"

"Course."

"I'll be there. Thanks."

I hung up and looked at Danielle. She was smiling.

"Fancy an evening of jazz?" I asked.

"I'm there."

CHAPTER THIRTY-FOUR

Ted's Jazz and Social Club sat behind a low-rent strip mall off West Sunrise Boulevard in Lauderhill. It seemed that Lauderhill was becoming my second home, and having developed a liking for jerk chicken in Jamaica, I had good reason to believe I'd be here more. Danielle and I left Ron at Bradley's and headed up A1A to Singer Island. We got in our gear and walked down to City Beach, across the paths through the sand hills, and onto the beach. Once we hit the hard stuff, she took the lead and picked up to a steady jog. I dropped in behind and enjoyed the view. We kept a good pace until we got to where the island thins out to a finger, and she stopped and stretched a little, and then we headed back across our footprints.

The sun was low in the sky when we got back to City Beach, and we stretched as we watched the guys packing up the sun loungers and umbrellas that were rented to hotel guests during the day. We walked at a good clip back across the island to my little rancher. We both took showers and got dressed, she in a little black dress, and me in a plain shirt and linen sports jacket. Then we killed time watching the sun disappear behind Riviera Beach until it was time to leave.

I parked in front of a nail salon that was doing a roaring trade despite the late hour, and we cut between the salon and a convenience store painted in the yellow, green, and black of Jamaica, down an alley that in other circumstances would have looked like a very stupid place to go. We found the sofa on the street outside the building, two old guys with generous smiles sitting in the cool evening, shooting the breeze. They both gave a nod and a *ma'am* to Danielle and a look of approval to me, and we stepped by an old, rusted sign that had been tacked into the wall with a nail: *Ted's Jazz and Social Club.* If it weren't for the sign, you might have thought you were walking into some stranger's home.

Inside it was already busy. These were not people who were fashionably late. They were fashionably on time, which suited me just fine. A throng of pine tables sat at the middle of the room, fronted by rows of stackable chairs. They were facing a small stage painted in a matte black, such that it looked like it was swallowing the light around it. We headed toward the rear of the room, where a congregation of folks were gathered around a small bar. They were all very well dressed, better than most people outfitted themselves at weddings these days. As was par for the course in Lauderhill, we were the only white faces in the room. It didn't bother me one bit and never seemed to bother them. A woman with a wartime hairdo saw us and gave Danielle a broad smile.

"I thought you'd forgotten about us," said the woman, looping her arm through Danielle's and dragging her toward the bar.

"It has been too long," said Danielle. "We just got back from Jamaica, actually."

"Do tell." The women left me for dead and headed for a thin guy with a pencil mustache who was mixing something amber in a glass shaker. I turned tail and went to the side of the stage where a door led to a hallway, where another door opened into a dressing room. It was filled with a mismatched assortment of furniture and a mismatched assortment of men. There was no uniform, no common theme to their look, except that each man held an instrument, save two, and I assumed them to be the piano player and the drummer. A guy in a deep sofa saw me and smiled.

"If it ain't screamin' cats. What is this I see? You wearin' grown-up clothes?" My previous visit had seen me blow my saxophone for the first time for Buzz, producing a sound that was less than human. I'd gotten some ribbing for it, and then I'd managed a decent note, and I'd gotten a lot of nods. These guys loved their music. Even the guy being consumed by the sofa. He had a black face and black shoes. The rest of his suit was yellow. The trousers, the shirt, the jacket, the tie. Last time

I saw the guy he was dressed like a zebra, so he certainly had some style about him.

"Me, I wear a suit like that if I want to go to a Halloween party as a banana," I said.

The banana gave me a broad grin. These guys liked to think they talked smack. I'd played football in college. This was a church picnic in comparison.

"Where's yo horn, brother?"

"I'm leaving the music to the pros tonight. Just dropped into say hi and break a leg."

"Break a leg? What the hell kind of thing is that to say?" said a trumpet player who was on a stool behind the sofa.

Banana looked up at him. "It's white man talk. Shakespeare or some crazy stuff. He means have a good show."

I nodded. "Yeah, that's what I mean. Is Buzz in?"

"He's havin' a smoke out back. Can you believe it? We can't even smoke in here no more."

"Welcome to the new Florida," I said. "Check your fun at the door."

"Amen to that, brother."

I made my way through the room, each man offering a smile as he worked on tuning his instrument, and I pushed open the door that led out into the back. It was a small courtyard, a single bulb enough to fill the space. Buzz Weeks was leaning on the wall, a lit cigarette between his fingers. He was stylish, in pleated trousers, a brown jacket and tie, and matching wing tips. He looked like something from *The Sting*.

"Hey, Buzz."

"Miami Jones." He leaned over and slapped me five, then put the cigarette to his lips. He wasn't a kid but he was younger than me, at least that was my guess. But he had old eyes, like he'd seen a lot more than he was telling. An old soul, my mother would have said.

"How're things?"

"All good, brother. You?"

"Not bad. So, you speak to Cool-aid?"

"Nah, man. I don't speak to Cool-aid. I know one of his guys. He says Cool-aid will be here. He's like a politician, though. He comes when he pleases, stays long enough to be seen, then leaves."

"Why does he come at all?"

"I told you before, he's looking for the cred. This ain't his crowd. We don't do that stuff, and he knows it. He wants to be seen as a big man around town. But he don't try to sell here, and he don't bother no one, so no one bothers him."

"Fair enough. You'll let me know before he leaves."

Buzz looked me up and down. "He'll know you're here, brother. I'm sure he won't leave without sayin' hello."

I nodded and made to leave Buzz to his cigarette. "Have a good show," I said.

"Thanks, brother. And hey, I like your look. Grown up."

I smiled. "So I'm told."

I wandered back through the green room and wished the boys the best, and then I went out to find Danielle. She was at a four-cover table with the woman from the bar, whom we had met before but whose name I couldn't recall. She was gracious enough to remind me it was Iris, and her man was LeBron.

"Miami," I said, shaking their hands.

"We know, honey. You're hard to forget."

She offered that thought with a handsome smile, so I took it as a compliment. LeBron skipped to the bar and brought back a couple of beers, and we clinked bottles.

"So, LeBron. Like the basketballer."

He nodded. "Yeah, The King, that's right."

"Can't be too many of those."

"Nah, I never heard of another. But at least now I don't gotta spell it out all the time."

"Good point."

We took a drink, and he pointed his bottle at me.

"So, Miami. Not too many of them."

"Ohio, Florida, and me. As far as I know."

He smiled and sipped his beer, and we chatted for a while until the band started drifting out. He was a mortgage broker, and Iris worked in customer service at Fort Lauderdale airport. They were smart and happy people, and I enjoyed their company. I grabbed another round before the lights dropped, and then we sat back and enjoyed the kind of show that comes with a fifty-buck cover and twenty-buck drinks in New York City. It was a joy to watch professionals at their trade, each a master of his instrument. But what struck me most was how much fun they had doing it. It was like watching a major league pitcher play catch with his kids on the front lawn. Just for the fun of it. We should all enjoy what we do so much, and do it so well.

As the band played, I noted a latecomer step through the door. He wasn't like anyone else. He was the same color, but that was where the similarities ended. This guy looked as if he had tripped over and fallen out of a time machine from the seventies. His afro was tight, and his suit was pure burgundy velour. I was also of a mind to believe a pirate had died to give up the shirt he was wearing. He looked around the room as though he owned it, until he saw me. Then his face dropped. I winked and then returned my attention to the show. I recalled that he might be the funniest-looking thing in the zoo, but he was also one mean hombre, whom it wouldn't pay to upset.

Unless I really had to.

CHAPTER THIRTY—FIVE

Buzz led us out into the rear courtyard. The breeze felt cool, and I knew the stars overhead would soon be covered by a blanket of cloud. I let Cool-aid go second, and his bodyguard go third. It was a respect thing. At least that's what I'd learned watching De Niro movies. I had about as much respect for Cool-aid as I did for Lance Armstrong, but I knew respect was important to people who never bothered to earn it, so I took the rear. Cool-aid walked like a snake might if it had legs, with a side-to-side motion that wasted a lot of forward momentum and looked like the Bee Gees were playing inside his head. Buzz dropped into the shadows, and Cool-aid spun on one toe to face me.

"Where's your little surfboard shirt?" He smiled at his own wit. I did not. "You know, 'cause last time you was wearin' a shirt with little surfboards on it, and now you is dressed like a man."

I nodded at his suit. "My neighbors had a sofa made of that material when I was a kid." I didn't want to poke the bear, but there was a limit.

"You what?"

I decided to get to the point. "I need your help."

This brought a big smile. The man had teeth that would be the envy of a Triple Crown winner, and he flashed them at all of us.

"Lemme git this straight. Last time you come here, you want a favor from Cool-aid." He wobbled his shoulders as he spoke, as if he were singing along at Woodstock. But there was nothing melodious about his voice. "And then you come here again, and you want my help again?"

"Are you all caught up now?" I wondered for a moment how such stupid people ended up so successful. It wasn't just in crime. I knew sportsmen, politicians, actors, even businesspeople who combined had the collective intelligence of a bonfire. Then reality sunk in. There was smart, and there was street-smart. And Cool-aid was the latter. He might have had a penchant for stating the blindingly obvious, but he knew when someone was about to stick him, and so far he'd always gotten his shank in first.

Cool-aid lost the smile. "Gimme one single reason why I should help you, surfboards."

"Let me ask you a question in return. Last time you helped me, was it good for your business?"

Cool-aid bobbed his head to the rhythm in his mind. "It didn't hurt. What's yo point, white man?"

"My point is I can help you out again. This time, much closer to home."

He bobbled again, considering his options. Then he decided, with a theatrical jutting of the jaw. "What you wanna know?"

"I need to know about two men."

"Two men?" His eyes went wide as if this was going to tax him beyond his brain's capability.

I ignored it. "First guy is called Cornelius Winston."

"Refresh my memory?"

"Jamaica Inter-Secondary Schools Sports Association."

"Yeah, okay. I know that cat. What about him?"

"He's all kinds of big news in Jamaica. I want to know what he's got going on here."

"Winston's chump change, man. He don't do no business."

"He's trying to get a very important role in Jamaican athletics. And he's doing something in the US to make that happen."

"Oh, that. Yeah, I heard about that. You talkin' about the Olympic thing." Cool-aid wasn't quick, but he listened well.

"That's right. So what's he doing here?"

"Brother's sellin' votes."

"For what?"

"You din't hear about the Olympic bid?"

"Yeah, I did. But how is Winston selling votes? He doesn't have the position yet. He doesn't have a vote to sell."

"Call it futures, man. See the old man who's in the seat now . . . What's his name?"

"Prestwich."

"That's him. That old guy, he's too clean for this stuff. I mean, those cats do everything first-class, you know it. But word is the old man votes on bids according to technical merit. *Technical merit*, man. Who does that?"

"You mean he can't be bought?"

"That either. But he's bailing out. *Re-tire-ment.* You know what I'm sayin'? So Winston is the man. He does the deals. That brother can deal. The honkies doing the bid here want Jamaica's vote, so Winston says he'll give it, in return for some of Uncle Sam's cold hard green. You know what I'm sayin'? In return, he uses some of his payola to fund the brothers back in Jamaica who are going to vote him in. It's win-win."

Cool-aid started his little dance again, and I thought about his words. Winston was buying his way to the top job using other people's money. It was clever, but it presented a problem. I didn't have any way to stop it. It was above my pay grade. Best I could do was inform Corporal Tellis and hope she could follow it up from her end. I wasn't even convinced that would get anywhere, so I turned to my more immediate problem.

"Okay, guy number two. Desmond Richmond."

Cool-aid stopped jiggling about and frowned. He looked like an old man squinting into the sun. "The bobsled brother?"

"That's him."

He started moving again, slowly at first, as if he had to work himself into it all over. "That brother is a different creature altogether."

"How so?"

"He in business. He not afraid to take a brother down."

"Tell me. What's he into?"

"What's he not into? He got all kind of merchandise."

"Does he have the kind of merchandise you have?" It never ceased to amuse me how these guys couldn't utter the word *drugs*. Perhaps every bushel held a wire.

"Yeah, man. But he works on the north side. My business is south, down to Plantation."

"So there's expansion opportunity."

Cool-aid turned his head and gave me the side-eye. "Go on."

"Richmond has threatened a friend of mine. An athlete. He gave the kid some shoes, and now he thinks he owns the boy."

"Yeah, I bet he got shoes to give like Santy Claus."

"What do you mean?"

He turned back and started a move that looked like the Supremes backing up Diana Ross. "Word is, he heisted a shipment of kicks from a warehouse in Georgia, Mississippi, someplace like that."

It sounded more likely than a sponsorship deal with Nike. "So he brought the shoes here? Where?"

"You seen his operation?"

"I've seen a lot of boarded-up storefronts."

Cool-aid held his hands out like a magician finishing a trick. Richmond's print store was in a building with another four or five units, all of which were buttoned up tight. Except for his. Plenty of room to store, well, anything.

"If you know this, how come the cops don't know?"

"Who says they don't know?"

"If they know, why don't they go in?"

Cool-aid tilted his head back to the sky and let out a laugh like a kookaburra.

"Point made," I said. "Where does Richmond hang out, apart from the print shop?"

He dropped his head and shrugged. "I don't keep tabs on the cat. But I tell you where he's gonna be tomorrow. Where every good Jamaican will be."

"Church?"

He did the flip-top head laugh again and came back down holding his chest from all the mirth. "Oh, man. You are a novelty. No, not church. The cricket, man. Richmond gonna be at the cricket."

"The Jamaica game?'

"Not Jamaica, man. West Indies."

"West Indies, right. And you think Richmond will be there?"

"You not listening. Every brother gonna be there."

"Then I'll be there too."

"You go, you might just run into old man Winston."

"He'll be at the game?"

"I tole you. Every brother be there."

I nodded and looked at Buzz, who was pretending he wasn't visible. "On with the show?" I suggested. Buzz nodded.

"One minute," said Cool-aid. "I done for you, now what you gonna do for me?"

I stepped to him so our noses were almost touching, and I could see his bodyguard twitching out of the corner of my eye.

"If Richmond's territory became vacant, would that be good for you?"

Cool-aid danced with his shoulders. "That would be nice."

"Well, I'm going to pull the rug from under Mr. Richmond. You make of that what you will."

CHAPTER THIRTY-SIX

I left Danielle in good company at Ted's and took off in the Boxster. Danielle was as game as most for an adventure, but she was also a sheriff's deputy and had a firm belief in the law and the process that went along with it. I saw those leather legal tomes more as guidelines, and my next activity wasn't going to blur them so much as cross them like Washington over the Delaware. I had no doubt that Danielle knew about my willingness to play outside the rulebook, but like the US Army of old, she operated on a *don't ask, don't tell* philosophy.

I parked the car a few blocks from Richmond's shop. The area was dark and silent. No street lamps were operating, and the clouds had pushed in off the water to cover any moonlight. I still felt like a beacon with my linen jacket and blond hair. I couldn't do much about the hair, but I pulled off the shirt and jacket and found a dark gray workout t-shirt in the trunk, along with a small backpack.

I walked up the opposite side of the street to survey the store and saw nothing. No light, no movement. One thing about breaking into a place that probably held illicit goods was the lack of security cameras and alarms. These guys didn't want the cops showing up for a stray raccoon. I crossed the road and did a lap of the strip. The only windows were in the print shop: the storefront and the two small ones at the rear by a rear door. All the other units were boarded up with ply and screws. All the units were the same size and configuration except the end unit, which had a roller door, like on a large garage. It was designed for deliveries from vans or small trucks. If these guys had any brains at all, that door was padlocked on the inside, and even if I could open it, it would make enough noise to wake up folks in San Francisco. There was an access door built into the garage roller door so someone could pass through without opening the whole thing. It was only about four feet high.

I dropped my backpack and pulled out a small leather wallet. My good friend Sally Mondavi had given it to me as a birthday present, about an even six months from my actual birthday. He thought it might come in handy and had shown me how to use the tools held in it. I dropped to my knees and took out a pick and a tension wrench. The lock was an older model tumbler lock. I inserted the pick and felt for the tumblers, getting two or three each time before they all fell back into place and I had to start again. It took a lot longer than in the movies, and I felt exposed. There was no cover, just parched asphalt parking lot behind me. But no one came, and eventually I got the pick in position and used the tension wrench to turn the barrel. The door snapped open with a sudden bang that sent a tinny echo across the lot. I pushed it open just enough to get inside, then grabbed my backpack and stepped through.

Pushing the door closed but not locking it, I grabbed a small flashlight from my pack. I panned the light across the dark room. The space was filled with wooden pallets of freight that stood five feet high and were shrink-wrapped. I moved through the pallets, counting at least a dozen before I found one that had its plastic wrap torn away. I shone the light on the boxes behind the wrapping, and an orange Nike swoosh glowed back at me.

I moved through the maze of wrapped shoeboxes toward the wall of the unit, where I found a connecting door to the next unit. It wasn't locked, so I moved through. I realized I was holding my breath, so I stopped and slowly took air in through my nose and let it out through my mouth. The next unit had shelving erected around its perimeter. I shone the light across the shelves and saw thin boxes with Sony logos on them. Boosted Blu-ray players. I thought about going further, but I had confirmed what I wanted to confirm, and I wanted to get back to Ted's before the show ended and people started asking questions. I edged back to the door between the two units and stopped when I heard the roller door rattle loudly. I killed my flashlight and blinked hard to adjust my eyes. The access door squealed open, and I saw the glow of a flashlight over the top of the pallets of shoes.

"See, it's open. I tole you," said a voice. It was young, a kid, and African American.

"Dis is a bad idea, homes," said a second voice, same approximate age.

"Hey, anyone here? Your door is open, man," called the first voice.

There was no one inside but me, and I wasn't answering, so the question bounced around in the silence for a while, and then the first voice spoke again.

"Ain't no one here, homes."

"Is still a bad idea. Dis Mista Richmond's stuff."

"He ain't gonna notice two pairs. Listen you wan' a pair a LeBrons or not?"

The response must have been physical because I heard no answer. The kids were light on their feet, and I couldn't hear them move about. I assumed they were scanning the pallets for their preferred design and size, like a late-night excursion to Foot Locker. After a couple of minutes I heard a whispered *here*, and then the sound of plastic ripping. It wasn't going to be quite as clean a break-in as they assumed, if they were ripping the shrink-wrap off unopened pallets, but maybe Richmond's inventory control wasn't that good.

"There. That's a nine," said one of the voices. I couldn't tell them apart anymore, but I knew they had big feet for kids.

"Find an eight. I'm an eight."

"Here's one."

I saw the flashlight drop and then point at the ceiling, and heard the muffled wump of butts hitting the ground. The lids were removed from the cartons, and I realized the little monsters were trying the shoes on for size. It was ballsy, but I guess if you're going to bother breaking in and stealing basketball boots, you don't want the discomfort of stealing the wrong size. Apparently it was all good, because I heard them stand and jump up and down on the spot, perhaps simulating a jump shots.

"Sick," said one voice.

"Kick," said the other.

The flashlight dropped again, and I heard them making their way to the door. They opened it, stepped through, and pulled it closed. I stood in the darkness for a couple of minutes, then turned on my light and wove my way through the pallets. I found the spot where the midnight shoppers had taken their bounty. They had left the open boxes lying on the concrete floor. At least they had taken their old shoes with them. I wondered what was going to happen when they appeared on the street with new sneakers and no credible explanation for how they had acquired them. It wasn't going to take much to connect them to the two empty boxes. I shook my head at the stupidity of youth. I hadn't broken into any warehouses as a kid, but I'd done my share of dumb things. I knew if they lived long enough, the kids would probably wise up some. It was the living long enough that was going to be the trick.

I left the boxes where they lay. Taking them would do nothing, and leaving them covered my tracks completely. I made my way back to the access door and gently pressed the handle down and opened the lock. As quietly as I could, I opened the door and then slipped out. I wasn't confident that the kids wouldn't be sitting right outside admiring their new footwear, but I couldn't see them. I pulled the door closed but didn't lock it, and then I skirted the side of the building until I hit the front. I crossed the street, casual as could be, just a guy with a backpack out for a walk in a dark neighborhood in the wee small hours. I made it back to the car, dropped my pack on the passenger seat, and headed back to see Buzz and the boys finish their set.

CHAPTER THIRTY—SEVEN

I told Danielle everything that Cool-aid had said. There was no doubt in my mind she had noticed that Buzz and Cool-aid had come back inside Ted's without me, but she didn't ask where I'd been. I made it back for the end of the set and had a beer, and we thanked everyone and headed out. On the drive home, I told her that Richmond had stolen Nikes in his warehouse. She said we needed to go to the police, and I told her that Cool-aid knew someone in the local precinct was on the take, and alerting them would only serve to alert Richmond. She sat in silence for a while, biting her lip. We were zooming through Delray Beach when she finally spoke.

"You said the shoes came from Georgia?"

"Georgia or Mississippi, he said. He wasn't sure."

"But not Florida."

"No, not Florida," I said.

"So they crossed state lines."

"Are you suggesting what I think you're suggesting?"

"FBI."

"Okay. Do we just call the Hoover Building? *Hey, we've got some missing Nikes.*"

"Well, actually you could. They have a tip line, but I've got a better idea. You remember that leadership conference I went to in Atlanta?"

"Yeah."

"I met the agent-in-charge of the field office down here. He's a good guy. I've got his card at the office."

So we got off the freeway at the airport and stopped off at the Criminal Justice Complex on Gun Club Road. The good thing about police stations is they're open 24/7. This was a huge office building that housed law enforcement of all varieties, and it looked closed for business when we pulled into the large lot. But the lobby desk was open, and Danielle dashed in and came back with a business card that bore the seal of the Federal Bureau of Investigation. I pulled back onto the freeway and headed home.

"You gonna call him now? It's late."

"No. There's nothing going down tonight. I'll call him first thing."

And she did. I was still in bed, but I don't think Danielle had slept much. Apparently neither did her guy at the FBI. They chatted, and then she brought the phone into the bedroom and put it on speaker.

"Miami, on the line is Agent-in-Charge Marcard. Agent Marcard, I have Miami Jones."

"Mr. Jones."

I always found those FBI titles so grandiose. Special Agent this and that. But I figured it was not the time to discuss it. "Agent," I said. He asked me to give him the lowdown, and I did. I didn't tell him my source, and he didn't ask.

"Is your source good?"

"One hundred percent," I said. "I'm sure the merchandise is there." I didn't add how I was so sure.

"Okay. Well, the hearsay of a crime figure, and I am assuming that your source is such, correct me if I'm wrong, won't stand up in front of a judge. We'll need more to get a warrant."

"Tomorrow, no, actually, later today, there is a cricket game being played at Broward Stadium. My source says Richmond will be there. The kid we brought out from Jamaica will also be there. I have reason to believe he might try to harm the kid."

"That's not an FBI matter."

"Unless Richmond kidnaps him."

"Is there a credible threat?"

I looked at Danielle. She shook her head. This was no time to make up stories.

"No, not really."

"Look, I'd like to help, Danielle, you know I would. But we have hearsay of a federal crime and speculation on a local one. We need more, and it needs to be within the FBI's remit for me to act."

"I understand," said Danielle.

"Look, I'll have someone check out the strip mall, look into this Richmond guy. If we can confirm a heist of this nature in either Georgia or Mississippi, then we can at least open a file."

I'm not the most comfortable person when it comes to bureaucracy. I understand that we are a group of states united under a common flag, rather than one federal entity, but I didn't suffer the demarcation malarkey well at all. I liked to just get the job done, and I wanted to tell this stuffed shirt exactly that. But I didn't. I bit my tongue, because this was Danielle's deal. It was her contact, and he might be important to her one day. And him doing nothing was where we were before she made the call anyway.

"If there's something federal in nature that is credible, just call," said Marcard.

"Sure. Thanks," said Danielle.

"Wait," I said.

"What is it, Mr. Jones?"

"It's Miami. Mr. Jones was my dad. Listen, do you guys handle corruption?"

"Every law enforcement body handles corruption. But again, we are federal in nature."

"So, like, if an Olympic bid were making illicit payoffs to foreign bodies in return for votes?"

There was a pause. "Yes, that would be us. What do you have?"

I told him about Winston, and about Lucia investigating his network, and how we had reason to believe he was getting payoffs in the US. And that he was here, right now. I didn't mention that the vital information had come from a hood named Cool-aid rather than a corporal in the Jamaican Constabulary Force, and Danielle didn't push me on it.

"All right. Let me check NCIC on that. I'll get back to you."

NCIC was the national law enforcement database, where cops could check on each other's investigations to see if someone was already involved in something they were about to walk in on. It worked in a broad, anonymous fashion, with minimal detail, so crooked cops couldn't source intel for the bad guys. If Agent Marcard found something, he would have to call the contact agent to explain his interest. He was good to his word, because twenty minutes later, he called back.

"Okay, Mr. Jones, you got a bite. We have a task force looking into corruption of national and international sporting bids. They're looking into everyone. Good, bad, or otherwise. FIFA, the NFL, the IOC. Anyone. They know your guy. They want to talk. Can you be in my office in Miramar in three hours?"

We could. Agent Marcard had brought in coffee and donuts, which seemed awfully cliché but tasted fresh and delicious. The FBI were housed in fresh, shiny digs way out where the last of the housing estates crushed up against the Everglades. It was still only nine o'clock, and the suburb was still. Miramar doesn't rise early. On hot days it doesn't rise at all.

We were joined in a conference room by a woman in a pinstripe suit who could have been a banker but introduced herself as Special Agent Kerns. She wore her long hair in a bun, and had an easy smile that didn't quite match the pinstripes. Marcard was also in a suit, which would have made me feel awkward about my palm tree-print shirt, if I gave a damn. Kerns gave us a high-level overview of her operation that didn't really tell us anything. Sometimes there was corruption in sporting organizations, just like everywhere else, and she was tasked with rooting it out. She had broad remit to investigate any organization she chose but only limited subpoena power. Some bodies, like the NFL, had provided open access, while others, like certain European organizations, had remained a closed book, open only to federal warrants.

"And all this is happening out of Miami?" I asked.

"No, Mr. Jones. I am based in Washington, DC."

"You came from DC this morning?"

She smiled. "No. I happened to be in Miami. We have information regarding irregularities with the athletics world championships bid. That was why I wanted to meet. Your information was timely."

"Well, I have solid intel that Winston will be in Lauderhill today. I don't know for sure that he'll be up to no good, but . . ."

"I'd like to watch him, all the same," said Special Agent Kerns. "And you say he'll be at a cricket game? So, at a public place. We don't need a warrant for that." She looked at Marcard, and he looked at Danielle.

"All right," he said. "I'll get a team together." He looked at me. "I know your other guy, Richmond, will be there. He is not of interest to this operation, unless he does something wrong. So we'll have eyes on him, but that's all. Winston is our focus. Okay?"

"Crystal."

"And I trust this intel is on the up-and-up. That Winston is what you say he is."

I leaned across the table toward him. "Agent Marcard, I don't like what either of these guys are doing, so if you take out one of them, I'm not fussed which one. I also know that Danielle is a great deputy who has a hell of a career ahead of her, and it won't do her any good to have me hoodwink the local FBI chief. Stuff like that sticks. I wouldn't do that to her, so I won't do that to you."

Marcard watched me but gave nothing away, and then he turned to Kerns. "Let's get our ducks in a row."

She nodded and looked at me. "What time is this game on?"

"Two o'clock."

"We have work to do. I need to make some calls." She stood, as did Marcard. I took that to be the end of the meeting. I stood, and Marcard turned to me.

"You stay. I'll get Special Agent Kerns a desk." The two FBI agents left us alone.

Danielle smiled at me. "That was nice, what you said. About my career."

"Nothing but the truth."

"It's nice anyway."

"Anytime, Deputy."

Agent Marcard came back alone and sat down.

"First, Mr. Jones, let me say I appreciate your candor. You're dead right. Deputy Castle isn't going to be a deputy for long. She's too good." He didn't look at Danielle and kept his gaze on me. "Second. I'm in charge of this operation, but I know you've been thinking about this for a while. So tell me. What's your plan?"

CHAPTER THIRTY-EIGHT

Central Broward Regional Park and Stadium was a large park and athletic area off West Sunrise Boulevard, smack-bang in the middle of Lauderhill. The stadium itself reminded me of a small-town minor league ballpark, one of those ones that had been bought out by a local private group and redeveloped with new facilities and a fun family atmosphere. I played in many parks like it, including two years at Port St. Lucie. But the Broward Stadium had one big difference. The playing area was an oval shape, and the game took place right in the middle of the space. The whole structure had that new-build feel to it that lots of places had in South Florida. An inviting and open boulevard swept toward an out-of-place clock tower, then beside it a grand pavilion that surrounded one half of the field. The crowd was bigger than I thought it would be. An attendant told me the stand held five thousand fans, and it looked as if they might fill it. It was like a community festival: lots of flags, mostly Jamaican but also other West Indian nations, like Guyana and Barbados; food trucks with jerk chicken and booths selling foam fingers and cricket caps that looked suspiciously like baseball caps; even a group dressed in black, drinking cans of beer and doing what I assumed was supposed to be the *haka*.

Danielle and I wandered up into the stands. There were trumpets and more flags and a lot of people, a throbbing mass of humanity, all waiting for the game to begin. Many of the eyes were pointed skyward, and the gray clouds that had come in overnight grew black. There was torrential rain to the south in Hialeah and north in Boynton Beach, and it was just a question of probability as to whether we saw a tropical downpour in Lauderhill. Cricket, like baseball, was not a game played in the rain, but it didn't feel as though a cancellation of the fixture would dampen the festive mood.

As we climbed the steps, we scanned for any faces we knew. I found Markus, and we made eye contact, so I waved and smiled, and he replied with a nod. Danielle slapped my shoulder and directed my attention to a spot high in the stands on the opposite side, where Desmond Richmond sat surrounded by a cordon of bodyguards and hangers-on, truly a man of his people.

I noted two crow's nests hanging off the roof of the stands. Cameramen were perched inside, taking shots of the vacant field, a sound engineer in each playing with cables and parabolic microphone dishes. I looked back to our side of the stands, and at the back I saw Cool-aid, bopping to his own tune, surrounded by his posse. He was on one side; Richmond was on the other. I was reminded of that childhood story about the two cities at war over which side of an egg should point up.

I didn't see any evidence of Cornelius Winston, but I didn't expect to. Not out here. Unlike Richmond, Winston was comfortable among a different class of folks. I gave Danielle the nod and she went to sit with Markus while I wandered back down the steps to the concourse. Behind the stand there was an administrative office and a section called the Field House. I had purchased access to the Field House with a two-hundred-dollar donation to the Broward Rotary, and I flashed my badge to gain access to the VIP lounge.

This was the kind of air that I figured Cornelius Winston would prefer to breathe. There were linen-covered cocktail tables and a bar, and well-dressed folks mingled around casual yet important conversations. While my palm tree-print shirt got a couple of sideways looks, it wasn't as many as I might attract anywhere else in the world. Large glass walls provided an excellent view of the ground and the plebs out in the stand.

I gave myself a wee mental pat on the back when I saw Cornelius Winston helping himself to a platter of sandwich rounds. I ambled up and grabbed a plate, picked up a turkey-and-cheese quarter, and feigned my surprise that I should end up standing next to old Cornelius.

"Mr. Winston," I exclaimed. "Fancy seeing you here."

"Indeed, Mr. Jones. I didn't realize you were a cricket fan."

"Oh, yeah. I'm a huge fan. Go All Blacks."

He nodded. "I think New Zealand calls their cricket team the Black Caps."

I shrugged. "Everything's black with them. What brings you to the US?"

"Official business," he said. "I have some important meetings."

I gave him my impressed face. "By the way, I owe you a debt of gratitude for your letter."

He looked rather pleased with himself. "I hope it was of use."

"Well, I don't think Mr. Richmond will be bothering Markus again."

"I'm glad."

I leaned into him. "Or anyone else," I said with a wink.

Winston frowned but didn't say anything, so I looked around the room like I was a spy in a Pink Panther movie. Still Winston said nothing, so I nudged him.

"You haven't seen Mr. Richmond in here, have you?"

"In here?" Winston scoffed. "I hardly think so. Why do you ask?"

"It's the whole Markus thing. The police are involved."

He didn't give much away. Not much, but enough. He'd have been a tough guy to beat at poker, but it was possible, because he had a tell. A subconscious tick, a raising of his left eyebrow that told me all I needed to know.

"The police?"

"Aha. They're here. All eyes on this pavilion, as long as he's in it. Apparently he's been up to all manner of no good here in Florida, and they're going to pick him up during the game."

"Is that so?"

"That's what I'm told."

He nodded and looked at the platter but decided against more sandwiches.

"Anyway, enjoy the game. And thanks again."

"Anything to help a Jamaican athlete." He smiled and turned away, and I wandered over to the window. The crowd started clapping as two teams of men took the field, one in burgundy uniforms and the other dressed in black. Not just their caps; head to toe. I glanced back and saw Winston put his plate down and fire up a cell phone. He made a call with a frown on his face, and then he ended the call and stayed at the back of the room, away from the game.

There's a rule in juggling bowling pins. You can throw one up in the air, but to juggle, you have to put all your pins in play. I had ruffled Winston's feathers, so I left him to do or not do as he would choose. I stuffed a couple of little sandwiches in my mouth and left the Field House, ventured back out onto the concourse, and turned away from where I had come, around the other side of the stands. People were streaming in, taking up their seats in preparation for the game. I got to the bottom of the steps leading up into the stands.

It looked like the burgundy team, which I took from the flags around me to be the West Indies team, were batting. Two of their guys walked out to the middle of the ground, wearing padding and helmets and carrying those bats that I remembered so well from my beating in a roadside ditch in MoBay. The black-clad team, New Zealand, was already on the field, waiting in a tight circle. The crowd cheered the batters onto the field with trumpets and drums and flags and noise to rival a Seattle Seahawks game. There was a lot more dancing than I usually saw at baseball games, save the seventh-inning stretch. The crowd was having a lot of fun, and I resolved to come and check out one of these games when I wasn't on the clock.

The batters made it to the middle and set up, one at each end of the pitch, and the crowd subdued some, a few people sitting down. The steel drums continued and showed no sign of stopping. I turned to the crowd and saw Markus chatting with his new college buddies. Danielle sat next to him, trying to hide a frown but failing, her eyes scanning the throng of faces for danger.

I headed up the steps at the side of the stands. Toward the back there was a cordon of thick-necked men, one of whom stepped in my way. He didn't look like most of the Jamaicans I'd met, who were predominantly thin and wispish. This guy was either from a different island, like Samoa, or he was the victim of the standard

American diet. He didn't smile either. In Jamaica, even the guys who wanted to smash my head with a cricket bat gave me a smile. I nodded toward where Desmond Richmond sat, and the big guy shook his head.

I didn't want to cause a scene, not yet, so I didn't push it. I just leaned against the railing and waited. I kept my focus on Richmond, while everyone else rose to cheer what I imagined was the first pitch of the game. I wished Garfield were there to explain it to me. I recalled the pitcher was actually called the bowler, and the batters were batsmen. The rest was Chinese arithmetic to me. It didn't matter—I wasn't watching it.

It took a minute, but eventually one of the cronies sitting with Richmond saw me. I wasn't the only white face in the crowd, but I was the only one with my back to the game. The crony slapped the arm of the guy next to him, who clocked me and then leaned and whispered into Richmond's ear. Richmond frowned and looked at me. I gave him my best Magnum P.I. cheesy grin. I didn't have dark hair or a mustache, so the effect was more an internal thing, but regardless, it was cocky as all hell. Richmond snarled but made no moves. He didn't invite me up, which was a bit rude, but he also didn't send anyone down to bang me on the head, so that more or less evened things out.

I was waiting for a text message, and I didn't understand cricket, so I really didn't mind standing with my back to the game, watching the crowd. It's a universal truth that most people don't like being stared at. A biker might start a fight over it, and an accountant might just get itchy in his seat, but no one enjoyed it. Richmond was no exception. He tried watching the game but just couldn't resist looking my way every so often to check if I was still looking at him. His bodyguard contingent started doing it too, until there was a line of them looking out, looking at me. Looking out, looking at me. It was like a Jackson Five routine. People in the crowd picked up on it, and others down near me, noticing that I was focused on the back of the stands, wondered what the hell I was looking at and turned in their seats to see. Half the section was twisted one way, half the other, all eyes focusing on Richmond, then back on the cricket, and then back on Richmond.

Richmond shifted in his seat. He liked the spotlight, but now he felt like a bug under a magnifying glass in the sun. He was getting seriously antsy, and I could feel the tension rise in the crowd. Then my phone buzzed in my pocket, and I took it out and glanced at it. I considered the message I had been waiting for, and then I looked one last time at Richmond. He was watching me so I gave him my little *I know something you don't know* grin. I had used it now and then on the pitching mound, and I knew it got in a lot of batters' heads and I had no reasons to suspect it wouldn't get into Richmond's. Then I spun and jogged down the steps and out of the stands like I had somewhere better to be.

CHAPTER THIRTY-NINE

The van sat on the outer concourse between the clock tower and the stands. It wasn't marked as a gardening services business or a television crew or something clever. In fact, it had no markings on it at all. A plain beige van with blacked-out windows. It looked ready to offer drugs out back after the game. The inhabitants of the van saw me coming because as I was about to bang on the back door, it swung open, and I got inside.

It looked like something out of the movies. Steel shelving had been installed on both sides, and on the shelving sat all manner of electronic surveillance equipment. What I realized was that in the movies they didn't really shoot inside vans. The space was cramped, just enough for four FBI agents and their stuff. I stayed against the rear door mostly because there was nowhere else to go.

"He's on the move," said Agent Marcard. "You think he'll bite?"

"He thinks we're all looking elsewhere right now," I said.

We watched a video monitor showing a picture from one of the cameras in the crow's nests hanging off the stands in the cricket ground. It drifted away from the cricket match to capture an older gentleman taking a walk. He sauntered away from the stand, eyes casually on the game, as he walked the perimeter fence. The camera followed him until he stopped on the far side of the field.

"He's not coming out this way," said Agent Marcard.

"Just keep the video on him," said Special Agent Kerns.

Winston looked across the cricket field and I was amazed how clear the picture was. I could see the pores on Cornelius Winston's face. From a distance he looked like he was watching the game, but in our close-up shot we could see that he was scanning from side to side, his body language forced casual, his eyes focused. Then something happened.

There was a roar from the crowd that we heard through both the audio equipment and the side of the van. The camera panned quickly back out, a wide shot, and we saw one of the West Indian batters walk from the middle of the field. Evidently he was out, and the crowd was making a hell of a lot of noise about it. A replacement batter was walking out. Special Agent Kerns sat in one of the small chairs, and she pointed at the screen.

"Winston," she said.

Agent Marcard spoke into the microphone attached to his wrist, Secret Service-style. "Back to Winston, back to Winston."

The camera zoomed back to the outfield shot and panned along the fence. Winston was gone.

"Find him," said Marcard, a tad redundantly, as the camera had already pulled back and was scanning the open space beyond the field. It was the area that in a minor league park would have been outfield bleachers and the scoreboard, and at a lot of stadiums either open space or the parking lot. Here it was more parkland, well-maintained tropical grass and white concrete sidewalks cutting paths alternately to nowhere or somewhere. Far beyond the boundaries of the cricket field was another red-roofed structure, matching the design of the stadium stands but much smaller. It looked like a gas station from a distance, high roof and open space underneath. Then I realized what it was.

"The picnic shelter, red roof," I said. Marcard repeated my direction, and the camera panned around as the operator searched for the building, then found it and zoomed in. It was part of the park facility, a roofed picnic shelter with rows of tables underneath and coin-operated grills available for public use. In the winter it was hired out for groups to enjoy picnics, and in the summer it could make you feel like you ended up on the losing side of a clambake. The camera moved in on a person walking toward the shelter. He looked skyward, and then started walking faster. Then I heard it on the roof of the van. I looked at Special Agent Kerns.

"Is that rain?" she said.

I nodded.

The camera now focused to show Cornelius Winston do that old-man fast-paced hobble, a run without using his knees, which looked less comfortable than actual running. He stumbled under the shelter. Barely a few drops had fallen, but where there was one, there were thousands, and around here they didn't arrive over the course of a few days. In Florida, rain really gets about its business. It dumps hard, and then it stops. No messing around.

"You got someone over there?" I asked Agent Marcard.

He shook his head. "He's got to come to the stadium, surely?"

"Not if it rains."

Marcard looked at me. He knew what I meant. Kerns didn't. She was from the Northeast, where they got their fair share of rain, but not the biblical stuff we got in Florida.

She smiled. "You guys get so much sunshine here that you're afraid of a little rain?"

Marcard didn't respond. He banged the wire mesh between him and the front of the van. "Get us around to the back of the stadium."

"I think that road's on the inside of the park," said the agent in the driver's seat.

"So?"

"So we're outside the park, sir."

"So get us inside the park. Now!"

I looked at the screen as the van started. Winston was standing under the shelter, watching another car pull up. It looked like a Lincoln Town Car. A man got out of the back and dashed across to the shelter. He reached Winston, brushed himself off, and they shook hands. The van wobbled as it turned a corner, and we all held onto the shelving. It was like watching television on a rollercoaster.

"You recording this?" I asked.

Marcard nodded. "Video and audio." He hit a button, and sound filled the van. We heard the *rat-tat-tat* of fat raindrops on the roof of the shelter like a slow drumbeat.

"What are we doing here, Cornelius?" asked the man.

"Precautions, Howard. Precautions."

We all went flying as the van hit the brakes.

"Dawkins, are you trying to kill us?" yelled Marcard.

"Sorry, sir. The gate is blocked."

"So crash through."

"It's blocked by concrete barriers. I'll need to go back and use the main gate."

"Then do it!"

I had hit the floor, so I stayed down. I grabbed my phone and called Danielle.

"MJ, the players are coming off. It's raining. What's happening?"

"Winston is in a picnic shelter behind the outfield. It's going down, but we're stuck outside the park."

"I'm there."

I looked up at the monitor. The man called Howard was handing a briefcase to Winston.

"The athletes of Jamaica thank you," said Winston.

"Yes, of course," said Howard. "And you'll be in position?"

"Absolutely. This will ensure my friends put me in charge, and soon. When the vote happens, well, let's just say the athletes of Jamaica look forward to competing in Miami."

The van skidded, but everyone was hanging on now, and it came to a halt. Dawkins rolled down the window and yelled at someone outside.

"FBI! Get that gate open. Now!"

There was a wait as I assumed the gate was being opened. Then Dawkins hit the gas, and we were thrown about again. On the monitor the man called Howard shook hands with Winston and turned to the edge of the shelter. A man got out of the front of the Town Car and hurried across with an umbrella, and he ushered Howard back to the car. Winston watched him go.

Then the heavens really opened.

More than once I had been on a freeway where every vehicle came to a complete stop from the rain. Now it came down so fast and so thick that we lost the picture on the monitor. It was like shooting video in a glass of milk. Dawkins slowed down and moved cautiously. I got up and looked through the wire mesh to the windshield. There was nothing to see. It was as if we had driven off the edge of a quarry and landed in a lake at the bottom. The whole view was murky gray, and the sound was deafening. The van shook from the force of the rain, and the noise was like dropping gravel from a plane. We couldn't see anything in the monitors, and Dawkins had slowed to about two miles an hour. He was driving like a pilot flies in a cloud, using the GPS screen stuck on his windshield to guide our passage. I hoped it was more accurate than mine. We all stood in the back, hanging on, all looking up at the roof of the van, like submariners waiting for the torpedo to hit.

Then, as suddenly as it began, it was gone. There are no geographical anomalies, a.k.a. mountains, in Florida, so there is nothing for clouds to gather around. Weather moves across the state pretty much unfettered, so it doesn't hang around. The sheets of rain moved across the park grounds, clearing at the picnic shelter first. The monitor showed doused grills and no sign of Winston or the Town Car.

"Dammit," said Marcard. "He's gone."

We were still in rain, so we couldn't go any faster until the downpour swept away from us as well and the vision started to clear, like driving out of a carwash. Dawkins hit the gas again, and we were thrust backward, and then we all slammed forward as he jumped on the brakes.

"Dawkins!" yelled Marcard. I was with him. They needed to redraw the straws on who did the driving.

"It's the Town Car, sir," said Dawkins as he leaped out of the van. Kerns moved fast too, pushing up and over me and out the back door. I flipped out and Marcard followed. We dashed around the van. The road was an inch deep in water, the curve of the asphalt running it off toward the grass. The Town Car was head on to the van, inches separating the bumpers. Dawkins had his weapon out, pointed at the driver. The driver had his hands on the top of the steering wheel as he had been directed, and he wasn't moving. Kerns ran to the back door, pulled it open, and dragged the occupant out. He was in a greatcoat and charcoal suit. The sun burst out from behind the clouds and hit the wet ground, and instantly the humidity rose, turning the whole park into a *bain-marie*. I was already uncomfortable, and I wasn't the one wearing a coat designed for Fifth Avenue in December.

"What is the meaning of this?" said the man called Howard. "Do you know who I am?"

"Howard Peeskill," said Kerns. "You are under arrest."

I saw the driver get out and get cuffed by Dawkins, and I turned to Marcard as he looked at me.

"Winston," we said at the same time.

Agent Marcard was a better driver, but in Dawkins's defense, the rain had stopped, and it was bright and sunny again. He maneuvered the van around the Town Car and screamed along the road that ringed the entire park. The two tech guys in the back were holding on for dear life again. I preferred the front seat and the comfort of a seat belt. We got to the picnic shelter, and Marcard skidded to a stop. All four of us jumped out, and the three FBI agents had weapons ready. My gun sat in a locker in my office. It was the safest place for it. I didn't think old Winston was armed. It didn't matter, because he was gone. We looked around the shelter and saw nothing.

"Maybe he headed back to the main gate?" said Marcard.

"Maybe."

We got back in the van and sped back around the perimeter road, stopping to collect Kerns and Howard, leaving Dawkins and the driver for a backup unit. We got to the main gate, expecting the chaos of a crowd leaving the stadium but finding only a few people venturing out for a corn dog or jerk chicken. Marcard stopped the van, and we marched through the gate.

"Should we split up?" asked Kerns.

"No," I said.

Marcard frowned. "Why?"

"Because." I pointed toward the side of the stands, and the two agents turned their attention to Danielle marching a very unhappy Cornelius Winston ahead of her. He was cuffed and moaning. Danielle gripped his wrists with one hand and held his briefcase in the other. She was so wet her clothes looked like a second skin. Steam was rising from her. She brought Winston to us with a sly grin.

"Not bad, Deputy," said Marcard.

"I'll say," said Kerns. "You ran over there in that rain?"

"No, ma'am," said Danielle. "I swam. He's all yours."

She pushed Winston to Kerns, and Winston growled.

"You can't do this. Do you know who I am?"

There seemed to be a bit of that defense going around.

"I do, Mr. Winston," said Kerns. "And I have no doubt that Deputy Castle has already Mirandized you, but I'm going to do it again, just for kicks. You are under arrest. You have the right to remain silent." Kerns dragged Winston away to the van, and I turned to Danielle.

"We need to get you home," I said. "Let's go find Markus."

We left Agent Marcard at the van and walked back into the stands. The players were warming up again as a man on a tractor drove around the edge of the field, a large rope being held in the middle of the ground, like a hand on a clock, pushing water off the grass. We scanned the seats. Not many people had left. They knew Florida weather, and I suspect they saw the cricket as an excuse to party anyway.

"I can't see him," said Danielle.

"Me either." Then I stopped, my eyes on the back of the stands. "Oh, no."

"What?"

"I don't see Richmond."

Danielle turned and took two steps up, scanning the crowd. Then a kid racing down the steps caught her attention.

"Miss, miss."

It was one of the student-athletes from the university.

"Miss," he said again.

Danielle grabbed the young guy by the shoulders. "Where's Markus?"

"He's gone."

"What do you mean he's gone?"

"He's gone. When the rain come."

"He left when the rain started?"

"No, miss. One of Mista Richmond's guys come and get him. Mista Richmond take him."

CHAPTER FORTY

I knew where Richmond had gone. At least I thought I did. I'd know for sure soon enough, but I didn't want to wait for confirmation, so I told Agent Marcard what I knew would get him moving. *Kidnapping* was the key word. It was a crime that got the FBI instantly involved, regardless of state lines or anything else. I told Marcard to follow me, and Danielle and I jumped into the Boxster and sped out of the park.

We weren't going far. The Sixteenth Street Shopping Center was only a couple of minutes from the stadium. It was a journey from the bright, recent-build Florida of wide sidewalks and fresh stucco to old Florida, of boarded-up windows and strip malls and businesses long gone bust. I parked outside a boarded-up storefront one street over from where Richmond's print shop was. The FBI van stopped behind me, and Agents Marcard and Dawkins got out of the front. The two techs got out of the back. Marcard had assured me they were agents first, techs second, and they seemed to know what they were doing at Howard's arrest, so I went with it.

"What are we doing here?" asked Marcard. "Where's Richmond?"

I looked at the roof of the storefront. It had once been a vacuum supply store, and the word *clean* had been rusted onto the wall from a sign that had been removed a long time ago. I called out.

"Lucas."

There was nothing in return, and I looked at Marcard. He frowned, so I tried one more time. "Lucas." I waited, and then a familiar face appeared over the edge of the roof. His dirty blond hair was matted to his head and his t-shirt clung to him.

"How are ya, mate?" He smiled and looked at everyone in the group.

"Been better. You get wet?"

"It was a good one, all right. Needed a shower anyway."

I nodded. "You see anything?"

"Yeah," he said. He spun around and dropped his feet off the edge of the roof, then wrapped his feet around a drainpipe and rappelled down to the sidewalk. Lucas gave everyone a smile, his white teeth beaming from well-tanned skin. "How are we all?"

"Who is this?" asked Agent Marcard.

"Agent Marcard, this is Lucas," I said. "Since you didn't have the probable cause to look into Desmond

Richmond, Lucas has been watching him for me." Lucas was the only guy I knew who would consider an afternoon lying on a rooftop in torrential rain a good time. "So?" I asked.

"Your man arrived a while ago with a little posse."

"Did he have a kid with him?" asked Marcard.

Lucas frowned. "A kid?"

"A teenager," I said. "The kid from Jamaica I was helping."

"That kind of a kid. Yeah, there was a young guy, maybe late teens. Didn't look happy about being helped inside."

"We need more than that," said Marcard.

He was a real stickler, old Marcard, and if he kept it up I wasn't sure I was going to be able to keep my trap shut for Danielle. I took out my phone and showed Lucas a picture of Markus that I had taken back in Jamaica.

"Yeah, that's him all right."

I raised an eyebrow at Marcard, which I thought was very restrained.

Marcard nodded. "Okay, where is he?"

Lucas began to shimmy back up the drainpipe. Marcard wasn't doing that in his nice suit. "Bring the van forward," he said. Dawkins moved the van up, and one of the tech guys opened the rear door. He used the end of the steel shelving as a ladder and climbed up onto the roof, then jumped up onto the top of the store. Lucas continued up the drainpipe. I took the van route. One of the techs stayed with the van, and the rest of us got up for a look. We could see clear across the wet parking lot to where a couple of large recent-model sedans were parked haphazardly. I couldn't decipher the make or model of the cars. They looked like all the other large sedans on the road these days.

"Ways in?" Marcard looked at Lucas. He hadn't bothered asking how Lucas fit into everything, but Lucas had that wiry look about him. A look that said he'd seen more than you ever wanted to and you'd best let it rest. And Marcard had.

"Not much. They went in the roller door, and that unit has nothing but boarded-up windows. There's a glass front to the print shop on the other side, but I can't say whether that's connected to the unit they went in."

"So the boy is in there, but we don't know where," said Marcard. "Should we assume these guys are armed?"

"Don't assume it," said Lucas. "I saw one handgun and two shotties, for starters."

Marcard sat back from the edge of the building and looked at his guys. He was drawing blanks. "It's a fortress," he said. "With a minor in there. We should contact hostage negotiation, and then make contact with Richmond."

"Hang on," said Danielle. "He doesn't know you're here. Let's not lose the element of surprise until we have to."

Marcard shrugged. "You have a better idea?"

"He's got to expect that Miami and I are going to notice Markus is gone, and plenty of people saw Markus leave with him. So he's got to think we'll come here."

"So?"

"So we should give him what he expects. One of us should go in. Then we'll know where Markus is."

"Are you volunteering, Deputy?" asked Marcard.

"I am."

"No," I said.

Danielle frowned. "You don't think I can do this?"

"Of course you can. But he knows you're a sheriff. He's not going to believe that you wouldn't call backup. And at least until we've got Markus, I'd rather he not focus on that."

"So who's going to go?" she said. "You?"

I dropped my shoulders. I wasn't excited about walking into a warehouse full of armed men, and the fact that I would be unarmed didn't make me any more enthusiastic. But that was the rub.

"Yeah, I guess I draw the short straw."

CHAPTER FORTY-ONE

Agent Marcard had the opposite opinion. He wanted a law enforcement officer to go in, not a civilian. The FBI top brass didn't take too kindly to civilians getting killed during FBI operations. I appreciated the point. It was nice to know they felt that way. But it wasn't working any other way, so he relented. He insisted that I wear a wire, so if things started to go bad, they would know. Marcard gave Lucas a radio so he could act as eagle eye, and the FBI guys and Danielle took positions around the building across the lot from Richmond. I got in my car and pulled out onto the street, then took the long block around to Richmond's unit.

I came in fast. The Boxster purred as if this was what she was made for, and I screamed into the lot like I was a man in a hurry. I was planning on skidding to a stop outside the roller door, announcing my presence loudly, but the Porsche's antilock brakes kicked in, and I just came to a sudden stop that almost had me head-butting the dashboard. I jumped out, strode to the roller door, and banged on it with an open palm.

"Richmond, I know you're there. Come on, man. This has gone too far. Let's talk. Let me in." I waited for a moment, hearing nothing. So I banged again. "Richmond!" The door rattled in waves, and it was loud on my side. It had to be deafening inside the warehouse. I waited a moment again, then I heard a rattle in the access door, and with a creak it opened. A black face popped out, squinting in the sunlight that had now permeated the day. The face blinked its eyes, looked around the lot, and then focused on me. He nodded his head, urging me in his direction. I walked over, keeping the pace slower now, not wanting to spook anyone and get shot.

I stepped through the small access door into the dark warehouse and was immediately pushed against the roller door with a metallic thud. The access door closed with a bang and I was searched for weapons in a very unfriendly manner. For a moment I was worried about them finding the wire, but the thing really was a tiny wire connected to a transmitter that was stuck down the front of my shorts. A guy had to be very comfortable in his own sexuality to frisk me there, and in my experience henchman types generally weren't.

Convinced that I was unarmed, they flipped me around and pushed me back into the door. I glanced around the room. It looked like they were moving. Pallets had been moved to the side to allow room for a small truck, like the kind people hire to move from one apartment to another. I could see four men carrying boxes of shoes, plus the guy at the door and the guy who had searched me—for a total of six. Richmond wasn't in the room, but he made seven.

And then there was Markus. He was in the midst of the guys carrying the shoes and had an armload himself. They were carrying them from a pallet, plastic wrap ripped open, to the van. They had used a pallet truck to put the shoes in the warehouse, but with the door closed there wasn't enough room to operate it, so they were working by hand. I nodded to Markus but he didn't nod back. He didn't look scared exactly. If I had to guess, and it was a guess, I'd have said he looked resigned. Resigned to the fact that his life had taken a brief, wonderful turn into the land of hope but then had snapped back to the despair it was always supposed to be in.

Richmond walked through the door from the room I had hidden in the night before while I was snooping around. He looked smug. I wanted to make fun of him, to ask him if he was hiding back there just because someone was banging on the door, but I didn't. He held the cards, and my objective was to play out this hand and hope my losses weren't too great, so when the next hand came around, I could nail him.

"Mr. Jones, you are a fool."

So we were dispensing with the pleasantries. "Feels that way," I said.

Richmond nodded. "You have caused me enough trouble, Mr. Jones. Both here and at home. I can't have any more trouble."

I shrugged, and Richmond nodded at the big guy who had searched me, who then dragged me by the collar over to Markus.

"You okay?" I asked him.

"No talking," said the big guy.

"Are you?" I said to Markus.

The big guy slapped my ear with the back of his hand. It was like being hit by my mother for cussing. I looked at Markus, and he shrugged again. I turned to Richmond.

"Look, Richmond. I can help you. I'll help you load. I'll even drive the damned truck to wherever you want it. Just let the boy go."

Richmond smiled. "You'll drive the truck? Where will you drive it, Mr. Jones? To your girlfriend, the police officer?"

"Come on, Richmond. There's seven of you and only two of us. I'll do what you want. Just let the kid go." I hoped the wire I was wearing was working and that Marcard had gotten the numbers.

"No, Mr. Jones. Markus has a lesson to learn. It was my fault for not teaching it earlier. A successful athlete has skin in the game. He runs for his life. Markus will help us load our merchandise. He will help us move it. And he will keep some of it to take back to Jamaica. Then he will have skin in the game, just like the rest of us.

As for you? You can help load. That's all. Unless you run fast? Do you, Mr. Jones? Do you run fast? No? Shame, then I have no use for you at all."

He nodded again, and the big guy gave me a shove. I had to admit I was getting pretty tired of him pushing me around. But I walked to the pallet and grabbed a few boxes of running shoes, and I carried them to the truck. I moved a little more quickly than the others. Not because I wanted to win employee of the month. I wanted to catch up with Markus without looking like I was doing that.

We started walking by each other, him to the truck, me away, and I gave him a wink, like I had everything under control. Fake it 'til you make it, that's what they say. I'd been on the mound more than a few times, clueless about what pitch to throw, so I'd given the batter a wink. It made me look like I was in control, like I had a plan, when I didn't. I caught up to Markus on my third load.

"Okay?" I asked.

He nodded.

"Good," I said, more for the benefit of those listening on the other end of the wire than for Markus. He looked the color of ash. So I turned my attention to the environment. Richmond was on the phone at the other side of the warehouse. The two lugnuts who had let me in and then searched me were over by the door. They were armed, one with a shotgun, the other wore a handgun in a holster like a cowboy. That left at least one other weapon unaccounted for. We were working on a pallet nearest the truck. The next pallet on that side of the truck was closer to the side wall. At the rear of it there was open space, but no line of sight to the armed guys. And the truck blocked that spot from Richmond's view.

We carried boxes, and I made a few comments about how hard it was, just to let Agent Marcard know we were still ticking. We finished the pallet, and then two of Richmond's henchmen pulled the wooden pallet to the side so we had a clear path to the next. I went to the pallet and started pulling at the shrink-wrap. It was thick and tight, but I didn't care if I opened it. I just wanted this to be the next pallet we worked on.

The two other henchmen joined me at that pallet, and one smiled and pulled out a switchblade. The others waited, and Switchblade ran his tool around the plastic, cutting through, and we stepped forward and ripped at the wrap. I watched the guy close the switchblade and put it in his hip pocket. I don't like knives anywhere except in a kitchen, and sometimes not even then. So I knew Switchblade was going to be the first to go down.

CHAPTER FORTY-TWO

We tore the shrink-wrap away and started shuttling the boxes to the truck. We were working on the side with an open view to Richmond, and I edged to the corner. On my next trip, I started on the side that was hidden by the truck. I directed Markus to work on my side. Then I carried an armful of boxes to the truck and glanced at Richmond. I gave him my poker face, like I had not a thought on my mind. He watched me through snake eyes, wary and cold. Then he spoke into the phone, and his attention shifted away from me.

I slowly walked back to my side of the pallet. Switchblade caught up to me, and I gently bumped my hip into his. It was almost no contact at all, not enough to make him angry or even aware, but enough to change his direction. He followed Markus around the end of the pallet, and I came in behind. We got behind the side of the truck, and he went for an armful of boxes. I went for his hip.

I slipped the knife out of his pocket, and he took a moment to realize what had happened. He took another moment to consider what to do with the armful of shoeboxes he carried. It was a moment too many. I held the knife out with one hand, attracting his eyes, and then with the other arm I drove an elbow into his nose. His face splattered like marinara sauce making a break for freedom, and he dropped to the concrete floor, the boxes of shoes landing on him. Markus's eyes were as wide as saucers. I held up my finger to tell him to stay put. Mercifully, the guy on the ground was whimpering but not screaming, so he wasn't attracting any attention. Yet.

I moved to the corner of the pallet and made a *what the?* face to the next guy and nodded to the rear of the pallet. He followed me, more curious than wary. They outnumbered us seven to two, so he wasn't too worried. Perhaps I'd found a pair of pink suede pumps among the Lady Nikes.

Not so. He saw his buddy on the floor and turned back, and I used his own momentum to drive his head into the corner of the truck's body. It was a hell of a thump, and it was going to hurt when he woke up. But for now he dropped like a bag of cement. On the downside, my advantage of surprise was gone. The truck shuddered under the momentum of the hit and attracted the attention of the last two loaders. They both came around the back of the truck fast, and as they reached the corner where the second guy lay on the concrete, one of them kept advancing toward me. The second cut along the side of the truck, heading for the cab. So now I knew where the missing weapon was.

Most fights in movies are like boxing matches. Loud punches, thrown ad infinitum as if the combatants had the endurance of an East African marathon runner. But in real life, most fights are like poorly choreographed wrestling events, two guys clenching and grabbing and holding, usually losing balance and ending up on the ground, rolling around like mating bears, until they very quickly run out of breath and the whole thing peters out. The result is that most guys look for the Hollywood version and never see the sucker punch coming. I needed to get to the cab. So when the guy came at me, I didn't have time for the Marquess of Queensberry rules. I took two steps toward the cab so the guy had to change direction slightly, and then I put my dukes up like a circus boxer from the eighteen hundreds. The guy saw the fists and focused on that. I kept moving, and he didn't see my left foot hook around and kick him hard in the side of the right knee. It didn't do any damage. My left foot isn't my kicking foot. But it did drop him to his knees. My left foot hit the floor and I pivoted, using my pace to spin me around like Brian Boitano, and I drove my right foot into the guy's Adam's apple. I was no punter, but I could kick a decent ball, and the guy flew back onto the concrete, gasping for air. I did a full spin, without the flourish, and kept moving to the truck cab.

The fourth guy was bent forward into the cab, grabbing for the shotgun that was tucked behind the seat. He was pulling it free when I arrived. I drove my body into his, my arms crossed and hitting the back of his head. His face thrust forward and smacked into the butt of the shotgun. It wasn't a big hit, but the butt of a shotgun is rock hard, and it dazed him a tad. Enough time for me to pull him back by the collar and drive his head into the side of the door. Again, not a lot of give there, and he dropped to the ground, not unconscious but not happy all the same.

Now I had to move. I had four guys down, any of whom could recover and come at me. And I could hear the armed thugs minding the door coming across the concrete. So I pumped the action and blew a shot into the roof. The sound was like the end of the earth. It rattled around the hard surfaces of the warehouse. I heard the door guys stop, probably behind one of the pallets, which put them in Richmond's direction. I ran behind the pallet where Markus was down on his backside, hands to his ears.

"Are you okay?"

He looked at me as though he didn't speak English anymore.

"Are you okay?" I repeated.

He nodded.

"Can you run?"

He frowned.

"Let me rephrase that." I got right in his face so he could have tasted the little sandwiches I had eaten in the Field House earlier that day. "How fast can you run?"

The life came into his face.

"How fast can you run?" I asked again.

"Dead fast," he said.

I pulled him up and pointed him in the right direction. He was facing the wall next to the roller door. There was room enough for a thin body to get between the pallet and the wall, and then an open stretch to the door. I pointed to the large rubber button on the wall by the door.

"How fast can you run?" I asked one last time.

"Dead fast," he said. Now he was getting it. He looked determined. He looked focused. But he'd never run under gunfire, so it was anyone's guess how he'd go.

"Marcard. We are go on three. One, two . . ."

I called *three* and flipped the gun up onto the pallet and aimed across the warehouse. I wasn't aiming for anything in particular. I didn't really want to hit Richmond or his goons, but at that moment, I wasn't overly fussed if I did.

I pumped and shot and pumped and shot. If they were smart, Richmond and his boys were staying down until the shells ran out, as they inevitably would. I shot again, pumping slower now, buying time.

Then the roller started rumbling and clattering and winding around itself, and up it went. It was only about a foot up when I heard the first call of *FBI*. Then there was *freeze* and more *FBI*. I dropped down behind the pallet of shoes and pumped the remaining shells out of the gun. I heard Danielle call *MJ*, and I slowly stood up, hands in the air like I was in a bank robbery. Danielle stood by the door, wearing a bulletproof vest with FBI emblazoned on it. She had her arm around Markus. The two FBI techs had the guys who had been guarding the door and who had wisely given themselves up. I saw Marcard, handgun in position, panning the room. Dawkins was moving between the pallet loads, sweeping the space. He got to the far corner and looked back to Marcard, and he shook his head. Marcard glanced at me.

"Richmond," I said. "Where's Richmond?"

We stood looking at each other for a moment, and then the truck started up. The exhaust sent a puff of black smoke into the warehouse, like a magician's trick, and it moved. Backward. It was the only way to go. I launched myself into the door of the cab as it accelerated by me. After grabbing the shotgun and taking out the last of the four guys loading the van, I had left the door ajar. As Richmond charged backward, the door flung open, so I grabbed on for dear life. The door flung all the way out, me hanging off the end like an orangutan, until the truck hit the roller door. It wasn't all the way up, and the top of the truck collected it, slowing the acceleration and jolting my door back toward the body of the truck. But not for long. Richmond hit the gas hard and pushed through, the garage door screeching and buckling as the truck ripped at it. The truck door made to swing away, so I grabbed the edge of the cabin and let the door go. We sped out into the parking lot, the sun falling low in the sky. Richmond kept going backward across the lot, and I saw Danielle and Markus standing under the mangled roller door, watching us careen away.

Richmond hit the brakes and spun the wheel, perhaps trying to dislodge me, which he almost did. My legs were flailing around the tire, and as the vehicle spun, my body hung off the cabin, my fingers holding on. Then Richmond straightened up, and hit the brakes, and crunched the gears. He should have driven all the way to Orlando in reverse. His change of direction pulled me back toward the cab and then catapulted me inside, the door crunching closed behind me. I was lying across the bench seat, and I looked up at Richmond and gave him a big smile. A kid-on-Christmas morning smile. Richmond snarled, and I saw his left hand bring up a shotgun. So he did have a weapon. There's always one more than you think. But it was a poor choice for such close quarters, and I didn't want to give him the chance to swing it across his lap and get a shot off. From that range I was Swiss cheese. But lying prone across the bench seat didn't give me a lot of options. So I did the only thing I could think of.

I pushed myself up into a starting position, like a sprinter low in the blocks. Arms straight like a push up, legs crouched, feet against the door. Richmond swung the shotgun up at the roof, so I launched myself forward like a torpedo. I drove straight at Richmond's head and made contact, my forehead to his jaw. It wasn't pleasant for either of us. I didn't tend to use my head for smashing stuff on a regular basis, and it hurt. But it was sacrificing my queen to take his king. It hurt him more than it hurt me. Richmond's jaw buckled and made a sickening crunching sound. He dropped the firearm and swerved. I doubted he could see. I couldn't. For a moment everything went fuzzy, and then it went white as the truck crashed into something and the airbag exploded in both of our faces.

The airbag deflated, and my head fell into Richmond's lap. I wasn't sure how mobile he felt or where the gun was. The doors to the cabin flew open, and I wondered if Richmond was making a break for it. Wondering was all I did because I couldn't get my brain to communicate to the rest of my body. Then Richmond disappeared from the cab, and I watched him go. I blinked hard a few times, looking at the sagging airbag droop across the steering wheel. My head lolled back toward the open door, and I saw an angel. If angels wore FBI flak jackets.

Danielle reached in to me, a glow surrounding her body, perhaps the sun setting behind her, or perhaps something more ethereal. I didn't know. She cupped my cheeks, and I thought she said everything was okay. Everything apart from the desire for my eyes to roll back in my head and the brain-splitting headache cutting like an earthquake across my mind.

"Richmon . . ." I managed to mumble.

The angel smiled. "We've got him." Her soft hands touched my cheeks, my mouth dropped open, and I looked at her beautiful face, and I decided that now was as good a time as any to go to sleep.

CHAPTER FORTY-THREE

Ron drove to the airport. I had spent the night in Broward General under observation for concussion. Desmond Richmond had also spent the night in Broward General under police guard, his jaw wired in three places. Evidently my head was harder than I thought, on the inside and out. Danielle was in my hospital room when I woke up that evening and still there the next morning. She was in the same clothes that she had gotten drenched in while arresting Cornelius Winston, but she had returned the bulletproof vest. She offered me a smile and ran her soft hand across my cheek again. It was its own medicine.

Hospitals were the growth business in Florida, and there were two kinds: those that worked on volume, turning the beds over like they were tables at a fast food restaurant, and those that charged plenty to look after you in old age until you passed on or ran out of money. Broward General was the former. The doctor came and ran some cursory tests designed to mitigate litigation should I fall in a heap after leaving the hospital, and then he discharged me. We were all happy about it. I still had a headache but plenty of ibuprofen, and the hospital wanted its bed back. Danielle needed a shower and a change of clothes, and probably a good night's sleep.

Ron came down from Palm Beach, and we collected Markus from the UM campus, where he had already attained cult status despite not yet being formally enrolled. Agent Marcard had taken a statement from Markus and then had driven him back to the campus, where he stayed the night in rooms reserved for visiting professors.

Ron pulled into the short-term parking lot, and we walked to the terminal. He asked if I needed a wheelchair, and I told him if he found one he'd end up in it. Danielle helped Markus check in, and we called Corporal Lucia Tellis to ask her to drop by the Swan house to let Mrs. Swan know Markus was on his way and to arrange for Garfield to collect him at Sangster International Airport. Lucia said she would pick up Mrs. Swan and take her to collect Markus herself.

Danielle arranged airside passes for us so we could go through security with Markus, and we sat at the gate lounge and talked about what he would do for the rest of the year. Danielle went pretty heavy on the *study hard* line, but Markus took the advice with good nature. He might not have been thrilled about the schoolwork, but he knew what he had to do. I went for a wander to the newsstand, where I bought a pennant flag emblazoned with the words *University of Miami Hurricanes*. I ripped the little stick off and handed the pennant to Markus, and he smiled. I think it was the first time I'd seen him do that away from the track.

"Keep it on you," I said. "At all times. Remember what the goal is this year. Finish school, get solid grades, get back here. Then you can run."

He nodded. "Thank you, Miami."

"Anytime, kid."

He folded the flag and put it in his pocket, and then he looked at me. "What will happen to Mista Richmond?"

"You don't need to worry about him. He's going to spend some time in a federal prison. Then he'll probably have his green card revoked and be sent back to Jamaica, where Corporal Tellis says they have some charges of their own."

He nodded, but this time he didn't smile. It wasn't a smiling matter. Sending bad guys to jail was never something to be happy about. Relieved, yes. But not happy.

The final call for the flight was made, and Markus shook hands with Ron and me, hugged Danielle, and headed for the boarding line. As he handed the boarding pass to the agent, he reached into his pocket and pulled out the pennant. I watched him stroke it. And he smiled. I thought of his mother, asking me why I was helping them, what I wanted. And right there, that was why. The agent returned the boarding pass to Markus, and he walked into the jetway. He didn't look back, which was a grand way to move on.

Agent Marcard had asked Danielle to bring me in to the office to complete formalities when I was up to it. Although the ringing in my ears had stopped, the headache persisted, but I didn't know when I would be up and about next, so we dropped by.

He welcomed us into the same conference room and slid some papers over to Danielle and me. He said he had taken the liberty of completing a report and asked us to read it. I didn't. I wasn't in a reading mood, and I was comfortable that his report would be honest to a fault and designed to nail Richmond. Then Special Agent Kerns joined us. She sat on the side with Marcard, and she slid a similar report over to each of us and asked the same question. I signed it too, equally confident that Winston would get what was coming to him at the end of Special Agent Kerns's big stick. Then Kerns turned to Danielle. She noted that Danielle had yet to change clothes.

"That was some fine work yesterday, Deputy," she said.

"Thank you, ma'am."

"Our international taskforce is ramping up. Winston is quite the scalp, but there's more to do. You wouldn't be interested in joining us in DC, would you?"

Danielle didn't smile or make any kind of face, but she took her time answering. "Thank you for the thought, Special Agent. But I feel like I'm needed down here."

Kerns nodded. "They're lucky to have you."

"If your task force is international, you might consider the officer who worked with us on the Jamaican end. Corporal Tellis, Jamaica Constabulary Force, Montego Bay. She's young, but she's as bright as I've seen."

Kerns made a note on her pad. "Tellis. Thanks. We can use someone good on that end." Kerns thanked us and left, and then Agent Marcard walked us to the parking lot, where Ron was waiting in his car with a coffee and the *Miami Herald.* Marcard stopped Danielle before she got in.

"If you're not interested in DC, perhaps you'll give some thought to joining my office."

"I'm happy where I am," she said.

Marcard shook his head. "I doubt that. You can do more, and you know it. But all I'm saying is, give it some thought." He handed Danielle a fresh version of his card, and Ron fired up the Camry. He drove us back to Broward General, where Danielle had left the Boxster, and we dropped her off. Then Ron pulled onto I-95 and headed north into another sunny South Florida day. The radio told us it was pouring cats and dogs across Okeechobee to Fort Pierce, but we saw no evidence of precipitation where we were. But that's the thing with Florida rain. It's a matter of being in the right place at the right time. Or the wrong place, depending on your point of view.

Ron cruised up I-95 without a word, and we both looked east as we shot by West Palm Beach and the turnoff that would have taken us toward Longboard Kelly's. He glanced back at me and smiled. Another day. We got to my house on Singer Island in good time, but unlike the last time when Ron had collected Markus and me from the airport, the Boxster already sat in the driveway. Ron didn't switch off the engine.

"I'll see you in the office tomorrow," he said.

"That you will."

"Take a few extra headache tablets. Lizzy's going to have quite a bit to say."

I smiled and got out of the car, then watched Ron turn and head away. I did the same, and found Danielle waiting at the front door. She still hadn't changed clothes.

"Okay?" she said.

I stopped in place. Palm trees wafted overhead, and the briny scent of the Intracoastal drifted on the air. I took in the blue sky, the temperature hinting at the summer to come. Looking back at Danielle, I nodded.

"All good."

I got settled on the living room sofa, and Danielle brought me some ice water.

"Can I get you anything else?" she asked.

"No. You need a long, hot shower, though, I'm sure."

"So do you."

I raised my eyebrows and made to get up, but she gently pushed me down.

"Easy, tiger. You can go later."

I feigned disappointment, but the attempt at standing had sent blood to my head, or taken it away, I didn't know which. Either way, it pounded for a good few minutes. Danielle went for a shower and I lay on the sofa and lamented the lack of a television, so I eased myself up nice and slow and took my water out to the back patio. I flicked the umbrella up so the loungers were in shade, and then I lay down and closed my eyes.

I must have dozed because I woke to find Danielle lying on her lounger next to me, sunglasses resting on her head, sipping a cup of tea, looking better than anyone deserved given the lack of sleep. I watched her for a while, her eyes dancing across the view of the water and Riviera Beach beyond. She must have sensed she was being watched, because she turned to me and gave me her half smile.

"Just like Jamaica," I said. "Without the rum."

"And the motorcycles," she said.

"The Porsche looks like the safest vehicle on the road in comparison."

Danielle shrugged.

"What?" I asked.

She wore a grin that suggested her mind was cooking up some kind of evil plan. "I think we need a new bet."

"Oh, save me. I just got out of the hospital because of the last bet, if you recall."

"But this one you can't lose."

"I thought that last time, but I have a knack for finding ways to end up getting cracked on the head. Go on, what's the bet?"

"You stay out of trouble for the next month."

"Define trouble."

"Someone wanting to or actually causing you bodily harm."

"I wish that every day. So if I lose, what do you get?"

"Nothing. You get rid of the Porsche."

"Why? It's the first car I've had that hasn't been smashed or bashed in I can't remember how long."

"But it's not you. You're a domestic car kind of guy."

"You think?"

She nodded.

"Okay. So what if I win the bet? What do I get?"

Danielle raised an eyebrow. "Me."

"You? Don't I already have you?"

"I'll make an honest man of you."

"Make an honest man of me? What does that mean?"

Danielle lay back in her lounger and flicked her sunglasses down over her eyes and turned to the water. "You give your bruised little brain some time to think about it."

I turned to the water as well. My bruised little brain wasn't in any shape to figure anything out, so I closed my eyes and listened to the *tink* of rigging on masts and the calls of the gulls, and felt the warmth of the sun on my face, and I thought about tourist brochures, and why people came to Florida in the first place, and in what ways I wasn't already an honest man.

GET YOUR NEXT BOOK FREE

Hearing from you, my readers, is one of the the best things about being a writer. If you want to sign up to my mailing list, we'll not only be able to keep in touch, but you can also get your next read free, as well as occasional pre-release reads, and free member exclusive ebooks that are only available to my list friends.

Join Now:
http://www.ajstewartbooks.com/reader

ACKNOWLEDGEMENTS

Thanks, as always, to all my readers who send me feedback. A huge thanks to Constance and Donna for their editorial and proofing expertise; all the beta readers, especially Heather and Lee; and the readers on my inner circle reading team. These books don't happen in isolation, so thank you.

Any and all errors are mine, especially but not limited to my approximation of the Jamaican patois, as picked up from Jamaicans all over the world, but especially at the Private Banks Cricket Ground in London, around Lauderhill in Florida, and in Montego Bay, Jamaica. A more joyful bunch of people you would have to travel a long way to find.

ABOUT THE AUTHOR

A.J. Stewart has lived in so many places it feels like he has a home team in every game he sees. Which explains why his wife begins any sports telecast with "who are we going for today?" A.J. and his family currently spend their time in Los Angeles and South Florida, but stay tuned, anything could happen.

You can find AJ online at www.ajstewartbooks.com, connect on Twitter @The_AJStewart or Facebook facebook.com/TheAJStewart.

Made in United States
Troutdale, OR
05/20/2025

31527713R00198